there
is
a
place

beyond the rainbow of consciousness,
a place without time or space or even
long-nosed Freudian critics. There,
anything is possible because just
thinking makes it so. Charles Beaumont
calls the place Yonder.

Opening this book constitutes a trip to
Yonder. Come as you are—because
where you're going there are millions
of things and people more bizarre-looking
than you. Not only that, but they've
got worse troubles—or maybe more fun . . .

YONDER

Stories

of

Fantasy

and

Science Fiction

by

Charles Beaumont

.

.

.

BANTAM BOOKS • NEW YORK

YONDER:
Stories of Science Fiction and Fantasy

A Bantam Book Published April 1958

This book is for BILL NOLAN,

A drifter of esses
at maximum speed;
A writer of excellent
stories, indeed.

Table of Contents

You Can't Have
Them All

U PON ENTERING the hotel room and glancing at its occupant, Doctor Lenardi assumed that hearty, cheerful manner which is characteristic of all physicians once they have abandoned hope. His eyes flicked over the luxurious appointments—the thick-piled rug, the hearth, the high fidelity phonograph—and across the towel-wrapped ice bucket, from which extruded a magnum of champagne, and the single guttering candle: then he smiled. He rubbed his hands together, professionally. "Well, now," he said, "and what seems to be the trouble here?"

The man in bed moaned, softly. "Women," he said.

"I beg your pardon?"

"Women," the man repeated, in a faint, almost inaudible whisper.

Doctor Lenardi sighed. He had come out of the rainswept streets like an angry raven, cursing, muttering; yet now he was ashamed. For he could not recall a time in his existence when he had been so instantaneously moved to pity. Why? The patina of weariness, of ineffable exhaustion, perhaps; the absolute incapacity that shone dully from the fellow's eyes . . . *Poor devil!* he thought.

Forgetting entirely the difficulty with his wife, an almost omnipresent burden on his mind these days, forgetting his own unhappy state, he walked briskly to the bed and began to unsnap his bag. "Can you understand me?" he asked gently.

The man nodded.

"Good. Then I want you to tell me this. Are you in any pain? Dizzy? Nauseated?"

"No." The man trembled. "That is, not exactly."

"I see." Doctor Lenardi uncoiled a stethoscope and applied it. He said, "Hmmm," and took from the bag a number of vari-sized articles with which he proceeded to peer, thump, prod, and listen.

Some minutes later he put everything away and sat for a time stroking his nose. Not even in Nairobi, during the

1

plague, had he encountered a human being whose thread with life seemed quite so frayed, whose *élan vital* and resistance had sunk to such abysmal depths. "Tell me," he said spontaneously, "if you can—how in the world did you manage to get yourself into this wretched condition, Mister——"

"Simms," the man said. "Edward Simms." He surrendered to a rather violent shudder, which sent his dressing gown to rippling like a troubled scarlet sea. His face was seamed and wasted; obviously once striking, the features had fallen into a mandarin desiccation. It was an old man's face, sure enough. "Well, you know, that's quite a question; yes. I called room service around seven, I think it was, and that's when the, the weakness came over me. A terrible weakness, in all my bones . . ."

Doctor Lenardi glanced at the two empty wine glasses on the coffee table. "Yes. Go on."

"That's all there is. I think that I just sort of blacked out, then. Must have knocked the phone off its hook." The man swallowed: it bobbled the knot of his white silk scarf. "Am I . . . all right?" he murmured.

"That," Doctor Lenardi said, making no effort whatever to conceal his astonishment, "is a moot question. There does not appear to be anything the matter with you, in particular——"

"Thank Heaven!"

"On the other hand, Mister Simms, I would say—and the opinion is based upon some twenty-five years of intensive practice—that you are, in general, the most singularly run-down human I've ever dealt with. There may be nothing wrong with you, but I give you my word that there is nothing right. May I ask your age?"

"Certainly," Edward Simms said. "I am twenty-eight."

"Please be serious."

"Twenty-eight is my exact age, I tell you. Here, look at my driver's license!"

Doctor Lenardi emitted a gust of wind. With difficulty he restrained himself from remarking that the patient looked closer to *forty*-eight. "Then," he said, "you are tremendously over-worked."

The man called Simms smiled strangely. "Perhaps." He glanced at his watch and made a futile effort to rise. "Doctor," he said, with considerable urgency, "I apologize for having detained you this long. I am perfectly all right now. If you will only give me a slight stimulant, something to get me ticking again, that is, I'll be much obliged."

"My dear chap, what you need is precisely the reverse. A sedative——"

"No, no!" Simms was looking at his watch again, and

shaking his head. "You don't understand. It's absolutely vital that I get a *stimulant*. Doctor——" His voice grew meaningful, edged with innuendo. "If I were to tell you that I am expecting a young lady, would that change your mind?"

Doctor Lenardi sat down abruptly. He gazed at the thin young man who did not appear to have the strength to pull himself off the bed, and tried to assimilate what he'd heard. He looked at the champagne. At the man's dressing gown . . .

"You're joking, Simms."

"Not a bit of it. See here now, I happen to be a man of science, too, and I know perfectly well what I need. I'm willing, if necessary, to *buy* what I ask. Name your price. Ten dollars? Fifty? A hundred?" Edward Simms reached out and grasped the other's lapels. *"Please,"* he said desperately; there was the fire of delirium in his eyes. The eyes searched for agreement, then hardened. "I'll—I'll tell you *exactly* why I need your help in this. Will you listen?"

Doctor Lenardi was about to answer in the negative, but he paused. It occurred to him, suddenly, that this man was familiar. In a peculiar, elusive way, familiar . . .

Well, let the fellow rave, let the poor wretch rave on, perhaps it would put him to sleep. "Very well, Mister Simms. But I will have to administer a sedative afterwards in any case."

"No; you'll see." The young man fell back against the pillows like a crumbling tower. "I've kept it to myself so long," he whispered, in a voice already distant; "So terribly long. It's good to be able to tell someone, at last, now that it's almost finished . . ."

Doctor Lenardi pulled his chair closer to the bed.

He removed his glasses.

"Go on, Mister Simms. I'm listening."

Beautiful women (the young man began, in muted tones) are my sickness; I know that now, but I did not always know it. Years ago, when I was terribly young and very naive, when life was hopscotch and marbles and jam sandwiches, and I had no glimpse of the adult world, I realized one thing: that boys and girls were *different*. And the difference disturbed me, though for what reason I could scarcely guess. I was one thing and girls were another, you see. But what? *How* were we different, in what way?

I used to wander about, turning the problem over in my mind. And it seemed to make no sense. But then I would catch sight of a particularly striking six-year-old with golden pigtails, and I knew that I must be right.

It was a thorny problem, but one which did not, apparently, concern my friends, or disturb them, so I tried earnestly to dismiss it. But I was not successful in this.

I found that while I went about my boyhood in a normal fashion, playing football and baseball and the like, my mind was ever ready to stray. I would be in the act of executing a forward pass, or bunting for a one base run, when my eyes would fall upon the smiling face of a beautiful girl, and I would be lost, lost.

Of course, later, in the private schools my parents sent me to, I learned that my earlier suspicions had been correct—there was indeed a difference between boys and girls—and the vaguely disturbed feeling became one of intense curiosity. But *a priori* knowldge was insufficient to quell my interest: you cannot appreciate the bouquet of a rare wine if it is forever sealed in the bottle. So I was more than pleased when a young coed named Bobbi indicated a fondness for me. She was an entrancing creature, 34-24-36, as attractive as she was cooperative, and we saw the stars up close. And that, I felt sure, was the end of my obsession. The bottle, so to speak, had been unsealed.

Time passed. I'd buried myself in my hobbies, which were science, mathematics and chemistry—with an occasional belt at electronics—as, I suppose, compensation for my obsessive curiosity; now I returned to them with vigor. All was well.

Then, on a day no different than any other, the terrible trouble began.

I'd set out for the parts house to purchase a coil of light wire, part of a perpetual motion experiment. I was crossing the street, with no other thought in my head, when, utterly without warning, I saw her walking toward me—a tall, slender yet curvesome female, regal as a goddess, with skin the color of white marble and hair the exotic tint of burnished copper; 35-24-36.

The old feeling had returned! I couldn't understand it. I had thought all my problems were solved. With Bobbi's sweet help, that feeling had been routed—for good, I'd thought. But *now!* . . .

I was deeply disturbed. That did not, however, prevent me from acting.

With what amounted to ferocity, I wheeled, overtook the girl, and, before I knew what was happening, made my overtures. They were rebuffed, needless to say, but I persisted, and (to spare you the details) it was not long before Clara and I had got to the hand-holding stage.

I think it was my relative inexperience that charmed her. Like a feminine Virgil, to my Dante, she seemed to take a grim delight in her role of guide, and would often laugh at my enthusiastic but hopelessly amateur stumblings. But whatever her shortcomings in matters of finesse, it must be said of Clara that she was thorough. I had entered the Undiscovered Country a stranger; now, thanks to her, I was a pioneer.

It was an enormously pleasant idyll, satisfactory in every sense.

Bobbi had begun my education, Clara had completed it. Surely now, I felt, I would be rid of the Feeling and could devote myself to other, less earthly, pursuits.

But——

Some weeks later, a very odd thing happened. On my way to Clara's apartment, I caught a glimpse of a blonde college girl. She was like the rest of them—young; uniformed in dark skirt and white sweater; approximately 36-24-36—but there was a then indefinable something about her that compelled me to stop in my tracks. The sway of her hips, perhaps; the jaunty bounce of her hair—I didn't know. I knew only that the Feeling was back, and in full force.

I started after her until she'd disappeared from view, then continued to Clara's. All evening I tried to analyze what it was that was wrong. Then, at a horribly ironic moment, I discovered the answer.

Clara was wonderful, she gave me all I could possibly ask and I could not have been fonder of her; yet, I wanted this stranger.

It was a crushing discovery and one which caused no little self-examination.

But I could no longer think of anything but that college girl, I tell you! She permeated my dreams. I saw her everywhere. She would not, absolutely would *not* leave me.

I am here to tell you that locating her was no easy task. But perseverance pays. I found her eventually at a malt shop, in the company of a dozen football players . . .

Well, Eunice and I began to see a bit of each other, as the phrase goes. I think it was my relative experience that charmed her. We traveled to remote picnic grounds, attended fairs and carnivals, and presently the Feeling, and my sadness at parting with Bobbi and Clara, abated.

Until I saw Carmen, 37-25-36 . . .

I spent an entire month and a great deal of my parents' money barraging this one with my attentions, and finally, with great reluctance, she granted me a date. We had no more than stepped out of her house, however, when I saw the flashing ankles of a honey blonde in a tight jersey. It all but drove me out of my mind. I could hardly wait to be done with Carmen and go after the blonde!

And so, I am afraid, it went.

A psychiatrist allayed my fears somewhat—and I had begun to wonder what the devil was the matter with me, anyway—by reporting that there was nothing really unusual in my case. "It is as if you owned an original painting by Rembrandt," he said. "It is beautiful. You love it. No other painting is more satisfying to you. But—there are other pictures in the gallery; and, because you are exceptionally sensitive to beauty, you cannot ignore them. You pass a Botticelli and your heart stops. You pause by a Van Gogh. Again the frustration. You see a fine Picasso . . ."

Shortly afterwards, my father offered similar diagnosis. "My son," he said, placing an affectionate hand upon my shoulder, "I know what you feel, believe me. And it's a terrible, terrible thing. But there's no way around it. You can't have them all."

Which seemed logical enough. At the time.

I waited for the calm acceptance to come, of course; for that moment when, fully matured, I would realize the patent impossibility of what must be my subconscious ambition and, like other men, content myself with a less rewarding arrangement.

Unfortunately, nothing happened.

Except that my condition, if we may refer to it as that, worsened. I was disturbed most of the time now, riddled with nameless hungers at the increasingly frequent sights of beautiful women. And whenever I would hear someone say, joshingly, "Well, remember, Simms boy, just remember now —you can't have 'em all!" I would find myself bristling.

At last, when I was sure that I could not continue to exist in the midst of such intolerable frustration, I sat down and took stock.

They say you cannot have them all, I thought.

And then I thought: Why not?

It was a beginning. In just such a way, I imagine, are most great advances made. One man asking himself: *Why not?*

The answer did not come exactly in a flash. I thought about it until my mind was all but paralyzed, and things looked very dark, indeed. In the first place, I ruminated, there were countless thousands—perhaps millions—of beautiful women on Earth. And even if I could locate them, what guarantee was there I would be uniformly successful? I was handsome enough then, charming enough, rich enough; but there would always be obstinate cases, there had been before. Also, counting time for courting, wooing, and what not, there would—and this was an important point—be *a new crop* before I had even made a dent in the first! Mathematically, it was far from encouraging.

Then, in the very act of loading the pistol that would disperse my woe, I asked myself the question that was to become, so to speak, the opening wedge.

I asked myself what I meant when I said *beautiful woman*. What did the term imply? Was it *really* as indefinable as all that?

I remembered the women who had attracted me and thought about them carefully, seeking a connecting link. There had to be one.

And there was.

You've heard the expression, "She may be pretty, but she's just not my type?"

It was this that gave me my greatest lead. Every man is attracted by a particular *type* of female; and there should be more-or-less consistent characteristics determining these types.

Things started to look up. This information meant that the field was unquestionably narrower than I'd thought. Three more questions remained, however; and they were not unimportant.

Number One: Exactly how many women of my type existed?

Number Two: Where were they?

Number Three: How could I get at them?

There was, you understand, no available method of answering these questions. But I knew that equally complex problems were being solved in the various universities and laboratories by electronic calculators, and—call it faith, call it desperation, or sheer naiveté—I was confident that a machine could be constructed to do the work.

However, such a machine would cost a large fortune, and I had but a small fortune, left to me by my parents, God rest them. So I was thrown upon the resources of my imagination. In time the answer came, though, I am proud to say.

At the local university, there was one of the largest and most modern electronic calculators in existence. It was an incredibly complex device, considerably more advanced than its rather primitive predecessors. It could do everything but dance a hornpipe, I was told, and they were working on that. So, in high fettle, and with respect for the instinct which had early turned me to a study of electronics, I immediately set to the problem of building what we may term an "extension" of the machine. Endless weeks passed, and failure after failure confronted me, but at last all that remained was devising a method of attaching the addition to the main body without calling the attention of officials or guards. It was a knotty business, but a way was found.

By now I knew to the last minute detail what sort of women I wanted—they had to be no younger than eighteen, no older than forty; they had to possess an intellectual potential; etc.—and had these specifications broken down in code upon

a series of tapes. My extension would be fed these data and
would then submit them to the giant calculator (which, in a
moment of whimsy, I had decided to call Procurer One).

Upon receiving the information, my machine lit up like
a grotesque Christmas tree and began to whine. It was almost
frightening, the noises it made; but after a few hours, it
quieted and was still and presently a scroll dropped into the
tray.

I breathed a silent hallelujah.

Procurer One had ingested my data and had ascertained
exactly the geographical and climatical, also the generic,
conditions likely to produce the type of women I sought.

It gave the number and the locations.

There were five hundred and sixty-three of them. Mostly
they were in America—which was no handy coincidence,
for I knew that however exotic and *interesting* the foreign
product might be, it was seldom more than that. There were
exceptions, of course, primarily in Sweden and Britain and
France; and a number of surprising contradictions—a Ta-
hitian, for example, was on the list; a total of four in Ran-
goon; and so on—but the bulk lay within the boundaries of
my own continent.

You can consider my delight.

I attacked the last phase of the project with something
akin to frenzy. Knowing the address of Tiffany's, I realized,
did not automatically put a diamond necklace about one's
throat. One must be able to afford the necklace, or—one must
be an accomplished thief.

In this connection, I eliminated all of the obvious answers
and reduced the matter to one incontrovertible equation:
Mutual attraction = Success of the plan. There could be no
slip-ups, no depending upon circumstances, and certainly no
unrealistic faith in my own charm, however devastating. No:
there must be, simply, a straightforward method by which
I could be absolutely assured of at least acquiescence to my
designs—a problem, as you can see, chockablock with
difficulties.

An aphrodisiac, of course, was what I needed. But in
what form? Perfume? Perhaps; but there would be imponder-
able drawbacks—an unruly wisp of breeze, for instance,
might throw everything off balance. One would have to be
sure to "hit the target," as it were, yet if the target happened
to be in a mixed crowd . . .

I decided at length upon a potion. Potions were once
very much the vogue, and a careful survey of Medieval literature convinced me that here was the one sure way; it
also convinced me that although we take it for granted that
the so-called Love Draught is a mythical and non-existent

form of wish fulfillment, it is nothing of the kind. As with stained glass, it is merely an art we had lost.

Reviving the art was not an easy matter, you may be sure, but I believe I mentioned that chemistry was one of my childhood loves. You will therefore not be shocked to learn that, in due time, I evolved sort of an herbal tea—I shan't become tiresome by going into the exact recipe—and that this brew sufficed for the purpose. One sip of it, in fact, was quite enough to engender *rapport* in the stoniest female heart, and two sips—ah well, enough to say that I was satisfied.

So, I must admit, were the first stray recipients of my experimentation.

But there was still work to be done. To go about it haphazardly would spell doom as surely as if nothing had been accomplished; for there was the unalterable fact that scores of *girls* would be leaping out of their chrysalises, so to say, and becoming *women*. As I've pointed out, nothing below the age of eighteen would do for me, but consider the sixteen and seventeen-year-olds all crouched, waiting to spring into the fray!

I therefore made up a schedule.

It was, as one might suspect, fantastically demanding. It granted me an absolute maximum of two days per case. Fortunately, there were certain areas where overlapping and doubling-up were feasible; otherwise I'd have been licked. In any event, it *could* be done. On paper, at least.

My work was now cut out for me.

I girded my loins, as they say, and began at once, enplaning the following morning for Europe. According to Procurer One, a ravishing brunette by the name of Françoise Simon, 37-25-36, lived on the outskirts of Montauban. She was married, without children, and of a generally sunny temperament. The machine, of course, had not been able to supply all of this information—I'd had to fall back on a number of private detectives—but I was certain of my facts. About the husbands, or similar ties, I knew nothing; but it didn't matter, particularly, as my system was sufficiently flexible to allow for contingencies.

I went straight to the village, located the cottage, and, making sure that the phial containing the potion was with me, rapped on the door.

It was opened by a young woman in a peasant blouse and full skirt.

Procurer One had not been whistling *Dixie!* From her frank Norman features there shone a warmth and honesty and fire that sent excitement flashing through me.

I recovered my aplomb and inquired, in French, the way to the nearest bus stop.

She told me that there were not such things as buses in this vicinity, but would I not step inside to take the chill off?

"Is your husband home?" I asked, noncommittally. She shook her head. I stepped inside.

Francoise blushed and made conversation about the weather but I could see that she was thinking of other things. When she leaned over to light my cigarette, I could almost feel the heat of her blood. "Monsieur," she said—actually it was "Monsieur l'Americain"—"would you care for a glass of brandy?" I nodded enthusiastically and, when the drinks were poured, managed to add a drop of my herbal tea to hers—though it did seem piling Scylla on Charybdis, or however that goes.

Upon the first swallow, Francoise lost even the vestigial reticence she had displayed and, literally, sprang across the room. I was not quite prepared, but I managed to catch her and soon it was raining clothes.

The whole thing was enormously pleasant. But my schedule did not permit of divertissement. I told her that she was exquisite, said "Merci beaucoup" or something like that and beat a hasty exit. From the way she sobbed and clung to my legs, I knew that I would have to cut down on the quantity of the draughts: even a single drop was entirely too powerful!

I seemed to hear her savage cries of woe all the way to my plane.

I proceeded to Boulogne, and there called upon a delightful creature named Laurette, 38-25-37: it was an equally satisfactory interlude. Laurette lived alone, fortunately, and so it did not require more than an hour, all told. Then I was off again, headed for Paris.

Procurer One had come through magnificently! With the foreign entries out of the way, I returned to America and settled down to a program of activity which, owing to its rigorousness, if not to its nature, would have impressed the most earnest toiler. Implacably I kept to the schedule, and there were not, I'm proud to say, more than a dozen occasions when the allotted time was exceeded. These were due to sudden moves, biological upsets over which no man has dominion, slight difficulties with relatives, and what have you.

Of course, there were problems with the philtre, particularly in the case of Mildred C., a teetotaler, but these were circumvented in divers ways. With Mildred, for example, it was necessary to tamper with the morning milk; whereas with Josie F., the hypochondriac, I was forced to modify the contents of her throat spray. Frequently I was thrown for a loss, but never for very long: nothing deflected me seriously from my course then.

Cutting a swath through California, an unusually rich vein, I began to work my way across the States. Albuquerque, Boise, Snohomish, Portland, Oklahoma City, Chicago, Wheeling, Detroit—these were the greatest concentrations, though there were hundreds of tiny outposts, some not even listed on the map, which yielded plenty, too. Tall ones, short ones, dark ones, light ones; the intellectual type with glasses and the innocent farm type; redheads, blondes, brunettes—they fell like wheat under the scythe. I left a wake of memorable evenings, and shattered reputations. True, some were more diverting than others: howbeit, I rolled on, relentless, dauntless, a veritable juggernaut. No power on Earth could stop me!

After a while, however, I must confess that some of the edge had gone out of the project. Not that I was tiring spiritually, you understand; but one is, after all, flesh and blood. Subsequent to number three hundred and seventy-four, I think there was less spontaneous joy than determination in it for me. To be brutally honest, I was becoming physically fagged of the whole thing—and I shudder now to think of the times when I came so close to throwing in the towel. Although I was in bed most of the while, I slept but little; and when I passed the four hundred mark, I found that my weight was dropping precipitously. From a robust one-ninety-six, I now weighed in at one hundred and fourteen pounds! My eyes had taken on their present glaze. I felt tired all of the time. Everything began to ache.

But Simmses are not quitters. When they start a thing, they finish it.

I went on.

The days melted into the nights. Each conquest became a supreme effort of will. I traveled like a somnambulist, dumbly carrying out my duties; and by the time the number had been whittled down to less than fifty, I was in the position of having to be constantly fortified with drugs, hormones, and other medications. I cannot describe to you the agonies of spirit and body I endured as the end approached. Logically I ought to have collapsed from overwork then; but, somehow, I was able to forge ahead.

Then, one day, as I lay gasping, I discovered a remarkable thing. I was down to ten. Ten more, and the project would be a *fait accompli!*

Despite my haggard look, and the fact that I was weak to the point of total exhaustion, I gathered together every last trace of my strength, and continued.

Isabella R., 39-23-35, number ten—Indianapolis—was shocked by my appearance but overwhelmed by my potion. In less than twenty minutes, she succumbed.

A practical nurse in Dubuque, Dorothy S., 40-25-37, offered to look after me, and in a way she did. A day for her.

Sondra the stenographer, Old Lyme, Conn., 41-24-38, was a pushover.

Then there was Ivy, formerly Miss Improved Ball Bearings and in 1953 voted "The Girl We'd Most Like to Retouch" by the Association of Commercial Photographers—42-25-37: a two day job.

Gloria the proper Bostonian, at an astounding 42½-24-34, followed; and the genuinely accomplished stripper Emma Samuelson (known professionally as "Peachy" Kean); and Pearl and Sally and Bertha. Then there was Detroit's Natasha, a fiery, mordant pseudo-intellectual with advanced views and retarded intentions. . . . Procurer One had shrewdly pierced her frosty exterior and added her to the list. I wasted no time.

But their names are unimportant. Important only that I was able to check them off.

It was at this point—this crucial, critical point—that an accident occurred. An accident that nearly ruined all my plans.

On my way to this city, where the remaining two women resided, the plane encountered foul weather. The pilot made the announcement: an announcement that was merely annoying to the other passengers, but which struck me with unnameable horror. He had been advised, by radio, to ground the plane at a small rural airport and wait for clearer weather . . .

Weak though I was, the news wrenched me to my feet, tore a cry of frustration and despair from my throat: *"Wait!? I cannot wait! I must be there on schedule! Time . . . is of the essence . . . my plans . . . all my plans . . ."* But the effort had proved too much for my weakened body. I blacked out, and I was soon to find myself marking time—precious, irrevocable time!—in a cheerless hotel in a cheerless town the name of which I never bothered to learn. Hours. Priceless hours! Do they seem unimportant to you, Doctor? Yes, they do, I am sure. But, you see—the nearer I drew to the end of my task, the more critical the time element became! One slip—such as this—one delay, and the delicate balance of the whole cycle might well be upset! The seventeen-year-olds would attain maturity, become eligible for my conquest, become part of the symbolic All that was now my *raison d'etre*, my obsession, my curse . . .

Do you understand? If this thing happened—if that immense armada of girls blossomed into womanhood before I completed my task—*I would have to begin all over again!* All over again: consider that, Doctor! Look at me, think of my condition, and then consider what that would mean. All over again? A wasted, spent, exhausted man, near death? Impossible! I waited six hours, but the weather did not clear. I asked about trains. There were no trains. And buses: I asked about buses. Yes, there was a bus . . . if you could call it that. It seems you took it to the adjacent county, where you transferred to another bus which took you to a place where you got a taxi (if you were lucky) which would transport you to the Greyhound station . . .

I looked once at the overcast sky, and took the bus. If you could call it that.

And, twenty-eight hours later, shaken to jelly, wracked with pain, held together only by tenacity and vitamin pills, I arrived here to make my last two conquests.

The first, a waitress over on Fifth Street, gasped when I entered the restaurant.

"What will you have, sir?" she asked, obviously uncertain whether to give me a glass of water or call an emergency clinic.

"What have you got?" I joshed, being careful not to chuckle. The drugs kept the pain down, and it hurt only when I laughed.

She leaned forward to place the silverware, and I felt like a tourist at the base of Mount Rushmore. "Poached eggs," I murmured, and when the meal was finished, I tucked half of a hundred dollar bill underneath my napkin, together with a note reading: "For the other half, meet me after work." A crude maneuver, perhaps, but generally effective.

We met and had cocktails. Then we went to my hotel. Poor creature, I think it was the first time she'd ever tasted good champagne . . .

When she left, I tried to sleep, but I could not sleep. How did Edison feel a few hours before he switched on the first electric light? Or Shakespeare, just before he dashed off *Hamlet?* I could only taste, again and again, the heady draught of Victory. One more, I kept saying, and the everlasting, long-enduring dream of my life would be realized! I'd be satisfied, for in essence I would have had every beautiful woman—beautiful, to me—on the list. All that existed when the list was made.

All.

The next morning I saw that in my excitement I had neglected to bring along the proper drugs, and even the vital hormones—but it didn't trouble me. I would need no artificial aids now. I therefore showered and shaved and dressed in one of my better-padded suits (so that I would not look quite so resurrected) and checked out.

Then, shaking with anticipation, I registered at a hotel hard by the site of Number Five Hundred and Sixty-three—this very hotel—and proceeded to the lady's house. It was a brownstone, very old and mellow-mossy. I opened the wicket gate and went to the heavy oak door and knocked.

It was opened presently by the queen of them all, a truly incredible woman. Short curly black hair, a Mona Lisa smile, blue-green burning eyes; 43-25-36, give or take a quarter-inch. She was clad in a dainty flowered house dress.

"What," she asked, in a throaty contralto, "can I do for you?"

I couldn't help smiling at that. "I represent a new firm, Kool-Kola, Inc.," I said, "and I have here a sample of our product. It is a dietetic soda pop, yet it has all the zest and effervescence of sweet drinks. Won't you try a taste?" I opened the bottle of pop and handed it to her.

"Well," she said, "if you'll leave it here, I'll be glad——"

"Please," I interrupted: this time I simply could not wait. "It's necessary for me to make a report, and I have a great many more houses to visit. Just a taste, just to tell me your reaction . . ."

She cocked her head to one side, and I was afraid I'd gone too far, then she laughed, shrugged, and put the bottle to her lips. She swallowed.

"Very nice," she said; then all but swooned. I'd put in four drops, to be doubly, or quadruply, safe: at this stage of the game, I could take no chances. There was no longer a margin for error. I had to attain this final one that night —or fail forever in my task.

I caught her and asked if I might come in. She told me no, this was impossible, as her husband was home and, she went on to explain, he was many years older than she and of a violently jealous nature. "I don't dare think of what he'd do . . ."

I said, "Very well, then it's up to you to make the necessary arrangements. I shall be waiting at this address."

She kissed me hard on the mouth, nodded and whispered: "I'll be there, tonight. Somehow. I promise!"

I returned to the hotel and spent the day trembling. At five-thirty I changed into my dressing gown. At seven I called room service for the champagne and candle.

Then I collapsed.

You know the rest . . .

Edward Simms was shaking like a blade of grass in a sirocco. He had spoken slowly and carefully, as if each word were a separate achievement; now he lay back, panting.

"So you see," he said, "why it is important for me to regain my strength. If I am the slightest bit tardy in this matter, everything will be thrown off. A new crop will spring up. And—you *do* understand?"

Doctor Lenardi, who had a somewhat dazed expression on his face, said, "Yes," in a voice equally dazed. "Yes, indeed."

"Then you'll do it? Now? At once?"

"Do it?" The elderly man shook his head and seemed to claw his way back to reality. "Mister Simms, you know, I think that from now on you're going to be rid of your troubles. Yes, now, I really think that."

"Thank you, sir!"

"Not at all." Doctor Lenardi's face had become a complacent mask. He got up and went to the telephone and mumbled something into the black mouthpiece. Then he returned and withdrew a hypodermic from the black bag. "Your arm, please."

"Doctor, you do believe me, don't you? I realize it's a pretty farfetched story, but it's essential that you understand I'm telling the absolute truth."

"Now, now. Your arm."

Simms lifed his right arm. "This is, I presume," he said weakly, "the stimulant——"

The physician grunted. He held the needle so that it hovered directly above the large vein. "As it happens, I had to phone down to the drugstore for what we need, but it'll be here in a jiffy. Meanwhile this will keep you calm. But first, you know, I would appreciate one last piece of information regarding your extraordinary adventure. Call it plain old scientific curiosity . . ."

"Yes?"

"This woman you're expecting—the one who'll, ah, round out the experiment . . . Do you recall her name?"

Edward Simms furled his brow and fell into deep concentration; then he snapped his fingers. "Alice," he said. "Alice Lenardi."

"Ah."

The needle descended.

The young man winced. Then he was quiet for many long minutes. "Doctor——"

There was a rap at the door. Doctor Lenardi leaped from his chair, crossed the room and returned with a small package in his hands. "Now, then," he said pleasantly, removing a bottle from the cardboard and pouring a quantity of the bottle's contents into a wine glass. "Drink this down."

Edward Simms blinked questioningly and gulped the odd fluid.

Once he'd finished, he said: "When will I begin to feel fit again?"

"Oh, I should say in about two weeks."

Simms' eyes widened. "T-two weeks! But——"

"You see," Doctor Lenardi said, chuckling, "I thought I recognized you, but I wasn't sure. When you grow old, that's what happens. You're not sure about things. I was in the living room when you called at our house, heard some of your talk, caught a glimpse of you; didn't think much of it at the time."

Now Simms' eyes threatened to leap from their sockets. The gaunt man struggled to rise from the bed and failed.

"I have, of course, known about you and Alice for a long while—that's why I made a point of returning home this morning unexpectedly. Eh? Oh, she's clever; always was; but . . . so am I." The physician chuckled again. "Thing is, I was only fifty when she married me, and for a while it looked as though it might work out; but now I'm sixty-two and she's barely thirty-five. And like all women in their prime, she's getting restless. Tied to an antique, an 'elderly gentleman'. Longing for strong, young arms—although I really don't quite see how yours qualify." Doctor Lenardi sighed; then he frowned. "I've known about the recondite meetings, Simms. The trips she made into town—to do the shopping!— and all the shoddy, sneaking ruses by which you both hoped to deceive me!"

"It isn't true!" Edward Simms made a strangulated sound. "You've got it all wrong. I never met your wife before this morning."

"Come, *come,* I'm not as old as all that. Nor am I naive!"

"But—Good Lord, do you think for a moment that I'd have told you my story if your suspicions were correct? Would I have——"

"Don't, please, take me for a fool, Simms. You got a room as near to Alice as you could without actually moving in with us. For reasons I'd rather not dwell on, you collapsed; and, since I am the closest doctor in the neighborhood, they naturally called me. Recognizing me, you thought fast and told me this fantastic tale, doubtless in the hope that I would consider you insane and therefore not liable. A low sort of dodge, boy, and an unsuccessful one."

The young man, who looked older than ever, moaned. His eyelids were coming together. "I swear to you," he whispered, "that every word was the truth. It was nothing personal; I'd never even laid eyes on your wife. As far as I was concerned, she was just Number Five Hundred and Sixty-three . . ."

Doctor Lenardi smiled. "You're a convincing actor," he said. "Really a remarkable talent—you should have gone on the stage! I don't, of course, believe you. But never let it be said that Leo Lenardi lacked vision. The injection I administered was a sedative, very powerful; the oral medication, on the other hand——"

Edward Simms was by this time a definition of terror, a synonym for fright; he stared out from frog eyes. "The oral medication ——" he croaked.

"Well," the older man said, "let's just say that it will keep you 'on the bench' for a couple of weeks. By which time, if there *is* anything to your story, a number of girls—a considerable number—will have celebrated their eighteenth birthdays. And then I suppose you'll have to start all over again. Except, you won't be in any condition for that, will you?"

Doctor Lenardi recognized the quick, tentative, feminine knocking at the door. He snapped his bag and rose.

"You see, Mister Simms," he said, "It's true. You *can't* have them all!"

Fritzchen

I T HAD once been a place for dreaming. For lying on your back in the warm sand and listening to the silence and making faraway things seem real. The finest place in all the world, for all the reasons that ever were.

But it had stopped being this long ago. Now, he supposed, it wasn't much more than a fairly isolated cove, really: a stretch of land bleeding into the river at one of its wide points, cut off like a tiny peninsula; a grey, dull place, damp and unnatural from its nights beneath the tidewaters—decaying, sinking slowly, glad to be eaten by the river. As Edna had put it: Just a lot of dirty wet sand. Not a place for dreaming anymore.

Mr. Peldo shifted his position and sighed as he remembered. He took from his mouth the eviscerated end of a lifeless cigar, flipped it away distastefully, watched as the mud whitened and oozed where it landed and the spiders lumbered clumsily away in fright.

The spiders made him think of his snakes. And soon he was thinking, too, of rabbits and goldfish and ooo wow-wow puppy dogs, all flop-eared and soft, common as a blade of grass—and his bread-and-butter. His living.

He was almost relieved to hear Edna's coarse voice beside him.

"Jake."

She would now make some complaint about the foolishness of this whole trip, adding that it made her sinuses runny.

"Yes, Chicken, what is it?"

"Go and see to Luther."

Go-and-see-to-Luther. Eight-year-old kid ought to be able to see to himself, by God.

"All right. Where'd he go?"

"Somewhere over in that direction, there by the trees. I'm worried he might think of going in the water or get lost."

Mr. Peldo grunted softly as he pulled his weight erect. Exertion. Oh well, that was all right. Soon he would have started with the frustration, thinking about the lousy pet shop and his lousy life. Better to hunt in the trees for spoiled brats.

18

It was hard going. Had to end in a few yards, of course, but still, it *was* . . . exciting, in a small, tired, remembering way. He pushed aside a drenched fern, and another, needles of wet hitting him.

"Luther."

Mr. Peldo continued for a few feet, until he could distinctly hear the current. A wall of leaves rose at the curve, so he stopped there, let the last of the thrill fall loose from him, then listened.

"Luther Hustle, boy."

Only the water. The vibrant, treacherous river water, hurrying to join the Sound and to go with it to the ocean.

"Hey, *Luu-therr.*"

Mr. Peldo stabbed his hands into the foliage and parted it. From the window, by peering close, he could see his son's back.

"Boy, when your father calls you, *answer* him, hear!"

Luther looked around disinterestedly, frowned and turned his head. He was sitting in the mud, playing.

Mr. Peldo felt the anger course spastically through him. He pushed forward and stopped, glared.

"Well?"

Then he glimpsed what his son had been playing with. Only a glimpse, though.

"Fritzchen!" Luther pronounced defiantly, shielding something in his hands. "Fritzchen—like I wanted to call Sol's birdie."

Mr. Peldo felt his eyes smart and rubbed them. "What have you got there?"

"Fritzchen, Fritzchen," the boy wailed. There was another sound then. A sound like none Mr. Peldo had ever heard: high-pitched, whiny, discordant. The sound an animal makes when it is in pain.

Mr. Peldo reached down and slapped at his son's mouth, which had fastened like a python's about the calf of his left leg. Then, by holding his thumb and forefinger tightly on Luther's nose, he forced him to drop the thing he had been hiding.

It fell onto the slime and began to thrash.

Mr. Peldo gasped. He stared for a moment, like an idiot at a lampshade, his mouth quite open and his eyes bulged.

A thin voice from across the trees called: *"Jake is there anything wrong? Answer me!"*

He pulled off his sport coat and threw it about the squirmy thing. "No, no, everything's okay. Kid's just acting up is all. Hold your horses!"

"Well, hurry! It's getting dark!"

Mr. Peldo blocked Luther's charge with his foot.

"Where did you get that?"

Luther did not answer. He glowered sullenly at the ground, mumbling. "He's mine. I found him. You can't have him."

"Where did it come from?" Mr. Peldo demanded.

Luther's lower lip resembled a bloated sausage. Finally he jerked his thumb in the direction of the river bank.

"You can talk!"

Luther whimpered, tried once again to get at the wriggling bundle on the sand, sat down and said, "I found him in the water. I snuk up on him and grabbed him when he wasn't looking. Now he's mine and you can't have——."

But Mr. Peldo, having recovered himself, had plucked off the coat and was staring.

A place for dreaming.

Roadsters that would go over two hundred miles per hour. Promontoried chateaus with ten bathrooms. Coveys of lithe young temptresses, vacant-minded, full-bodied, infinitely imaginative, infinitely accessible . . .

"JAAAAke! Are you trying to scare me to death? It's cold and my sinuses are beginning to run!"

Luther looker at his father, snorted loudly and started for the trees.

"He's Fritzchen and he's *mine!*" he called back as he ran. "All right—I'll get even! You'll see!"

Mr. Peldo watched the small creature, fascinated, as all its legs commenced to move together, dwarfed, undeveloped legs, burrowing into the viscous ground. Shuddering slightly, he replaced the coat, gathered it into the form of a sack and started through the shrubbery.

Edna's nose had turned red. He decided not to show Fritzchen to her, for a while.

"Got no empties," Sol said slowly, eying the bundle Mr. Peldo held at arms' length. Sol didn't care for animals. He was old; his mind had fallen into a ravine; it paced the ravine; turned and paced, like a contented baboon. He was old.

Mr. Peldo waited for Edna and Luther to go around to the living quarters in the back. "Put the capuchin in with Bess," he said, then. "Ought to have a stout one. Hop to it, Sol, I can't stand here holding this all day."

" 'nother stray?"

"You—might say."

Sol shrugged and transferred the raucous little monkey from his carved wood cage to the parrot dome.

Then he looked back. Mr. Peldo was holding the jacket-bundle down on a table with both hands. Whatever was inside was moving in violent spasms, not the way a dog moves or a rabbit. There were tiny sounds.

"Give me a hand," Mr. Peldo said, and Sol helped him put the bundle, jacket and all, into the cage. They locked it.

"This'll do for a while," Mr. Peldo said, "until I can build a proper one. Now mind, Sol, you keep your mouth strictly shut about this. Shut."

Sol didn't answer. His nose had snapped upward and he held a conched hand behind his ear.

"Listen, you," Sol said.

Mr. Peldo took his fingers off the sport coat, which had begun to show a purplish stain through.

"First time it ever happened in sixteen years," Sol said.

The silence roared. The silent pet shop roared and burst and pulsed with tension, quiet electric tension. The animals didn't move anywhere in the room. Mr. Peldo's eyes darted from cage to cage, seeing the second strangest thing he had ever seen: unmoving snakes, coiled or supine, but still as though listening; monkeys hidden in far corners, haunched; rabbits— even their noses quiet and frozen—; white mice huddled at the bottom of mills that turned in cautious, diminishing arcs, frightened, staring creatures.

The phlegm in Mr. Peldo's throat racked loose.

Then it was quiet again. Though not exactly quiet.

Sol quit his survey of the animals and turned back to the occupant of the capuchin's cage. The sport jacket glistened with stain now and from within the dark folds there was a scrabbling and a small gurgling sound.

Then the jacket fell away.

"Tom-hell, Jake!" Sol said.

The animals had begun to scream, all of them, all at once.

"Not a word to anyone now, Sol! Promise."

Mr. Peldo feasted. He stared and stared, feeling satisfaction.

"What in glory is it?" Sol inquired above the din.

"A pet," Mr. Peldo answered, simply.

"Pet, hey?"

"We'll have to build a special cage for it," Mr. Peldo beamed. "Say, bet there ain't many like this one! No, sir. We'll have to read up on it so's we can get the feeding right and all . . ."

"*You* read up." Sol's eyes were large. The air was filled with the wild beating of birds' wings.

Mr. Peldo was musing. "By the way, Sol, what you suppose it could be?"

The old man cocked his head to one side, peered from slitted eyes, picked out the crumpled sport jacket quickly and let it fall to the floor. It dropped heavily and exuded a sick water smell. Sol shrugged.

"Cross between a whale," he said, "and a horsefly, near's I can see."

"Maybe it's valuable—you think?" Mr. Peldo's ideas were growing.

"Couldn't say. Most likely not, in the face of it."

The chittering sound rose into a sort of staccato wail, piercing, clear over the frantic pets.

"Where in thunder you get it?"

"He didn't. *I* did." It was Luther, scowling, in his night-clothes.

"Go to bed. Go away."

"I found Fritzchen in the water. He likes me."

"Out!"

"Dirty stinking rotten lousy rotten stealer!"

Sol put his fingers into his ears and shut his eyes.

Luther made a pout and advanced towards Fritzchen's cage. The sobbing noises ceased.

"He hadda lock you up. Yeah. *I* was gonna let you loose again." The boy glared at his father. "See how he loves me." Luther put his face up to the cage, and as he did so the small animal came forward, ponderously, with suctionlike noises from its many legs.

Mr. Peldo looked disinterested. He inspected his watchstem. Neither he nor Sol saw what happened.

Luther stamped his foot and yelled. The right side of his face was covered with something that gathered and dripped down.

"Luther!" It was Mr. Peldo's wife. She ran into the room and looked at the cage. "Oh, that nasty thing!" She stormed out, clutching her son's pink ear.

"Damn woman will drive me crazy," Mr. Peldo said. Then he noticed that the shop was quiet again. Sol had thrown the damp jacket over Fritzchen's cage. There was only the sobbing.

"Funny!"

Mr. Peldo bent down, lifted the end of the coat and put his face close. He jerked back with abnormal speed, swabbing at his cheek.

There was a sound like a drowning kitten's purr.

Luther stood in the back doorway. Hate and astonishment contorted his features. "That's all he cares about me when I only wanted to be good to him! Now he loves *you*, dirty rotten—."

"Look, boy, your father's getting might tired of—."

"Yeah, well, he'll be sorry."

Fritzchen began to chitter again.

When Mr. Peldo returned to the shop after dinner, he found a curious thing. Bess, the parrot, lay on her side, dead.

Everything else was normal. The animals were wakeful or somnolent but normal. Fritzchen's cage was covered with a canvas and there was silence from within.

Mr. Peldo inspected Bess and was horrified to discover the bird's condition. She lay inundated in an odd miasmic jelly which had hardened and was now spongey to the touch. It covered her completely. What was more, extended prodding revealed that something had happened to Bess's insides.

They were gone.

And without a trace. Even the bones. Bess was little more than skin and feathers.

Mr. Peldo recalled the substance that had struck his face when he examined Fritzchen's cage the last time. In a frenzy he pulled off the tarpaulin. But Fritzchen was there and the cage was as securely locked as ever.

And easily twenty feet from the parrot dome.

He went back and found the capuchin staring at him out of quizzical eyes.

Luther, of course. Monster boy. Spoiled bug of a child. He had an active imagination. Probably rigged the whole thing, like the time he emasculated the parakeet in an attempt to turn it inside out.

Mr. Peldo was ungratified that the animals had not yet gotten used to Fritzchen. They began their harangue, so he switched off the light and waited for his eyes to accustom themselves to the moonlight. Moonlight comes fast to small towns near rivers.

Fritzchen must be sleeping. Curled like a baby anaconda, legs slender filaments adhering to the cage floor, the tender tiny tail tucked around so that the tip rested just inside the immense mouth.

Mr. Peldo studied the animal. He watched the mouth especially, noting its outsized relationship to the rest of the body.

But—Mr. Peldo peered—could it actually be that Fritzchen was *larger?* Surely not. The stomach did seem fatter, yet the finely ground hamburger, the dish of milk, the oysters, sat to one side, untouched. Nor had the accommodating bathing and drinking pool been disturbed.

Then he noticed, for the first time, that the mouth had no teeth. There did not appear to be a gullet! And the spiny snout, with its florid green cup, was not a nose after all, for the nose was elsewhere.

But most curious of all, Fritzchen had grown. Oh, yes, grown. No doubt about it.

Mr. Peldo retired hours later with sparkling visions of wealth. He would contact—somebody appropriate—and sell his find for many hundreds of thousands of dollars. Then he would run away to Europe and play with a different woman every night until he died of his excesses.

He was awakened a short time later by Sol, who informed him that the bird of paradise and one dalmatian pup had died during the night. He knew because he'd heard the racket from clean across the street.

"Oh, not the ooo wow-wow," said Edna. "Not the liddle puppy!"

Luther sat up in bed, interested.

"How'd it happen?" Mr. Peldo said.

"Don't know. No good way for definite sure." Sol's eyelids almost closed. "Their innards is gone."

Edna put her head beneath the covers.

"Fritzchen?"

"Guess. Y'ough't'a do somethin' with that crittur. Bad actor."

"He got out—that it?"

"Hey-up. Or somebody let him out. Cage is all locked up tight as wax, 'n it wailin' like a banshee."

Mr. Peldo whirled to face his son, who stuck out his tongue.

"See here, young fellow, we're going to get to the bottom of this. If I find out that you—."

"Don't think t'was the lad," Sol said.

"Why not?"

"Wa'l . . . that there thing is thrice the size t'was yesterday when you brung'er in."

"No."

"No nothin'. Stomach's pooched out like it's fit to bust."

Mr. Peldo got up and rubbed his hand over his bald head.

"But look, Sol, if it didn't get out, and—Luther, you didn't let it out, did you?"

"No, ma'am."

"—then how we going to blame it? Maybe there's a disease going around."

"*I* know, *I* know," Luther sang, swinging his feet in the air. "His nose can go longer."

"Be still, boy."

"Well, it *can!* I saw it. Fritzchen did it on the beach—hit a bird 'way out over the water and he didn't move out of my hands."

"What happened to the bird, Luther?"

"Well, it got stuck up with this stuff Fritzchen has inside him, so it couldn't do anything. Then when it was all glued, Fritzchen pulled it back closer to him and shot out his nose and put his nose inside the bird's mou—"

Mr. Peldo felt his cheek, where the molasses had gathered that time. Both he and Luther had thought of it as an affectionate gesture, no worse than a St. Bernard leaping and pawing over you, raking your face, covering you with friendly, doggy slobber.

That's why Luther had gotten angry.

But Fritzchen wasn't being affectionate. It didn't work only because Fritzchen was too small, or they had been too big.

Mr. Peldo remembered Bess.

Edna poked her head out of the covers and said, "You listen to that! The neighbors will kill us!"

The sounds from the shop were growing stronger and louder and more chaotic.

Mr. Peldo dashed to the hall and returned with a telephone book. "Here," he said, tossing it to his wife, "get the numbers of all the zoos and museums."

"He's mine, he's mine!" Luther screeched.

Sol, who was old, said, "Jake, you never you mind about that. You just fished up something quaar, is all, and the best thing you can do is chuck 'er smack back where she come from."

"Edna—. Get those numbers, do you hear me? All the museums in the state. I'll be back."

The wailing had reached a crescendo now.

And Luther had disappeared.

Mr. Peldo put on a robe and hurried across the frosty lawn to the back door of the shop.

"Luther!"

The small boy had a box of kitchen matches, holding a cluster of these in his hands, lighting them and hurling them into Fritzchen's cage. The fiery sticks landed; there was a cry of pain and then the matches spluttered out against moist skin.

"Luther!"

"I wanted to be good to you," Luther was saying, "but then you hadda take up with *him!* Yeah, well, now you'll see!"

Mr. Peldo threw his son out the door.

The painful wail became an intermittent cry: a strange cry, not unmelodious.

Mr. Peldo looked into the great jeweled milk-white eyes of the creature and dodged as the snout unrolled like a party favor, spraying a fine crystal glaze of puce jam.

Fritzchen stood erect. He—it—had changed. There were

antennae where no antennae had been; many of the legs had developed claws; the mouth, which had been toothless the day before, was now filled with sharp brown needles. Fritzchen had been fifteen inches high when Mr. Peldo first saw him. Now he stood over thirty inches.

Still time, though. Time for everything.

Mr. Peldo looked at the animal until his eyes hurt; then he saw the newspaper on the floor. It was soaked with what looked like shreds of liquid soap-jelly, greenish, foul with the odor of seaweed and other things. On it lay a bird and a small dog.

He felt sad for a moment. But then he thought again of some of the things he had dreamed a long time ago, of what he had now, and he determined to make certain telephone calls.

A million dollars, or almost, probably. They'd—oh, they'd stuff Fritzchen, at all odds, or something like that.

"Dirty rotten lousy—."

Luther had come back. He had a crumpled-up magazine saturated with oil and lighter fluid. The magazine was on fire.

The monkeys and the rabbits and the mice and the goldfish and the cats and birds and dogs shrilled in fear. But Fritzchen didn't.

Fritzchen howled only once. Or lowed: a deep sound from somewhere in the middle of his body that seemed to come from his body and not just his mouth. It was an eerily mournful sound that carried a new tone, a tone of helplessness. Then the creature was silent.

By the time Mr. Peldo reached the cage, Luther had thrown inflammable fluid from a can. The fire burned fiercely.

"I *told* you," Luther said, pettishly.

When the fire was pulled and scattered and trampled out, an ugly thing remained in the cage. An ugly blackened thing that made no noise.

Luther began to cry.

Then he stopped.

And Mr. Peldo stopped chasing him.

Sol and Edna in the doorway didn't move either.

They all listened.

It could have been a crazed elephant shambling madly through a straw village . . .

Or a whale blind with the pain of sharp steel, thrashing and leaping in illimitable waters . . .

Or it could have been a massive hawk swooping in outraged vengeance upon the killers of her young . . .

The killers of her young!

In that moment before the rustling sound grew huge; before the windows shattered and the great nightmarish shadow came into the shop, Mr. Peldo understood the meaning of Fritzchen's inconsolable cries.

They were the cries of a lost infant for its mother.

Last Rites

Somewhere in the church a baby was shrieking. Father Courtney listened to it, and sighed, and made the Sign of the Cross. Another battle, he thought, dismally. Another grand tug of war. And who won this time, Lord? Me? Or that squalling infant, bless its innocence?

"In the Name of the Father, and of the Son, and of the Holy Ghost. Amen."

He turned and made his way down the pulpit steps, and told himself, Well, you ought to be used to it by now, Heaven knows. After all, you're a priest, not a monologist. What do you care about "audience reaction"? And besides, who ever listens to these sermons of yours, anyway—even under the best of conditions? A few of the ladies in the parish (though you're sure they never hear or understand a word), and, of course, Donovan. But who else?

Screech away, little pink child! Screech until you—no.

No, no. Ahhh!

He walked through the sacristy, trying not to think of Donovan, or the big city churches with their fine nurseries, and sound-proof walls, and amplifiers that amplified . . .

One had what one had: It was God's will.

And were things really so bad? Here there was the smell of forests, wasn't there? And in what city parish could you see wild flowers growing on the hills like bright lava? Or feel the earth breathing?

He opened the door and stepped outside.

The fields were dark-silver and silent. Far above the fields, up near the clouds, a rocket launch moved swiftly, dragging its slow thunder behind it.

Father Courtney blinked.

Of course things were not so bad. Things would be just fine, he thought, and I would not be nervous and annoyed at little children, if only—

Abruptly he put his hands together. "Father," he whispered, "let him be well. Let that be Your will!"

Then, deciding not to wait to greet the people, he wiped his palms with a handkerchief and started for the rectory.

28

The morning was very cold. A thin film of dew coated each pebble along the path, and made them all glisten like drops of mercury. Father Courtney looked at the pebbles and thought of other walks down this path, which led through a wood to Hidden River, and of himself laughing; of excellent wine and soft cushions and himself arguing, arguing; of a thousand sweet hours in the past.

He walked and thought these things and did not hear the telephone until he had reached the rectory stairs.

A chill passed over him, unaccountably.

He went inside and pressed a yellow switch. The screen blurred, came into focus. The face of an old man appeared, filling the screen.

"Hello, Father."

"George!" the priest smiled and waved his fist, menacingly. "George, why haven't you contacted me?" He sputtered. "Aren't you out of that bed yet?"

"Not yet, Father."

"Well, I expected it, I knew it. *Now* will you let me call a doctor?"

"No—" The old man in the screen shook his head. He was thin and pale. His hair was profuse, but very white, and there was something in his eyes. "I think I'd like you to come over, if you could."

"I shouldn't," the priest said, "after the way you've been treating all of us. But, if there's still some of that Chianti left . . ."

George Donovan nodded. "Could you come right away?"

"Father Yoshida won't be happy about it."

"Please. Right away."

Father Courtney felt his fingers draw into fists. "Why?" he asked, holding onto the conversational tone. "Is anything the matter?"

"Not really," Donovan said. His smile was brief. "It's just that I'm dying."

"And I'm going to call Doctor Ferguson. Don't give me any argument, either. This nonsence has gone far—"

The old man's face knotted. "No," he said, loudly. "I forbid you to do that."

"But you're ill, man. For all we know, you're *seriously* ill. And if you think I'm going to stand around and watch you work yourself into the hospital just because you happen to dislike doctors, you're crazy."

"Father, listen—*please*. I have my reasons. You don't understand them, and I don't blame you. But you've got to trust me. I'll explain everything, if you'll promise me you won't call *anyone*."

Father Courtney breathed unsteadily; he studied his friend's face. Then he said, "I'll promise this much. I won't contact a doctor until I've seen you."

"Good." The old man seemed to relax.

"I'll be there in fifteen minutes."

"With your Little Black Bag?"

"Certainly not. You're going to be all right."

"Bring it, Father. Please. Just in case."

The screen blurred and danced and went white.

Father Courtney hesitated at the blank telephone.

Then he walked to a table and raised his fists and brought them down hard, once.

You're going to get well, he thought. It isn't going to be too late.

Because if you are dying, if you really are, and I could have prevented it . . .

He went to the closet and drew on his overcoat.

It was thick and heavy, but it did not warm him. As he returned to the sacristy he shivered and thought that he had never been so cold before in all his life.

The Helicar whirred and dropped quickly to the ground. Father Courtney removed the ignition key, pocketed it, and thrust his bulk out the narrow door, wheezing.

A dull rumbling sifted down from the sky. The wake of fleets a mile away, ten miles, a hundred.

It's raining whales in our backyard, the priest thought, remembering how Donovan had described the sound once to a little girl.

A freshet of autumn leaves burst against his leg, softly, and for a while he stood listening to the rockets' dying rumble, watching the shapes of gold and red that scattered in the wind, like fire.

Then he whispered, "Let it be Your will," and pushed the picket gate.

The front door of the house was open.

He walked in, through the living-room, to the study.

"George."

"In here," a voice answered.

He moved to the bedroom, and twisted the knob.

George Donovan lay propped on a cloudbank of pillows, his thin face white as the linen. He was smiling.

"I'm glad to see you, Father," he said, quietly.

The priest's heart expanded and shrank and began to thump in his chest.

"The Chianti's down here in the night-table," Donovan gestured. "Pour some: morning's a good enough time for a dinner wine."

"Not now, George."

"Please. It will help."

Father Courtney pulled out the drawer and removed the half-empty bottle. He got a glass from the bookshelf, filled it. Dutifully, according to ritual, he asked, "For you?"

"No," Donovan said. "Thank you all the same." He turned his head. "Sit over there, Father, where I can see you."

The priest frowned. He noticed that Donovan's arms were perfectly flat against the blanket, that his body was rigid, outlined beneath the covering. No part of the old man moved except the head, and that slowly, unnaturally.

"That's better. But take off your coat—it's terribly hot in here. You'll catch pneumonia."

The room was full of cold winds from the open shutters.

Father Courtney removed his coat.

"You've been worried, haven't you?" Donovan asked.

The priest nodded. He tried to sense what was wrong, to smell the disease, if there was a disease, if there was anything.

"I'm sorry about that." The old man seemed to sigh. His eyes were misted, webbed with distance, lightly. "But I wanted to be alone. Sometimes you have to be alone, to think, to get things straight. Isn't that true?"

"Sometimes, I suppose, but—"

"No. I know what you're going to say, the questions you want to ask. But there's not enough time . . ."

Father Courtney arose from the chair, and walked quickly to the telephone extension. He jabbed a button. "I'm sorry, George," he said, "but you're going to have a doctor."

The screen did not flicker.

He pressed the button again, firmly.

"Sit down," the tired voice whispered. "It doesn't work. I pulled the wires ten minutes ago."

"Then I'll fly over to Milburn—"

"If you do, I'll be dead when you get back. Believe that: I know what I'm talking about."

The priest clenched and unclenched his stubby fingers, and sat down in the chair again.

Donovan chuckled. "Drink up," he said. "We can't have good wine going to waste, can we?"

The priest put the glass to his lips. He tried to think clearly. If he rushed out to Milburn and got Doctor Ferguson, perhaps there'd be a chance. Or—He took a deep swallow.

No. That wouldn't do. It might take hours.

Donovan was talking now; the words lost—a hum of locusts in the room, a far-off murmuring; then, like a radio turned up: "Father, how long have we been friends, you and I?"

"Why . . . twenty years," the priest answered. "Or more."

"Would you say you know me very well by now?"

"I believe so."

"Then tell me first, right now, would you say that I've been a good man?"

Father Courtney smiled. "There've been worse," he said and thought of what this man had accomplished in Mount Vernon, quietly, in his own quiet way, over the years. The building of a decent school for the children—Donovan had shamed the people into it. The new hospital—Donovan's doing, his patient campaigning. Entertainment halls for the young; a city fund for the poor; better teachers, better doctors—all, all because of the old man with the soft voice, George Donovan.

"Do you mean it?"

"Don't be foolish. And don't be treacly, either. Of course I mean it."

In the room, now, a strange odor fumed up, suddenly.

The old man said, "I'm glad." Still he did not move. "But, I'm sorry I asked. It was unfair."

"I don't have the slightest idea what you're talking about."

"Neither do I, Father, completely. I thought I did, once, but I was wrong."

The priest slapped his knees, angrily. "Why won't you let me get a doctor? We'll have plenty of time to talk afterwards."

Donovan's eyes narrowed, and curved into what resembled a smile. "You're my doctor," he said. "The only one who can help me now."

"In what way?"

"By making a decision." The voice was reedy: it seemed to waver and change pitch.

"What sort of a decision?"

Donovan's head jerked up. He closed his eyes and remained this way for a full minute, while the acrid smell bellied and grew stronger and whorled about the room in invisible currents.

"'. . . the gentleman lay graveward with his furies . . .' Do you remember that, Father?"

"Yes," the priest said. "Thomas, isn't it?"

"Thomas, He's been here with me, you know, really; and I've been asking him things. On the theory that poets aren't entirely human. But he just grins. 'You're dying of strangers.' he says; and grins. Bless him." The old man lowered his head. "He disappointed me."

Father Courtney reached for a cigarette, crumpled the empty pack, laced and unlaced his fingers. He waited, remembering the times he had come to this house, all the fine evenings. Ending now?

Yes, Whatever else he would learn, he knew that, suddenly: they were ending.

"What sort of a decision, George?"

"A theological sort."

Father Courtney snorted and walked to a window. Outside, the sun was hidden behind a curtain of gray. Birds sat black and still on the telephone lines, like notes of music; and there was rain.

"Is there something you think you haven't told me?" he asked.

"Yes."

"About yourself?"

"Yes."

"I don't think so, George." Father Courtney turned. "I've known about it for a long time."

The old man tried to speak.

"I've known very well. And now I think I understand why you've refused to see anyone."

"No," Donovan said. "You don't. Father, listen to me: it isn't what you think."

"Nonsense." The priest reverted to his usual gruffness. "We've been friends for too many years for this kind of thing. It's *exactly* what I think. You're an intelligent, well-read, mule-stubborn old man who's worried he won't get to Heaven because sometimes he has doubts."

"That isn't—"

"Well, rubbish! Do you think I don't ask questions, myself, once in a while? Just because I'm a priest, do you think I go blindly on, never wondering, not even for a minute?"

The old man's eyes moved swiftly, up and down.

"Every intelligent person doubts, George, once in a while. And we all feel terrible about it, and we're terribly sorry. But I assure you, if this were enough to damn us, Heaven would be a wilderness." Father Courtney reached again for a cigarette. "So you've shut yourself up like a hermit and worried and stewed and endangered your life, and all for nothing." He coughed. "Well, that's it, isn't it?"

"I wish it were," Donovan said, sadly. His eyes kept dancing. There was a long pause; then he said, "Let me pose you a theoretical problem, Father. Something I've been thinking about lately."

Father Courtney recalled the sentence, and how many times it had begun the evenings of talk—wonderful talk! These evenings, he realized, were part of his life now. An important part. For there was no one else, no one of Donovan's intelligence, with whom you could argue any subject under the sun—from Frescobaldi to baseball, from Colonization on Mars to the early French symbolists, to agrarian reforms, to wines, to theology . . .

The old man shifted in the bed. As he did, the acrid odor

diminished and swelled and pulsed. "You once told me," he said, "that you read imaginative fiction, didn't you?"

"I suppose so."

"And that there were certain concepts you could swallow—such as parallel worlds, mutated humans, and the like—, but that other concepts you couldn't swallow at all. Artificial life, I believe you mentioned, and time travel, and a few others."

The priest nodded.

"Well, let's take one of these themes for our problem. Will you do that? Let's take the first idea."

"All right. Then the doctor."

"We have this man, Father," Donovan said, gazing at the ceiling. "He looks perfectly ordinary, you see, and it would occur to no one to doubt this; but he is not ordinary. Strictly speaking, he isn't even a man. For, though he lives, he isn't alive. You follow? He is a thing of wires and coils and magic, a creation of other men. He is a machine . . ."

"George!" The priest shook his head. "We've gone through this before: it's foolish to waste time. I came here to help you, not to engage in a discussion of science fiction themes!"

"But that's how you *can* help me," Donovan said.

"Very well," the priest sighed. "But you know my views on this. Even if there were a logical purpose to which such a creature might be put—and I can't think of any—I still say they will never create a machine that is capable of abstract thought. Human intelligence is a spiritual thing—and spiritual things can't be duplicated by men."

"You really believe that?"

"Of course I do. Extrapolation of known scientific advances is perfectly all right; but this is something else entirely."

"Is it?" the old man said. "What about Pasteur's discovery? Or the X-Ray? Did Roentgen correlate a lot of embryonic data, Father, or did he come upon something brand new? What do you think even the scientists themselves would have said to the idea of a machine that would see through human tissue? They would have said, It's fantastic. And it was, too, and is. Nevertheless, it exists."

"It's not the same thing."

"No . . . I suppose that's true. However, I'm not trying to convince you of my thesis. I ask merely that you accept it for the sake of the problem. Will you?"

"Go ahead, George."

"We have this man, then. He's artificial, but he's perfect: great pains have been taken to see to this. Perfect, no detail spared, however small. He looks human, and he acts human, and for all the world knows, he *is* human. In fact, sometimes even he, our man, gets confused. When he feels a pain in his heart, for instance, its difficult for him to remember that he has no heart. When he sleeps and awakes refreshed, he must remind himself that this is all controlled by an automatic switch somewhere inside his brain, and that he doesn't *actually* feel refreshed. He must think, I'm not real, I'm not real, I'm not real!

"But this becomes impossible, after a while. Because he doesn't believe it. He begins to ask, Why? *Why* am I not real? Where is the difference, when you come right down to it? Humans eat and sleep—as I do. They talk—as I do. They move and work and laugh—as I do. What they think, I think, and what they feel, I feel. Don't I?

"He wonders, this mechanical man does, Father, what would happen if all the people on earth were suddenly to discover they were mechanical also. Would they feel any the less human? Is it likely that they would rush off to woo type-writers and adding machines? Or would they think, perhaps, of revising their definition of the word, 'Life'?

"Well, our man thinks about it, and thinks about it, but he never reaches a conclusion. He doesn't believe he's nothing more than an advanced calculator, but he doesn't really believe he's human, either: not completely.

"All he knows is that the smell of wet grass is a fine smell to him, and that the sound of the wind blowing through trees is very sad and very beautiful, and that he loves the whole earth with an impossible passion . . ."

Father Courtney shifted uncomfortably in his chair. If only the telephone worked, he thought. Or if he could be sure it was safe to leave.

". . . other men made the creature, as I've said; but many more like him were made. However, of them all, let's say only he was successful."

"Why?" the priest asked, irritably. "Why would this be done in the first place?"

Donovan smiled. "Why did we send the first ship to the moon? Or bother to split the atom? For no very good reason, Father. Except the reason behind all of science: Curiosity. My theoretical scientists were curious to see if it could be accomplished, that's all."

The priest shrugged.

"But perhaps I'd better give our man a history. That would make it a bit more logical. All right, he was born a hundred years ago, roughly. A privately owned industrial monopoly was his mother, and a dozen or so assorted technicians his father. He sprang from his electronic womb fully formed. But, as the result of an accident—lack of knowledge, what have you —he came out rather different from his unsuccessful brothers. A mutant! A mutated robot, Father—now there's an idea that ought to appeal to you! Anyway, *he* knew who, or what, he

was. He remembered. And so—to make it brief—when the
war interrupted the experiment and threw things into a general
uproar, our man decided to escape. He wanted his individual-
ity. He wanted to get out of the zoo.

"It wasn't particularly easy, but he did this. Once free, of
course, it was impossible to find him. For one thing, he had
been constructed along almost painfully ordinary lines. And
for another, they couldn't very well release the information
that a mechanical man built by their laboratories was wander-
ing the streets. It would cause a panic. And there was enough
panic, what with the nerve gas and the bombs."

"So they never found him, I gather."

"No," Donovan said, wistfully. "They never found him. And
they kept their secret well: it died when they died."

"And what happened to the creature?"

"Very little, to tell the truth. They'd given him a decent
intelligence, you see—far more decent, and complex, than
they knew—so he didn't have much trouble finding small jobs.
A rather old-looking man, fairly strong—he made out. Needless to say, he couldn't stay in the same town for more than
twenty years or so, because of his inability to age, but this
was all right. Everyone makes friends and loses them. He got
used to it."

Father Courtney sat very still now. The birds had flown
away from the telephone lines, and were at the window, beating
their wings, and crying harshly.

"But all this time, he's been thinking, Father. Thinking and
reading. He makes quite a study of philosophy, and for a time
he favors a somewhat peculiar combination of Russell and
Schopenhauer—unbitter bitterness, you might say. Then this
phase passes, and he begins to search through the vast theological and metaphysical literature. For what? He isn't sure.
However, he is sure of one thing, now: He *is*, indubitably,
human. Without breath, without heart, without blood or bone,
artificially created, he thinks this and believes it, with a fair
amount of firmness, too. Isn't that remarkable!"

"It is indeed," the priest said, his throat oddly tight and
dry. "Go on."

"Well," Donovan chuckled, "I've caught your interest, have
I? All right, then. Let us imagine that one hundred years have
passed. The creature has been able to make minor repairs on
himself, but—at last—he is dying. Like an ancient motor,
he's gone on running year after year, until he's all paste and
hairpins, and now, like the motor, he's falling apart. And
nothing and no one can save him."

The acrid aroma burned and fumed.

"Here's the real paradox, though. Our man has become

religious. Father! He doesn't have a living cell within him, yet he's concerned about his soul!"

Donovan's eyes quieted, as the rest of him did. "The problem," he said, "is this: Having lived creditably for over a century as a member of the human species, can this creature of ours hope for Heaven? Or will he 'die' and become only a heap of metal cogs?"

Father Courtney leapt from the chair, and moved to the bed. "George, in Heaven's name, let me call Doctor Ferguson!"

"Answer the question first. Or haven't you decided?"

"There's nothing to decide," the priest said, with impatience. "It's a preposterous idea. No machine can have a soul."

Donovan made the sighing sound, through closed lips. He said, "You don't think it's conceivable, then, that God could have made an exception here?"

"What do you mean?"

"That He could have taken pity on this theoretical man of ours, and breathed a soul into him after all? Is that so impossible?"

Father Courtney shrugged. "It's a poor word, impossible," he said. "But it's a poor problem, too. Why not ask me whether pigs ought to be allowed to fly?"

"Then you admit it's conceivable?"

"I admit nothing of the kind. It simply isn't the sort of question any man can answer."

"Not even a priest?"

"Especially not a priest. You know as much about Catholicism as I do, George; you ought to know how absurd the proposition is."

"Yes," Donovan said. His eyes were closed.

Father Courtney remembered the time they had argued furiously on what would happen if you went back in time and killed your own grandfather. This was like that argument. Exactly like it—exactly. It was no stranger than a dozen other discussions (What if Mozart had been a writer instead of a composer? If a person died and remained dead for an hour and were then revived, would he be haunted by his own ghost?) Plus, perhaps, the fact that Donovan might be in a fever. Perhaps and might and why do I sit here while his life may be draining away . . .

The old man made a sharp noise. "But you can tell me this much," he said. "If our theoretical man were dying, and you knew that he was dying, would you give him Extreme Unction?"

"George, you're delirious."

"No, I'm not: please, Father! Would you give this creature

the Last Rites? If, say, you knew him? If you'd known him for years, as a friend, as a member of the parish?"

The priest shook his head. "It would be sacriligious."

"But why? You said yourself that he might have a soul, that God might have granted him this. Didn't you say that?"

"I—"

"Father, remember, he's a friend of yours. You know him *well*. You and he, this creature, have worked together, side by side, for years. You've taken a thousand walks together, shared the same interests, the same love of art and knowledge. For the sake of the thesis, Father. Do you understand?"

"No," the priest said, feeling a chill freeze into him. "No, I don't."

"Just answer this, then. If your friend were suddenly to reveal himself to you as a machine, and he was dying, and wanted very much to go to Heaven—what would you do?"

The priest picked up the wine glass and emptied it. He noticed that his hand was trembling. "Why—" he began, and stopped, and looked at the silent old man in the bed, studying the face, searching for madness, for death.

"What would you do?"

An unsummoned image flashed through his mind. Donovan, kneeling at the altar for Communion, Sunday after Sunday; Donovan, with his mouth firmly shut, while the others' yawned; Donovan, waiting to the last moment, then snatching the Host, quickly, dartingly, like a lizard gobbling a fly.

Had he ever seen Donovan eat?

Had he seen him take even one glass of wine, ever?

Father Courtney shruddered slightly, brushing away the images. He felt unwell. He wished the birds would go elsewhere.

Well, answer him, he thought. *Give him an answer. Then get in the helicar and fly to Milburn and pray it's not too late . . .*

"I think," the priest said, "that in such a case, I would administer Extreme Unction."

"Just as a precautionary measure?"

"It's all very ridiculous, but—I think that's what I'd do. Does that answer the question?"

"It does, Father. It does." Donovan's voice came from nowhere. "There is one last point, then I'm finished with my little thesis."

"Yes?"

"Let us say the man dies and you give him Extreme Unction; he does or does not go to Heaven, provided there is a Heaven. What happens to the body? Do you tell the townspeople they have been living with a mechanical monster all these years?"

"What do you think, George?"

"I think it would be unwise. They remember our theoretical

man as a friend, you see. The shock would be terrible. Also, they would never believe he was the only one of his kind: they'd begin to suspect their neighbors of having clockwork interiors. And some of them might be tempted to investigate and see for sure. And, too, the news would be bound to spread, all over the world. I think it would be a bad thing to let anyone know, Father."

"How would I be able to suppress it?" the priest heard himself ask, seriously.

"By conducting a private autopsy, so to speak. Then, afterwards, you could take the parts to a junkyard and scatter them."

Donovan's voice dropped to a whisper. Again the locust hum.

". . . and if our monster had left a note to the effect he had moved to some unspecified place, you . . ."

The acrid smell billowed, all at once, like a steam, a hiss of blinding vapor.

"George."

Donovan lay unstirring on the cloud of linen, his face composed, expressionless.

"George!"

The priest reached his hand under the blanket and touched the heart-area of Donovan's chest. He tried to pull the eyelids up: they would not move.

He blinked away the burning wetness. "Forgive me!" he said, and paused, and took from his pocket a small white jar and a white stole.

He spoke softly, under his breath, in Latin. While he spoke, he touched the old man's feet and head with glistening fingertips.

Then, when many minutes had passed, he raised his head.

Rain sounded in the room, and swift winds, and far-off rockets.

Father Courtney grasped the edge of the blanket.

He made the Sign of the Cross, breathed, and pulled downward, slowly.

After a long while he opened his eyes.

Place of Meeting

It swept down from the mountains, a loose crystal-smelling wind, an autumn chill of moving wetness. Down from the mountains and into the town where it set the dead trees hissing and the signboards creaking. And it even went into the church, because the bell was ringing and there was no one to ring the bell.

The people in the yard stopped their talk and listened to the rusty music.

Big Jim Kroner listened too. Then he cleared his throat and clapped his hands—thick hands, calloused and work-dirtied.

"All right," he said loudly. "All right, let's us settle down now." He walked out from the group and turned. "Who's got the list?"

"Got it right here, Jim," a woman said, coming forward with a loose-leaf folder.

"All present?"

"Everybody except that there German, Mr. Grunin—Grunger—"

Kroner smiled; he made a megaphone of his hands. "Grüninger—Barthold Grüninger?"

A small man with a mustache called out excitedly: "Ja, ja! . . . s'war schwer den Friedhof zu finden."

"All right. That's all we wanted to know, whether you was here or not." Kroner studied the pages carefully. Then he reached into the back pocket of his overalls and withdrew a stub of pencil and put the tip to his mouth.

"Now, before we start off," he said to the group, "I want to know is there anybody here that's got a question or anything to ask?" He looked over the crowd of silent faces. "Anybody don't know who I am? No?"

It came another wind then, mountain-scattered and fast: it billowed dresses, set damp hair moving; it pushed over pewter vases and smashed dead roses and hydrangeas to swirling dust against the gritty tombstones. Its clean rain smell was gone now, though, for it had passed over the fields with the odors of rotting life.

Kroner made a check mark in the notebook. "Anderson," he shouted, "Edward L."

A man in overalls like Kroner's stepped forward.

"Andy, you covered Skagit valley, Snohomish and King counties, as well as Seattle and the rest?"

"Yes, sir."

"What you got to report?"

"They're all dead," Anderson said.

"You looked everywhere? You was real careful?"

"Yes, sir. Ain't nobody alive in the whole state."

Kroner nodded and made another check mark. "That's all, Andy. Next: Avakian, Katina."

A woman in a wool skirt and grey blouse walked up from the back, waving her arms. She started to speak.

Kroner tapped his stick. "Listen here for a second, folks," he said. "For those that don't know how to talk English, you know what this is all about—so when I ask my question, you just nod up-and-down for yes (like this) and sideways (like this) for no. Makes it a lot easier for those of us as don't remember too good. All right?"

There were murmurings and whispered consultations and for a little while the yard was full of noise. The woman called Avakian kept nodding.

"Fine," Kroner said. "Now, Miss Avakian. You covered what? . . . Iran, Iraq, Turkey, Syria. Did you—find—an-y-body a-live?"

The woman stopped nodding. "No," she said. "No, no."

Kroner checked the name. "Let's see here. Boleslavsky, Peter. You go on back, Miss Avakian."

A man in bright city clothes walked briskly to the tree clearing. "Yes, sir," he said.

"What have you got for us?"

The man shrugged. "Well, I tell you; I went over New York with a fine-tooth comb. Then I hit Brooklyn and Jersey. Nothin', man. Nothin' nowhere."

"He is right," a dark-faced woman said in a tremulous voice. "I was there too. Only the dead in the streets, all over, all over the city; in the cars I looked even, in the *offices*. Everywhere is people dead."

"Chavez, Pietro. Baja California."

"All dead, señor chief."

"Ciodo, Ruggiero. Capri."

The man from Capri shook his head violently.

"Denman, Charlotte. Southern United States."

"Dead as doornails . . ."

"Elgar, David S. . . .

"Ferrazio, Ignatz . . .

"Goldfarb, Bernard . . .

"Halpern . . .

"Ives . . . Kranek . . . O'Brian . . ."

The names exploded in the pale evening air like deep gunshots; there was much head-shaking, many people saying, "No. No."

At last Kroner stopped marking. He closed the notebook and spread his big workman's hands. He saw the round eyes, the trembling mouths, the young faces; he saw all the frightened people.

A girl began to cry. She sank to the damp ground and covered her face and made these crying sounds. An elderly man put his hand on her head. The elderly man looked sad. But not afraid. Only the young ones seemed afraid.

"Settle down now," Kroner said firmly. "Settle on down. Now, listen to me. I'm going to ask you all the same question one more time, because we got to be sure." He waited for them to grow quiet. "All right. This here is all of us, every one. We've covered all the spots. Did anybody here find one single solitary sign of life?"

The people were silent. The wind had died again, so there was no sound at all. Across the corroded wire fence the grey meadows lay strewn with the carcasses of cows and horses and, in one of the fields, sheep. No flies buzzed near the dead animals; there were no maggots burrowing. No vultures; the sky was clean of birds. And in all the untended rolling hills of grass and weeds which had once sung and pulsed with a million hidden voices, in all the land there was only this immense stillness now, still as years, still as the unheard motion of the stars.

Kroner watched the people. The young woman in the gay print dress; the tall African with his bright paint and cultivated scars; the fierce-looking Swede looking not so fierce now in this greying twilight. He watched all the tall and short and old and young people from all over the world, pressed together now, a vast silent polyglot in this country meeting place, this always lonely and long-deserted spot— deserted even before the gas bombs and the disease and the flying pestilences that had covered the earth in three days and three nights. Deserted. Forgotten.

"Talk to us, Jim," the woman who had handed him the notebook said. She was new.

Kroner put the list inside his big overalls pocket.

"Tell us," someone else said. "How shall we be nourished? What will we do?"

"The world's all dead," a child moaned. "Dead as dead, the whole world . . ."

"Todo el mund—"

"Monsieur Kroner, Monsieur Kroner, what will we do?"

Kroner smiled. "Do?" He looked up through the still-hanging poison cloud, the dun blanket, up to where the moon was now risen in full coldness. His voice was steady, but it lacked life. "What some of us have done before," he said. "We'll go back and wait. It ain't the first time. It ain't the last."

A little fat bald man with old eyes sighed and began to waver in the October dusk. The outline of his form wavered and disappeared in the shadows under the trees where the moonlight did not reach. Others followed him as Kroner talked.

"Same thing we'll do again and likely keep on doing. We'll go back and—sleep. And we'll wait. Then it'll start all over again and folks'll build their cities—new folks with new blood—and then we'll wake up. Maybe a long time yet. But it ain't so bad; it's quiet, and time passes." He lifted a small girl of fifteen or sixteen with pale cheeks and red lips. "Come on, now! Why, just think of the appetite you'll have all built up!"

The girl smiled. Kroner faced the crowd and waved his hands, large hands, rough from the stone of midnight pyramids and the feel of muskets, boil-speckled from night-hours in packing plants and trucking lines; broken by the impact of a tomahawk and a machine-gun bullet; but white where the dirt was not caked, and bloodless. Old hands, old beyond years.

As he waved, the wind came limping back from the mountains. It blew the heavy iron bell high in the steepled white barn and set the signboards creaking and lifted ancient dusts and hissed again through the dead trees.

Kroner watched the air turn black. He listened to it fill with the flappings and the flutterings and the squeakings. He waited; then he stopped waving and sighed and began to walk.

He walked to a place of vines and heavy brush. Here he paused for a moment and looked out at the silent place of high dark grass, of hidden huddled tombs, of scrolls and stone-frozen children stained silver in the night's wet darkness; at the crosses he did not look. The people were gone; the place was empty.

Kroner kicked away the foliage. Then he got into the coffin and closed the lid.

Soon he was asleep.

A World of Differents

A-B-C-D-E-F-G-H-I-J-K-L-M-N-O-P-Q-R-S-T-U-V-W-X-Y-Z.

Now these are the symbolkeys to what I am saying. What is Earthword TELEPATHY doesn't work because I think out and nobody hears me. All the time I think. It is maybe that I am alone of the livers, if that's the story then I send this message by my last cone that wasn't shot to hell (and it was a farrago hiding it from them). *Figure out the language, figure it out.* Of course it isn't easy but you can try, *I* tried and I ain't no scientist. To make help I am (*Earthword*) deatomizing (?) a book which contents all words and send this with message. Study the book it is FINNEGANS WAKE BY James Joyce. It is where I learned Earth language also from when I listen to the Earthman who captured me talk.

The reason that it is I don't send this message with our ciphers is this: that, What has happened to my body, for crying out loud? O gig goggle of gigguels. I can't tell you how! It is too screaming to rizo, rabbit it all! Why I can't walk or hold a writing stick to make our symbols or anything else already. *Helpless!* I can't hardly work this machine but that I watched the Guard (he calls it a *tripewriter*) who uses it when it is late and dark. You stare at it for hours and then you hit key and say damn-goddamn-it and when it is a long time the *words* come out on paper. But there are only Earthwords on tripewriter. So you work hard to understand me, you get the drift? It is no good if they catch me, then it is pain, I know. Thats what happens they are so cruel.

Now listen I'm no scientist. All I know is we were traveling out of formation to study more on atmosphere and I was damn pilot, we were going to rejoin the group later on in the day. Atmosphere near water which you call LAKE. But when we are nearly through, What is it? Something has gone wrongo with the ship. I can't control it and we fall into the drink only it is that I get the door opened and while the ship is sinking I crawl out. But there is no time for suiting!

What a luckyness I don't die you bet your sweet ars.

Well its blacking up in my head. I crawl out of the LAKE and the ship is gone. I remember what I thought it was I AM THE FIRST OF OUR RACE TO BE ON EARTH BY THE GREAT HORNED TOAD! Then I see I have only got one cone left.

When I am awake finally I try to walk, but, What's up with my legs? Different something. WHAMBO! I am a pratfall. So it was late and no sun and hard to see. No more any of my clothes are left: then, mothernaked, I sampood myself with galawater and fraguant pistania mud, wupper and lauar, from crown to sole. So it is not so cold but to breathe is a horse of another color. O Mother that took the cake to breathe. What will I: die? All alone, thinks me, and theres nobody nothin nohow and I'm alone on Earth . . .

I thought if a planet inhabitant will come along maybe I can explain our mission its friendly see and we ain't a-aimin to cause no trouble, that we are just looking for a new place into which to live. *But maybe he will be afraid of me,* I thought, *or I will be afraid of him!*

Well when I figgered that the (*Earthword*) jig is up I saw this Earth man. Great God Amighty I said what a strange basteed! Four legs this creature and a long tail with the horns on the head. Describe it? Hustle along, why can't you? Spitz on the iern while it's hot. I wouldn't have missed it for irthing on nerthe. Not for the lucre of lomba strait. Oceans of Gaud, I mosel hear that! Ogowe presta! Ishekarry and washmeskad, the carishy caratimaney? Sez I crawling up near it and told him my name saying, Heres what happened old podnuh. But I can't talk very good and the Earthman is eating and only one word very hard to spell, Moooooooooo.

Then I saw other Earthman and some were like this big sonuvabitch but others were smaller with four legs and some by (*Earthword*) MAGIC were flying in the atmosphere like ships and no machines in them. Wings! With so many different.

I ain't no scientist. All I could do is drive my craft before nobody told me about Earthmen being all different. Or that you could live without suits, thats why you have to understand this: no suits. You can breathe the air only no fun pops.

Well nobody pays attention to me and I am going to

starve to death or something. So I cry out for help, me alone, the first and with only one cone. "Somebody help me!" I think, "My name is—" (*Earthword*) etc. (?)

Thats when the giants came. Holy Scamander, I sar it! Ocis on us! Seints of light! Zezere! They are in a machine the machine going stop and here are the giants getting out and givin us a looksee. I'm making sounds and afraid what if they're not friendly! And I can't stop throat sounds: Subdue your noise, you hamble creature! Deataceas!

O am I so afraid when I see them close. Big just ain't the word. Ah, but one was the queer old skeowsha anyhow, trinkettoes! And sure he was the quare old buntz too, foostherfather of fingalls and dotthergills. But here is the funny part they are horrible but not like the way we are taught, like completely different. No. Thats the scorcher. Hair, tendrils, on their heads and they are (*Earthword*) anthropomorphic (?) and built like brick outhouses, no less. Stretch me, pull me out of shape, make it six times as long, and ugly? Ouch!

Well I'm pretty brave. So I clambered right up to them and telepathed hello there, my name is etc. I am part of a patrol from Zaras, we have to move and we were sort of lookin her over. My ship crashed and I thought maybe you'd take care of me until I can get word through to my buddy-buddies.

They didn't scream. They just looked at me that layed on the wet grass and I knew they didn't dig my conception. Of course I couldn't understand them either then, but of nature I remember what they said, they said:

—*Hank, it's a miracle!*

—*Now for God's sake, don't go jumping the gun! We'll have to look into this.*

—*It's a miracle, I tell you! Just as I'd prayed, Hank!*

—*Just got lost, or abandoned, or . . .*

I thought: Our civilization is a thousand years more advanced nor yours, folkses, and we want to be friends, if poss, we'll share and share alike, kay, keeds?

No intelligible response: to make the Gripes hear how coy they are (though he was much too schystimatically auricular about *his ens* to heed her). Giant Hank reaches down and picks up me and the other, also Giant but two fat-hills in front, long hair on head, bigger buttinsky, says:

—*Owww-poor-ittle-feller-izums'al-wosted?*

No sense here! (They got them two languages, one I figured out, this; but another that they talk most of the time to me just do not come through. Nemmine.)

Well brother am I gullible. Scared and hungry I figured to let them take over me. I let them pick up me—practically there is no (*Earthword*) gravity—and I trusted. Tired, get what I mean and hungry wow. And pains all over so that what it was I did I went to sleep before I could be finding out even wha's wha.

Did somebody say Earth people friendly? Let me at him is all because I am just one single Zarasan and heres what happened to *me*.

Incredible! Semperexcommunicambiambisumers. (Poor little sowsieved subsquashed me! Already I begin to feel contemption for them!)

Its got me beat how much time there went by right then. But always they're saying, He's sick, he's sick, and the black kept getting in my head hard to get used to. Natural? When I'm conscious in moments I begin TELEPATHY (no answer) and I look to see how the land lays. With another one Giant all the time its:

—*Hes gotta blong tuh somebody, for Cry Eye.*

And:

—*We've checked everywhere. I can't lose him!*

Well they put me in a cage first. Yes in a prison. I wake up and where am I? Behind bars. No clothes still but a white clothy thing I don't know what the hell. The ground in the cage is soft BWAAANG! but then I see there is something in the cage there with me. With the arms and the legs. And furry. I thought wow whats this!

Well I'm pretty brave. So when this liver wouldn't talk I challenged him in custom and we fought very hard, yes. Whatta fight! While that Mooksius with preprocession and proprecession, duplicitly and displussedly, was promulgating ipsofacts and sadcontras this raskolly Zarasan he had allbust seceded in monophysicking his illsobordunates . . . and his babskissed nepogreasymost got the hoof from my philioquus right in the snoot! Its insides came out dry and it was still. We'll see now, is what I thought, then whos bossman. We'll see now.

Then the Giant Earthman with the fat-hills and long hair came in and stood by my cage.

—*Iz-tzums-aw-wet?* the Earthman said and picked up me and did unspeakable things so bad I can't talk about them. Back home you do what he did to me thats all, you get the bis in the gretch. Humiliation! Jing.

I tried to fight but it wasn't no dice on because Earthman like the Giants are superstrength. I said, See here, is this how you treat visitors? Is this how a Guest is treated by Earth-dwellers in the name of Pete?

—*Him'th-talkin'* he said. Such tongue!

Then you don't know, you just don't know. Great things they put in my mouth and tubes places if I told you you would say I'm lying, it's so doity, and tried to smother me. Tortures like this all the time. When I sleep its wake up and when I try to talk what is it? Go to sleep.

And worse. Well Lord knows how long this rebop went on. No communication, *Quas primas*—but 'tis bitter to compote my knowledge's fructos of. Tomes. They pretend they do not understand me or maybe they are so jerkhead they cannot translate even now. And every day I talk to them and say who I am and why are they torturing me, what have I ever done to them?

I have surprise they didn't take away my cone, they found it finally, then where would I be? Once they tried but I screamed threats and they said,—*Iddumswiddah-pwaysing?* (Meaning?) And let me have it back.

I was thonthorstrok that time.

Well this Earthman who is my Guard and maintorturer is what they call WRITER. When it is light and I am too tired to walk—impossible! Whooth!—he will leave alone me. Maybe come in and say,—*Quite a set of lungs boy givin em a rest?* But the other Earthman who is what they call a chick or doll-type housewife, never. Always it is that this one hits and ounches me and holds me up in her giant hands and does these unspeakable things. Always she says,—*So glad he can be ours, so glad, Hank, I knew we didn't do wrong, we asked around, we watched the papers didn't we?* (—*We're kidnapers,* says another one Giant.)

Well I tried to make a message to home but my hands have trouble to work. A writing stick they gave me but it would not god-damn. Halfway through my dispatch, what did they do? They took it away and said,—*See the widduh wabbit him him dwawed?* But all right you couldn't have read it anyway.

Then what I saw is Writer working this machine. I stopped to fight and was quiet for long and watching. The language I learned, then when I watched, I can see what to operate. Writer now he is very cool,—*Here,* he says *this is how the tripewriter works, baby.* And when he caught me with his books, he says,—*Here, try some Joyce, kid maybe you can make some sense out of it.*

My captors have beat it for a short while. Writer is at what is called a Library doing research for novel, but I can hear the voice of Giant Shewife at near place: Nextdoor-neighbors. I escaped my cage and am finishing now hurry-up in case they see: that would be bad. Then they hit you. But pretty clever of me for being no scientist?

I will get free tonight (snakes in clover, picked and scotched, and a vaticanned viper). After they torture me with what they call (*Earthword*) BOTTLE and go asleep then I will climb out of this cage that Shewife calls CRIB and, fast, because I learned how. Fool them. Then I will make a twist on what they never let me touch, a device thing they always say,—*Don't ever play with that, that's the gas-heater, don't ever touch that its dangerous.*

So you come pronto but forget all that jazz about being friendships for these are vicious warlike creatures.

Try friendships and you know what they'll give you? They'll give you prison and torture like the kind O I can't even start to tell you.

Bring weapons—Perkodhuskurunbarggruauyagokgorlayor-gromgremmitghundhurthrumathunaradidillifaititillibumullun-ukkunun!—the big ones. But watch out for me, I'll be in a field away from the falling buildings, you know what I mean. And Amen brothers, you bet.

Anthem

I

TITLES

FADE IN

1 CLOSE SHOT—PAINTING—COVERS SCREEN

This is Brueghel's THE FALL OF ICARUS.

> VOICE O.S.:
> > (Fake Mountain Ballad style,
> > with guitar)
>
> When Ick saw the birds
> And how they flew,
> And said to himself,
> "I'll do it, too!"
> And got out his feathers
> And got out his glue—
> The Dream wasn't new.

> SECOND VOICE O.S.:
> Not even then?

> FIRST VOICE O.S.:
> Not even then.

Camera moves leisurely over painting, pausing at
the Flemish plowman and the shepherd.

> SECOND VOICE O.S.:
> Wait a minute! Where is he?

> FIRST VOICE O.S.:
> Who?

> SECOND VOICE O.S.:
> Icarus! The guy who wanted to fly to the stars—
> the guy with the old dream.

Camera moves into picture for EXTREME C. U. of a pair of legs sticking out of the water.

FIRST VOICE O.S.:
Well, something went wrong. You see, the sun got too hot, and—

SECOND VOICE O.S.:
He never made it.

FIRST VOICE O.S.:
That's right. He never made it.

FADE OUT

II

FADE IN

2   PAN SHOT—THE UNIVERSE:

In all its starry magnificence. (Process; or footage from INTOLERANCE—come on, Mr. Lamberger, you can do it, if you try!)

VOICE O.S.
(Ook it up a la Corwin;
March-of-Timsey)
This is what we're talking about.
Look! Look!

SECOND VOICE O.S.:
Hey, is it true that they twinkle?
I mean *really*.

FIRST VOICE O.S.:
Sure, they twinkle, And don't
let anybody tell you different,
little guy!

We diddle around Orion, getting good comp. This drives the kids wild, Mr. Lamberger, see—*science fiction!* We sneak the message in right under their noses. You idiotic poop.
Okay: strings up; *schmaltzissimo!*

VOICE O.S.
(Get Presley for this)

Ever since Man crawled
Out of the slime
And looked at the time
And said, "It's late!"
He started to dream;
He started to hate . . .

SECOND VOICE O.S.:
What'd he dream about?
What'd he hate about?

FIRST VOICE O.S.:
This! Don't you get it,
Mac? Man wanted *out!*

SECOND VOICE O.S.:
How come?

FIRST VOICE O.S.:
Now you're talking like my
boss Lamberger who thinks
I am working on INVASION FROM
THE STARS.

SECOND VOICE O.S.:
You're drunk. You've been
writing movies for five years
now, and you still think they're
gonna do a *good* s.f.'er. You're
drunk.

FIRST VOICE O.S.:
On with the script!

SECOND VOICE O.S.:
Some script. You'll get
fired. Well, okay: *How come?*

FIRST VOICE O.S.:
                    (What the hell does O. S.
                    mean?)
How come we flopped out of the
water and died and did it again
and wouldn't rest until we could
walk in dust up to our derrieres?
How come we don't just sit down
and drop the whole thing? Life,
I mean.

SECOND VOICE O.S.:

I dunno.

The planets and the stars are on fire now; they're like the dust from an immense diamond suddenly struck by a great hammer; and their dust is alive on a field of dark velvet. (Got that, Mr. Set Designer?)

FIRST VOICE O.S.:

But it takes more than
dreaming. Look: We're
locked in a closet. It's
filling up with garbage.
The air's going out of it.
It's on fire. But we
won't reach out and turn the
key.

CHORUS OF ONE THOUSAND
BRUNETTES O.S.:

Why?

FIRST VOICE O.S.:

Because our fingers are frozen
in prayer and our heads are
filled with fear; because we're
covered with the crust of
burial grounds and our hands
are dripping wine.

SECOND VOICE O.S.:

We ever gonna make it? We
ever gonna get to the stars?

FIRST VOICE O.S.:

A good question!

FADE OUT

III

FADE IN

3 RICHMOND BLAST-OFF AREA—EXT.—DAY—
MED. SHOT
Professor Isaac Gold, fortyish, and Professor Fred

Inman, somewhat younger, are standing together, bare-headed, on the rim of a platform. The dawn is steel-gray and damp. They are in heavy coats.

> PROF. GOLD
> (looking O. S.)
> . . . y'know, Fred, twenty years
> from now they'll be calling her
> a pig. Put her in a museum
> along with *The Spirit of St. Louis,*
> and all the snot-nosed brats will
> laugh at her.

> PROF. INMAN
> It's taken a long time.

> PROF. GOLD
> They'll forget. We'll be
> paragraphs in text-books,
> Freddie—us and Myerson and
> Scott and . . . all of us.
> Historical data. They'll never
> write about—well, about *this*
> morning. Look, Freddie,
> goddamnit, look at her!

They look upward and CAMERA ASSUMES THEIR POINT OF VIEW. The rocket gleams dully, a smooth metal giant pointing straight toward the stars.

> PROF. GOLD
> I wish we could be aboard.

> PROF. INMAN
> Yeah.

They circle the platform, hands in pockets.

> PROF. GOLD
> I was afraid we wouldn't make it,
> you know?

> PROF. INMAN
> Well, we did make it, sir.
> Next week she'll go to the Moon;
> then we'll see Mars.
> Venus, maybe. After that—O

hell, the sky *isn't* the limit.
There'll be no limit. We'll go
everywhere!

PROF. GOLD
(thoughtfully)

Everywhere . . .

PROF. INMAN
I was walking by the barracks
last night. I passed your window.
Thought I saw something . . .
Professor Gold, you were praying.

PROF. GOLD
(turning to his friend)

Was I?

They look a long while at the rocket. Then they turn
and walk back across the empty field, on past the
guards and sentries. The CAMERA SWINGS BACK
TO THE ROCKET, BACK TO THE STARS.

FADE OUT

IV

FADE IN

4   INSERT—NEWSPAPER

The headline, dated 1980, reads:

WAR DECLARED!

CAMERA MOVES THROUGH to paragraph at end
of paper. C.U.

. . . due to the declaration of a national emergency, the scheduled experimental flight of the
moon rocket AD ASTRA has been indefinitely
postponed. It will be weather-treated and will
remain under constant guard at Richmond Arena,
until such time . . .

FADE OUT

V

FADE IN

5 BATTLE MONTAGE—(Stock; any old World War II stuff)

Bombs exploding in N.Y.C.; planes strafing boy scout picnics; etc., etc.

6 EXT SHOT—RICHMOND ARENA—MED

A bomb has demolished the shed housing the AD ASTRA. There is movement nowhere. Guards have been dismissed. The rocket stands nakedly alone in the middle of the battered field, her weather-covering blowing in rubbery shreds in the cold wind.

FADE OUT

VI

FADE IN

7 (Production Note: Conceive quick method of getting across passage of fifteen years without resorting to calendar bit. Also, through montages, blend in gradual deterioration of rocket—it's stripped by adventurers and kids, it rusts, it begins to fall apart.)

8 MED SHOT—EXT RICHMOND ARENA— TWILIGHT

(Possibly delete scene of Prof. Gold and Prof. Inman standing at ravaged rocket, discussing futility of persuading gov't to resume Moon Project. War is over now; work that in, too.)

9 MED CLOSE—EXT RICHMOND ARENA—DAY

The rocket is being loaded into a number of big trucks. Make truckdrivers beautiful dames in flesh tights. (Got to work in sex *somehow*.)

QUICK CUT TO

10 BIG CLOSE UP—HARRY LAMBERGER

He is a weasel-faced, sharp-eyed, heartless, soulless huckster who doesn't give a damn whether we ever get to the moon. He's just out for the doller-oos. (Your big chance, Lamberger; now you can make like Hitchcock and play in your own film. Or is it type-casting?)

He grins widely as he watches loading procedure.

11   MONTAGE

Showing trucks taking rocket from town to town, setting up of tents, crowds gathering to gawk as, OVER-SCENE, we hear:

> VOICE:
>   (barker type)
> Built in 1980 at a cost
> of *sev*eral million dollars,
> this here space ship could
> have flown to the moon!
> But fuel cost money and the war . . .

                    QUICK CUT TO

12   MED CLOSE SHOT—INT CIRCUS WAGON—
     HARRY & WIFE

Harry is drooling into a tankard of suds.

> HARRY
> O brother! And you din't
> think th' idea would work!
> 'Rocket ships, who wants
> to see rocket ships?'
> Ha-haaa-aa-a!

> EMMA
> What wife, I'm asking, likes
> any idea that includes shelling
> out five hundred G's?

> HARRY
> Sweetheart, baby, if you will
> kindly make another count of
> today's take? Every bum in
> this whole country is
> dyin' to pay his $2.50

for a guided tour through
th' only rocket ship in the
world. Hey, hoo-boy, now, I'm
tellin' ya—leave it to ol'
Lamberger . . .

FADE OUT

VII

FADE IN

13   (Production Note: More years pass. Make Lamberger
      older.)

14   CLOSE SHOT—SIGN READING "STARBURGERS"
      —DINE IN THE STARS!

      CAMERA PULLS OUT and wanders through the
      rocket ship, now an exclusive, though somewhat down-
      at-the-heels, restaurant. All port holes are painted
      with phony stars. Place is jammed. Old Lamberger
      beams.

FADE OUT

VIII

15   (Production Note: Attn: Special Effects Dept.: This
      has got to be short but clear. One, another war—
      super bomb. Two, Passage of time—use *clever* gim-
      mick. Maybe shoot back for L.S. universe, from time
      to time. You figure it out, you're getting paid more
      than I am.)

IX

FADE IN

16   LONG SHOT—FOREST

      It is the forest primeval. Trees bigger and uglier than
      any trees we know today; vines a lá Tarzan hanging
      around. It's green and wet and quiet, except for the
      chatter of monkeys or something slithering through

the underbrush. Real atmospheric: feeling of doom
everywhere. (Production Note: It had better be damn
clear what has happened to Earth.)

In the midst of this, we DOLLY IN on the AD ASTRA,
upright once again. Pretty miserable condition, but
still majestic, still suggestive of her appearance when
Professors Gold and Inman were slobbering over her.
This could have been our solution.

It's a good day. The sun is out and picks up the
few unrusted spots on the ship's hull, making it glint
and shine. We see all sorts of animals clambering
around her. When we TRUCK INSIDE, we can't even
recognize the restaurant—it's a shambles. Piles of
junk. CAMERA MOVES slowly, picking up signs that
this was once a mighty space ship. Control panel—
left intact by shrewd old Lamberger—is acrawl with
spiders. CAMERA MOVES IN for close shot large
port hole, the painted stars twinkling . . .

FADE OUT

X

FADE IN

17   MED SHOT—INT CAVE

A fire blazes in the center of the cave. Neanderthal-
type men and women, and a couple mutants, plus
maybe a panther-girl, are seated around a fire, tearing at a slab of raw meat. Over in a corner, others
are tearing at themselves—stylistic, bloody fight.
(Shoot up their nostrils.) CAMERA DOLLIES IN for
MED C.U. lone cave-man. He's standing at mouth
of cave.

18   DIFFERENT ANGLE

This particular cave-man is not so toothy and dirty
and repulsive as the others in the cave, but he is not
Robert Taylor, either. In the b.g., shadowed by immense trees, the ruins of cities coming suddenly to
view out of the phantasmagoric aspect (!), is the AD
ASTRA—almost fallen to pieces now.

The cave-man looks at his fellow creatures eating and

fighting inside. Then, slowly, he lifts his head and—CAMERA FOLLOWING—stares at the clear night sky, black-velvet black and filled with all the stars and all the planets that one universe can hold.

They seem to be on fire now, these stars and planets: vibrant and alive, shimmering, dancing holes of brightness.

(Production Note: If possible, Sid, this constellation should be given a *mocking* and at the same time *beckoning* appearance. Can do?)

FADE OUT

XI

FADE IN

19 MED SHOT—INT HOLLYWOOD STUDIO—WRITER'S OFFICE

Writer, resembling cave-man at mouth of cave, hangs himself with thirty-five dollar hand-painted tie.

FADE OUT

THE END

In His Image

I WAITED, MISTER," the old woman said. "For thirty years; yes sir." She smelled of hospital corridors, pressed ferns, dust: age had devoured her. Now there was nothing left, except the eyes which flashed.

The tall young man did not smile. His hands were almost fists, but the fingers were loose.

"All my life, since I was a little girl, can you imagine? Then it came, out of a clear sky, while I was ironing. Ironing on a Sunday, God save me. It came."

"What did?" the man said, because he had to say something, he couldn't just walk away or ignore her.

"The good Lord's Own sweet breath, that's what," the old woman said. "Like an electricity shock. I was revelated. Praise God, Mister, and praise His good works."

The man looked quickly away. The station was deserted. Its floor sparkled fiercely and this gave the impression of movement, but there was no movement. And there was no sound, either, except for the miles away roar of the train, and the old woman's voice, whispering and whispering.

Please lady!

"Mister, I wonder if you'd tell me something."

The young man did not answer. *Please!*

"Do you read the book?" She cocked her head and arched and smiled.

"What book is that, ma'am?"

"Why," her eyes blinked, "the *good* book, of course."

His fingers laced together, tightly. "Yes," he told her. "All the time."

She nodded, then raised one hand. It was thin and the flesh was transparent. "You're sure you're telling the truth now? We may be a mile underground, but He hears *every word.*"

"It's the truth."

Suddenly the old woman leaned forward. Her face was sharp bones and dry flesh and tiny white hairs. "All right," she said. "All right." The smile altered. Then, almost hissing: "Leviticus; Chapter Five; Verse Two!"

Where are the people!

"Well?" She was clucking her tongue. "Well, Mister?"

The young man rose from the bench and walked to the edge of the platform. In either direction there was darkness. He stood there, watching the darkness, listening to the growing thunder of the train.

It's got to come. It's got to come soon!

The old woman's shoes rang along the cement. She looked feeble and very small. About her shoulders an orange fox lay curled, its head beneath her chin, its eyes beady with cunning.

Train!

" 'Or if a soul touch any unclean thing, whether *it be* a carcass of an unclean beast, or a carcass of unclean cattle, or the carcass of unclean creeping things, and *if* it be hidden from him; he also shall be unclean, and guilty.' "

"Go away."

"Mister," the old woman said. She reached out and touched the young man's arm. It was hard and well-muscled, as the rest of him was.

He jerked away. "Leave me alone!"

"You want His infinite love, don't you?"

"No, goddamn it, no," he shouted. "Please, lady, get away from me."

"He forgives His sheep, Mister. Maybe you're afraid it's too late but you're wrong." She moved in front of the young man. "We are all His lambs . . ."

Her words became lost in the hollow roar, growing.

Jess!

The single headlight appeared, an immense, blinding circle of sharp brilliance.

The old woman's hands were fluttering. She blinked behind thick lenses and opened and closed her cracking lips.

The first car appeared.

The young man pulled his head around. The station was still deserted. It sang piercingly, and trembled, and shook loose flaming splinters of pain.

The old woman had stopped talking.

She stood there, smiling.

The young man took a step backwards and put his hands about the old woman's shoulders.

Her eyes widened.

He waited; then, as the Express burst out of the blackness, its dark metal tons lurching and jolting along the tracks, he released his hold and pushed.

The old woman fell over the edge of the platform.

"Good-bye, Walter!"

The train scooped her up and flattened her against the headlight and held her there for half an instant like a giant moth. Then she came loose.

The young man turned around and ran up the stairs.

Outside, the streets were crowded . . .

The door was opened to the length of its chain by a girl who was mostly shadow.

Peter Nolan put his hands behind his back and smiled. "Well, ma'am," he said, "see, I'm a member of the Junior Woodchucks—"

"The what?"

"—and all I got to do is sell one more subscription to get my genuine toy dial typewriter. What do you say?"

The girl said, "No," and closed the door.

Then she opened it again. "Hi, Pete."

"Hi." He stepped inside. The apartment was thick with heat. Through the drawn shades he could see the beginnings of sunlight. "Ready?" he said.

"And willing," the girl said. "Are you disappointed?"

"Just a little surprised." He put his hand on the back of the girl's neck and pulled her gently. He kissed her.

"Pete! I've told you, there are lines I just don't cross."

"I was going to wait till after we got married, but then I figured what the hell." He touched her nose.

She wriggled out of his arms. "How come so late?"

"What am I, three minutes off schedule?"

"That's close. You miss by only half an hour."

He walked over to the couch, lay down, and groaned theatrically. "I keep telling you to get rid of that sun dial!"

"Okay, so you overslept," the girl said. "God knows leaving at six o'clock wasn't *my* idea."

He lit a cigarette. "I did not oversleep. I left the hotel at four-thirty A.M., got on a subway, got off the subway, and came directly here. Therefore—"

"Therefore, you're nuts. It's now five past six."

He sat upright, pulled back his coatsleeves, glared at a small Benrus.

"Don't worry about it, dear," she said, patting his knee. "I'm just glad I found out now."

She sniffed. "Oh-oh."

"Oh-oh what?"

"I think I smell the maid burning." She rushed across the room and into the kitchen. "You said you wanted to bring some food along, didn't you?"

"Sure."

"So I roasted us a chicken. We can have sandwiches."

He rose and walked into the kitchen. "You," he said, "are only the wildest."

She did not turn around.

He leaned against the refrigerator. "I know what you mean," he said. "It's too good."

"No." Jess did busy things with the chicken. "It's just that I'm happy—understand? And that's enough to give any girl the creeps this day and age."

He watched her work and was quiet for a while. Then he said, "Maybe you ought to change your mind."

She tried to press her hand against his mouth.

"I mean it. Do you really know what the hell you're doing?"

"Of course I do. I—a twenty-eight-year-old spinster, of sound mind and body—am going to run away to a town I never even heard of for the purpose of marrying a guy I've known exactly seven days. Is there anything odd about that?"

"I'm serious, Jess. Shouldn't you know a little more about me, or something?"

"Like what? I know that your name is Peter Nolan. I know that you live in Coeurville, New York, in a big white house surrounded by rose bushes and trees. I know that you do scientific research on a bomb—"

"Not a bomb," he smiled. "A computer. Electronics. See, you're romanticizing me already."

"Don't interrupt. You are visiting New York City for the pure morbid pleasure of it, currently rooming at the Chesterfield Inn. You make five hundred dollars a month, but have saved nothing—which tells me a good deal more about you than I care to know. But—let me finish! Apart from the libertine side of your personality, you are moderately intelligent—and immoderately handsome—kind to small dogs and old chestnut vendors but cool towards the rest of humanity. You prefer Basie to Bach, Grandma Moses to Van Gogh and _____ Above all, you're lonely and in desperate need of a woman five feet nine inches tall with black hair answering to the name of Jessica." She exhaled. "Now, is there anything important that I've missed? Not counting the multitudes of dark women out of your past, of course."

He picked up the wicker basket. "Okay," he said. "You got me dead to rights."

"In that case, let us away—before you start asking questions about *me*."

He kissed her very hard and held her.

"You'll like Coeurville, Jess," he said, "I know you will."

"I'd *better*, if I expect you to make an honest woman out of me! That town is rough competition."

"It's a good town."

She took the basket and waited for him to gather up the suitcases. "Homesick already," she murmured, "after not even two weeks away."

"You'll see," he said. "It's quite a place."

She nodded and looked around the apartment. Then she closed the door and locked it.

"Come on," she said, "let's go make it legal."

Fire!

A bright leaf on the rotted curtain first and then two leaves and three, and then the curtain falling and the leaves turned into blazing yellow ivy, reaching up the wall, across the floor, over all the tables and chairs, growing—

"Walter!"

—a forest of flame, hungry . . . and the man with the bandage quiet, still and quiet, waiting to be eaten . . .

Peter Nolan opened his eyes, quickly. The dream lingered a moment, and vanished.

"Has nightmares," Jess said, "screams, twitches, talks gibberish. *This* you didn't tell me."

The dream was gone. He tried to remember it, but it was gone. "Must have been the pastrami," he said, yawning, vaguely aware of the heat inside his skull. "Pastrami doesn't care much for me."

"I'd say it hates your guts." She whistled. "And who, may I inquire, is Walter?"

"Who is who?"

"You kept yelling Walter."

"Well," he said, "this is a poor time to be telling you, I suppose, but . . . he happens to be my brother."

"What?"

"Yes. We keep him in the cellar. I don't like to think about it."

"Pete."

"I don't know any Walter."

"Really?"

"Not that I can remember, anyway. Maybe he's the Father-Symbol . . . or would that be the Mother-Symbol?"

"Probably," Jess said, "it's the Sex-Symbol. Walter is your repressed libido, and he's champing at the bit."

The highway sloped gently and curved past an immense field of wild growth. Beyond the field there were farm houses and straggles of horses and wide shade trees, small and bright in the clear air. The thunder of rockets rumbled distantly.

Peter Nolan stretched and yawned again. "Want me to take over?"

"If you want to." Jess stopped the car and they switched seat positions.

"Which reminds me," she said, "just how far is this rustic paradise?"

"Well . . ." He studied the countryside. "I *ought* to know, but I generally come through at night . . ."

"Pretty country, anyway," she said.

"The prettiest." He squinted, leaned close to the windshield. "I know where we are now. See that scatter creek?"

"Yup."

"Used to play there when I was a kid. Every time I ran away from home, this is as far as I got. Water's ice cold."

"Good old Scatter Creek!"

He nudged her. "Don't be so damn big-city. I intend to acquaint you with every square inch of Coeurville, and you're going to love it."

"Aye, aye," she said, sleepily.

"Over there's Lonely Yew Lane. Great place for sparking with the girlies."

"How would you know?"

"Among sparking circles," he said, "I was referred to as *The Electrode*."

She made feline movements against him. "I'll just bet you're the best known figure in town."

"Only one of the best," he admitted. Then, "Lean your head on my shoulder—we've got an hour anyway."

She closed her eyes. In a tired, contented voice she whispered, "Pete Nolan, you have the sharpest, boniest, damndest shoulders in all the world."

He slipped his arm around her, and they drove in silence for a while. Things, he thought, are very good. Things are about as good as they can be. If they were any better, I would go berserk.

He thought of how he and Jess had met, only a week before. It had been late at night, and he had been walking . . . where? Somewhere. And he was in the middle of the street, when the light changed to red. Then something happened—he couldn't figure out what, or why. Shock, maybe. Anyway, suddenly he was lying on his back, with the bumper of a car less than three feet from his head. This car. And Jess, standing there, whitefaced and trembling. *'Are you hurt, Mister?' 'You never laid a wheel on me.' 'In that case, I don't mind telling you, buddy, you have reduced me to a nervous wreck.' 'How about a drink?' 'A drink would be fine.'* . . . .

The field gave way to lawns and small houses and freshfruit stands.

Peter Nolan eased off the accelerator. They passed a sign which read: *You are entering Coeurville, N. Y.—Pop. 3,550.*

Then the houses multiplied and soon there were stores and motels.

"Mah plantation," he boomed. "Fur as th' eye kin see!"

It was a very small town, and very narrow, pressed by grassy knolls and shaded by giant poplars which burst from the sidewalks. The streets were white and clean. Above the streets banners announcing a fair drifted calmly in the breeze, all reds and greens. There were a lot of women, but also a number of old men.

Peter Nolan smoothed the powerful turbines down and dropped rapidly from 114 miles-per-hour to a calm 40. He sighed. "There's the New Brunswick," he gestured. "Got an ice cream parlor and a magazine shop. You can get cigarettes there, too, if you can prove you're over twenty-one—Mr. van Brooks is very strict about that."

"I shouldn't have too much trouble."

"Over there's the Foodbag grocery where we trade. Depot's over to the right, you can't see it now. And—"

He narrowed his eyes.

He looked at a large red office building on the corner.

"Come on, don't stop now."

He shook his head, almost imperceptibly. "—library's down Elm Street, there—"

A red office building in Coeurville?

As he tried to place it, a clothing store glided slowly past the car window. Helmer's Men's Wear. Wide glass front, yellow plastic shade, perfectly ordinary and not in the least peculiar— except, he couldn't recall any Helmer's Men's Wear.

It was brand new to him.

Brother, you're an observant one, all right. Too much work . . .

Town could burn down, you wouldn't know it.

Burn down . . .

"Pete, do me a favor."

"Sure."

"Let's get a quick one before meeting the gang, huh? Just one quick one."

"No can do," he said. "Have to go into Temple for liquor. That's four miles away."

"I thought I saw a bar back there on the main drag."

"Not in Coeurville you didn't." He frowned, felt a tenseness spring into life inside him. "How about coffee?"

"Okay."

He nosed the car onto a shoulder and cut the engine.

Burn . . .

"Hey."

They walked past a dry goods store and a motion picture theatre and a drugstore.

And entered a small hotel lobby.

"Pete, what's biting you?"

He dropped the frown. "Nothing. The nervous bridegroom is all."

"Maybe we ought to get married right away," Jess said. She looked around the deserted lobby. It was dark and musty. "You want to get coffee here?" she said, dubiously.

"Down the street," someone said. Jess turned and faced an amiable old man in a blue suit. He was standing behind a desk. "Four stores down. Kelsey's Cafe."

Peter Nolan walked over to the man. "This is the Imperial, isn't it?" he asked, and thought, Of course this is the Imperial. What a stupid question.

"Sure is, Mister."

Sure is, Mister. Who is this old bird anyway?

"You close up your coffee shop?"

"Nope. Never had a coffee shop. Just the hotel."

The tenseness increased. "That's certainly very interesting," he told the man, remembering the five hundred or more times he'd eaten lunch here.

He snorted and walked across the lobby. It looked the same. Even the dust looked the same. He returned to the desk. "Is this a gag?"

The old man took a step backwards. "Beg pardon?"

Jess laughed. "Come on," she said, "they're probably using it for an orgy, stag only."

"But—"

Outside in the sunlight, Peter Nolan looked at the building carefully.

"It was here," he said, pointing to the brick wall. "At least, I think it was. Or else—did he say Kelsey's Cafe?"

"That's what he said."

"I never heard in my entire life of a Kelsey's Cafe." He turned his head, peered up and down the street. It was the same, and yet, somehow, it wasn't the same.

"You sure we're in the right town, Petesey?" Jess said. "I know how absent-minded you scientific men are."

"Of course I'm sure."

"Well, don't snap at me . . ."

"Look, Jess—let's go on home, get something there. I think maybe I'm a little upset. All right?"

"Sure."

They went back to the car.

"Is it far?"

"Just a few blocks." He felt the tenseness growing. As the houses passed, it grew. He thought about the red building, the bar Jess said she'd seen, and now this ridiculous business with the coffee shop . . . Just a mix-up, of course, that and his natural nervousness.

No. Something was wrong. He knew it, he could feel the wrongness all around him.

"That's it, isn't it?" Jess said. She was looking at a large square white house.

"Yeah." The familiarity of the house restored his spirits.

The feeling drained away. "Your future home, Miss Lang." He stopped the car.

"It's beautiful, Pete. Really."

He got out of the car.

"Think I better go in first," he said. "The shock would be too great for Aunt Mildred."

"I thought you'd written her."

"I did, but I forgot to—" He took the letter from his inside coat pocket, and grinned.

"God, and you worry about forgetting coffee shops!"

He walked across the porch and tried the door.

It was locked.

He removed a key from his pocket and inserted it. It didn't work.

The feeling came back, sickeningly. He twisted the key first one way and then the other, and examined the chain to see that he'd not made a mistake.

The door opened.

"What is it?" A fat man with a fat red face stood glaring.

Peter Nolan glanced at the house numbers: 515. He glared back at the man. "Who are you?"

The fat man closed one eye. An old friend of Mildred's, probably—Mildred had so many screwy friends. Or a plumber, maybe. "Look, my name's Nolan. I live here. I own the house."

The fat man scratched his chin. He said nothing.

"Where's Mildred?"

"Who?"

"Mildred Nolan! Say, what the hell are you doing here, anyway?"

"It's none of your business," the fat man told him, "but I happen to live here. I've lived here for nine years, bought the place from Gerald Butler, got the deed to prove it. There ain't nobody named Mildred here and I never saw you before in my life." He started to close the door. "You got the wrong house."

"Look, fella, you're headed for a lot of trouble. I mean it. Now open up, and—"

The fat man slammed the door hurriedly.

Peter Nolan walked back to the car. He turned and stared. "What's up?" Jess asked.

He looked at the house. At the curtains he'd never seen, and the *fresh* white paint, and the green doormat . . . He thought about the key that didn't fit the lock.

"Pete."

Goddamn it, what was happening? This was his house, all right, there wasn't any doubt of that. No doubt at all. None.

He looked at Jess, opened his mouth, closed it, and walked quickly across the street.

He went up the steps of a brown shake bungalow, and rapped on the door.

"Mrs. Cook! Hey, Jennie!"

A young girl appeared at the open window. "Who'd you want?" she said.

"Mrs. Cook. I've got to talk with her."

The girl leaned on her elbows. "Mrs. Cook died," she said. "Didn't you know?"

"What . . . did you say?"

"Three years ago. You aren't her cousin from Chicago, are you?"

"No," he said, dazedly. "No, I'm not. Sorry." He walked slowly back across the street and got into the car.

Jess was frowning, searching his face. "What is it, Pete?" she said. "Don't you think you better clue me in?"

"I don't—" He ran a hand through his hair. "The kid over there claims Mrs. Cook has been dead for three years."

"So what?"

"I had lunch with Mrs. Cook just before I left for New York . . . a week and a half ago."

For a long time now he had driven in silence, gazing directly ahead at the road, his hands tight about the steering wheel. The tachometer needle was hovering around the danger mark.

Jess sat close to the door. The smile that usually played about her face was gone. She looked different, just as everything looked different, and she no longer had the sixteen or seventeen year old's look.

For Peter Nolan the tension was now like a steel rail bent almost to the breaking point. It would snap at any moment, he felt sure. Because there was no suspecting now, only knowing, knowing absolutely. They'd driven from his house—*that* house, he wasn't sure whose it was any longer—to the city hall. Fred Dickey would clear things up, make the proper explanations, good old Fred. Except good old Fred hadn't recognized him. Neither had Bert Zangwill over at the sheriff's office—Bert, who used to tell him stories, who was a hero to him! And the others, the friends he had known all his life— all dead, or gone away, or unable to remember him . . .

But not completely unable. That was the strangest thing of all. The way they would stare and seem about to greet him and then shake their heads . . .

He felt like screaming now, as he remembered how Jess' face had changed in the past two hours, how her eyes had changed, how she looked at him, the suspicion and the wonder only too obvious.

God, maybe I am nuts, he thought, maybe I really am. Then, No, dammit! This is Coeurville and this is my home and I know every foot of it. That tree over there, the strawberry patch we're passing, everything. I do!

Jess was rubbing the back of her neck. "Pete—"

"Yes?"

"You said something a little while ago, back in town . . . You said it was as though Coeurville had aged twenty years. Didn't you?"

"That's right. Twenty years—in a week and a half."

"Maybe not," she said.

"What do you mean?"

"I'm not really sure, but—this is going to sound corny. I just mean, what if it's true? What if twenty years actually have gone by?"

"Rip van Winkle?"

She shrugged. "Well, why not? At least it's a possibility."

"No," he said "I thought of it, but it doesn't hold up. For a lot of reasons. One, it would make me at least forty-five—unless I left at age ten. Which couldn't very well be, because I went to high school and college here. And that," he sighed, nervously, "brings us to the real beaut. There are no records of my having attended Coeurville High. Remember?"

She nodded.

"And the university I work for, dear old Coeurville U., it doesn't even exist. It never existed." He thought of the feeling in his chest when they'd driven out onto that unbroken field of grass which had been a campus, had been, he knew, had to have been. "And what about Mildred?"

Jess shivered slightly.

"Mildred was the head of the Garden Club," he continued. "She got around town like a visiting Congressman, all the time. Everybody knew her. And now there isn't a single trace of evidence to show that Mildred Nolan ever lived in Coeurville, New York."

"Okay, so it won't work. It was an idea."

The berry patches became fields once more, golden brown and dark, almost black, green. Peter Nolan turned down a small gravel road and decelerated sharply and drove the road that wound through the fields.

He hit the brake at a curve and slid to a stop.

"Wait here," he said.

He got out of the car and walked through the rusted wire gate of the cemetery. It was a small place, and very old. The gravestones were ornate carvings of fat children with wings or great scrolls or filagreed crosses, all grimed with age.

He walked across the raised humps of neglected lawn, toward the east end of the cemetery. Beyond the fence was rich grass, dairy cows grazing in utter silence, and a dark stream crossed by a trestle.

Peter Nolan approached two marble tombstones, and remembered with every step the sadness he had felt when he
had stood exactly here, in the foul rain, and watched them
lower his mother's casket, down close to the father he had
never known.

The memory was alive and strong. It was the one thing he
was sure of, now.

He knelt and stared at the twin epitaphs on the tombstones.

And felt the steel bar of tenseness inside him snap and
explode into a million white-hot fragments.

The epitaphs read:

MARY F. CUMMINGS

1883 - 1931

and

WALTER B. CUMMINGS, SR.

1879 - 1909

The sky was a deep red stain now. Jess pushed hard on the
pedal, keeping it at a steady 140. Her lips were dry.

"We'll be home in a little while," she said, softly, "and then
it'll be okay. Go on, pass out again. Rest."

The speed lane merged with the narrow highway and the
traffic thinned and disappeared. Barns and farmhouses flashed
past the window in a darkening blur.

Peter Nolan sat very still. He clutched his knees.

The pain that was not precisely that vanished and returned
and grew and diminished. He fought it with all of his strength.
But it would not stay away. Nothing he did would make it
stay away.

Memories skirted close, and he kept reaching for them.

Fire. A man with bandages. A house.

He reached and sometimes came very near, and always
missed. No. It would take something more than reaching. But
what? And for what?

The car pulled into a service station and he shut his eyes
against the sudden brilliance.

What was she trying to do, anyway, blind him?

And who the hell did she think she was to order him
around?

He looked at Jess. She smiled.

Then he remembered that she had used the word *doctor*.
Why? To cure him, or—to get rid of him, quietly?

Of course. One of her doctor friends would slip him a
needle and that would be that. Never mind the reason. Women
have their own reasons.

He waited until the sky had turned almost completely
black, then he said, "Jess, would you please stop the car?"

She pulled over onto the dirt. "You going to be sick?"

"Yeah," he said. "I'll be back in a minute. I don't feel so good."

He went outside, leaped the shallow ditch, and walked into the dense foliage.

His shoe scraped. He bent down and patted the ground and closed his fingers about a large jagged stone.

Good. We'll see about doctors now.

"Jess!" he called. "Could you give me a hand?"

A pause. Then the sound of the metal door opening and slamming and the sound of movement in the brush.

Jess walked over to him and touched his arm.

"Is it better?" she asked.

"Yes."

Her eyes moved to his hand.

He raised the stone, stood there with it raised, staring; then he turned and threw the stone into the foliage in back of him.

"What is it, Pete?"

"Stubbed my damn toe." He moved toward Jess and pulled her close. "Stubbed my toe on the rock." The pain was leaving. It had torn across his mind like a sheet of flame, until there had been only a dancing blackness. Now it was leaving.

Jess put her fingers against his face, gently. "Come on back to the car," she said.

He took his hands from her.

"Come on, Pete."

"All right. You go on—I'll be there in a minute."

She looked at him helplessly, then she walked back. When she was gone, when he heard the door again, Peter Nolan closed his eyes. He waited for the pain to return, but it did not return. He tried to hang on to the memories that had been flying quickly through his brain, but they were elusive. Something about an old woman, something about a train, they were, and fire, and—

He realized, suddenly, why he had picked up the stone.

He had meant to kill Jess.

Why?

He bunched his fingers into fists and drove them, hard, into a tree, again, and again.

Then he stopped. The moon slid out of a clump of blackness, and spilled light over the land—cool, soft, clear light.

Peter Nolan looked at his hands. He turned them over and looked at them.

They were white and dry.

The tree bark had torn away small strips and pieces of flesh, but there was no blood.

He carefully pulled a flap of skin down three inches below the wrist, and focused his eyes.

Beneath the flap of skin, where veins ought to have been, and cartilage, and bone, were hundreds of tiny flexible rods, jointed and gleaming, and infinitesimal springs, turning, and bright yellow coils of wire.

He looked at his wrist watch for a long time. Then he wrapped a handkerchief around the torn section, and went back to the car.

Jess was waiting. "Better now?" she asked in the same genuine, unfrightened tone she had used before.

"Better," he said. Everything was returning now. Like relays clicking into place. Everything.

He threw his head back. "Drive to your apartment," he said, expressionlessly. "Let me off when I tell you to, then drive to your apartment and wait for me."

Jess said nothing. She started the car.

Soon they were in the outskirts of the city.

He walked up the circular driveway and stood for a moment, looking at the house. It was fat and sprawling and ugly: a little of 1860 and a little of 1960, brick and wood, gabled windows, false pilasters. Its color was gray. Where once had been white paint was now only this grayness. The age-bulged slats were pocked and cancered, held by crumbling nails.

He walked to the machine-carved door.

The knocker put out deep sound.

He waited, knocked again.

The door opened.

"Hello, Walter."

The tall man with the bandaged face sighed. "Pete," he said, extending his hand. "I've been waiting for you."

Peter Nolan walked with the tall man into a large room.

There were hundreds of books in this room, all shabby and worn, a few heavy pieces of furniture, mostly ancient, fancy letter openers, dark lace curtains.

"Sit down," the tall man said. "Over there." He walked over to a small cupboard and poured whiskey into a glass. "You've been to Coeurville, haven't you?"

"Yes. Tell me about it, Walter."

"But you know already. How else could you have come here?"

"I asked you to talk. Please."

The tall man paused, then shrugged. "All right." He reached up and tore loose from his forehead the upper strips of adhesive tape.

The bandage fell.

Peter Nolan stared at an exact duplicate of himself. Except for the stitched scar running from just below the left eye to the mouth, the face was a mirrored reflection.

"As you can see, you nearly blinded me with those scissors."

"From the beginning, Walter."

"But this *is* the beginning," the tall man said. Then, "All right. Your name is Peter Nolan—you know that."

"Yes."

"And you know that you were born eight days ago. I made the delivery: Doctor W. B. Cummings, Jr., Ph.D. I'm your mother. I'm also your father—and every single one of your ancestors, too, unless we count the first adding machine."

"You're drunk."

"Aye. Drunk as an owl. Drunk as a lord. Care to join me? It's quite possible, and I guarantee no hangover—"

"All I want is for you to stow the colorful dialogue and tell me things."

The tall man tilted his glass. "You've been to Coeurville, so you've learned that Peter Nolan never lived there. You also know that you've been behaving—oddly—of late. And from the handkerchief around your hand, I should judge you know about that, too. With this information what can *I* tell you?"

"Who am I?" The heat was beginning again.

"You're nobody," the tall man said. "You're nobody at all."

"Stop it, Walter."

"Who is this watch I'm wearing? Ask me that. Who is the refrigerator in the kitchen? Don't you understand?" The man's eyes glinted briefly. "You're a machine, Pete."

Memories took solider form. They came into focus.

But not entirely. Pieces were missing.

"Go on."

The tall man pulled his dressing gown closer about his unshaven throat. He seemed to talk to himself alone.

"You were born a long time ago, actually," he said. "Inside my head. All kids have dreams, don't they? You were mine. The others thought about ice cream mountains and success with the F.B.I. and going to Mars, and swapped their dreams, and finally forgot them. I didn't. I thought about one thing and longed for one thing, always; just one: a *perfect* artificial man. Not just a robot, but a duplicate of a human being." He laughed. "It was harmless—and not even terribly imaginative for a child. I became an adult—only, I didn't forget my dream."

Peter Nolan picked up one of the letter openers. It was sturdy and sharp.

"All right," the tall man said, "I made you. Is that straight enough? It took a lot of years and a lot of money, and more failures than I like to think about. But I was patient. I studied, I read, I experimented. I'd already built a man—also Peter Nolan: I like the name: no reason—but he was nothing. A crude job. So I started all over again from scratch, duplicating from every manner of material the physical elements of the human body. People helped me, but they didn't know what it was for. Some of them solved problems I could never have solved. But—don't you see? I wanted to give my man a brain that worked like a brain; and emotions; and intelligence." He refilled the glass, took another swallow. "All that—I dreamed. Of course, intelligence was the most difficult. You have no idea how difficult. My man had to have memories, he had to have reasoning power—abstract reasoning power—a past, a personality—millions of intricate facets multiplied by millions to make up *intelligence*. Inventing these things from whole cloth would have taken forever. So I worked and found the answer. I would use myself. On certain cells I made certain impressions. My own memories went into the cells. Some of my talent. Some of my knowledge. Bits and pieces, of myself. It took a long time . . . a very long time."

They were silent for a time. Peter Nolan gripped the letter opener and struggled against the heat.

"You were perfect, I felt," the tall man went on. "But I had to be sure. Ten years ago you would have been impossible: since the discoveries in plastics, however, you were merely improbable. My plastic felt like flesh to *me,* and I had cushioned the mechanical parts so that they felt exactly like human bones when touched, but—it would be the final test: to let you mingle with crowds, and observe closely their reactions. I blocked out—or tried to—all memory of me and your actual construction. You were Peter Nolan, research scientist, in New York on a sabbatical . . ."

"You lived in Coeurville?" The question leapt out.

"Of course. For your past, I gave you my memories of the town. Some of them were probably quite inaccurate and incomplete—I left Coeurville many years ago. Going there must have been an experience . . ."

"It was." Peter Nolan closed his eyes. "What about the University?"

"Fictitious. I had to give you a job."

"And Aunt Mildred?"

"A conceit. All the old women I've known in one. I worked out your relationship with her very carefully—not at all necessary, I suppose. The female conquests, by the way, are also —I regret to report—imaginary." He shook a cigarette loose from a pack. "That's about all," he said. "You can fill in the rest. Up to last week, anyway."

"What about last week."

The tall man shook his head. "I wish I knew," he said. "Something went wrong, something mechanical . . . I couldn't tell. You attacked me with a pair of scissors and I couldn't stop you. As you know, I've been unable to find you since."

"What's wrong with me?"

"I'm not sure. But—look, Pete. You're me. Everything you know or feel or think reflects some portion of myself, Walter Cummings. If you wished to kill—I've read the papers, I know about it; the conductor caught a glimpse of you—it could only mean that there is some part of me that wished to kill. *My* own death-wish, inverted. Everyone has it. I mean, we're all potential suicides or murderers or rapists or thieves. We all have the seeds of paranoia, schizophrenia, or worse, lying inside us, somewhere—from the moment we're born to the moment we die. But—and here's the thing—if we're normal, we're protected. We're protected by our inhibitions. These instincts are never given a chance to get out of hand. We may *want* to kill the loudmouthed woman downstairs, or we may *want* to commit suicide at times—but usually we don't."

"So?"

"So, Pete, it would appear that my own 'seeds' are more developed than I'd realized. In you, they are. In giving you parts of myself, I also gave you—although unintentionally—my latent psychoses. Big ones. Big enough to break through . . ."

There was a long silence.

"To put it even clearer," the tall man said, "you're insane."

Peter Nolan rose from the couch and walked over to the window. The night pressed, moved, tugged at the branches of dead trees.

"Can I be—fixed?"

The tall man shrugged.

The heat dripped faster, melting into pain. Whirlings and bright dots and pain. "Can I?"

"I don't know."

"Why don't you know?"

"Because . . . much as I hated to admit it, luck had a great deal to do with your success." The man stared at the letter opener in Peter Nolan's hand. "Skill alone wasn't enough. There were so many failures before, they should have made it clear—but they didn't. I was obsessed."

"What are you saying?"

"That you were an accident. I was a blind man with a machine gun, Pete. I kept shooting and reloading and shooting and finally I hit the target; but it was off-center. I don't know that I could even come close again."

Peter Nolan fought the pain, grasped at the picture of an old woman falling toward dark tracks.

The tall man smiled, wanly. "But that's the story of my

life, right down the line. A long series of failures. I told myself that I wanted to make an artificial man, but I think my real aim was simply to build another Walter Cummings, Only, without the shyness, without the frustration—a reverse Jekyll and Hyde. All I wished I was. The 'real' me . . ."

Peter Nolan turned. "I came here to kill you," he said.

The tall man nodded.

"I was going to kill you and set fire to the house."

"I know: I felt like doing it myself. It's what I'd do if I were in your shoes."

"There's a girl, Walter."

The tall man raised his eyebrows; then he lit another cigarette, slowly, off the old one.

"Does she know?" he said.

"No. I took her with me to Coeurville; we were going to get married there; and she thinks I'm probably nuts—but she doesn't know. She's in love with me."

"Pretty?"

"And intelligent. And lonely—something you ought to be able to understand. She's got a fine life all mapped out, for her and me, together."

"That's—too bad," the tall man said. He pressed his fingertips into his temples. "I'm truly sorry, Pete."

"Her name is Jessica Lang. She has old-fashioned ideas about virtue: that's why she never found out, I imagine," Peter Nolan gripped the edge of the chair. "That would have been a nice scene."

"No," the tall man said. "You're perfect. It would have gone all right—that is, if she's a virgin. It would seem strange, but then, it always does. Or so I've heard."

The pain jabbed in and out, fire-tipped needles, jabbing.

The tall man rose from the couch-arm on which he had been seated. "Well," he said, "what are we going to do?"

"You can't fix me for sure?"

"No."

"You can't stop me from killing. You can't make me grow old, either—I'll always be like this. I'm insane and I'll stay insane, until something goes out—then I'll die. Is that it?"

"I'm sorry, Pete. I wanted you to be all the things I wasn't; that's the truth. If I'd known—"

Peter Nolan put his hands out. "She'd learn about it, some day," he said.

"Yes. She would."

"She'd find out, or I'd kill her—I almost did, tonight. I might kill Jess."

"You might."

The two figures were very quiet for a time. The wind beat

against the loose window panes, and against the shutters of the house.

They were quiet, listening.

Then Peter Nolan said: "Do you want to make it right, Walter?"

The tall man clenched his fists. "I would give anything to do that."

"Are you telling the truth?"

"Yes."

"Then listen to me carefully. You're going to build another Peter Nolan—"

"What?"

"That's right. You're going to build another me, and it's going to be right, this time, and you're going to do it tonight. This Peter Nolan is going to marry Jess; and he's going to be happy, for the first time in his life."

The tall man stared.

Understanding came into his eyes, slowly.

"It's something you can do—*now*—isn't it?"

"I think so."

"Then let's get to work, before I jam this letter opener into your chest."

"Pete—"

"Come on."

Together, they walked into the hall and down the long flight of stairs to the laboratory below.

Hours later one of them returned to the study.

The door was opened to the length of its chain by a girl who was mostly shadow.

The tall man put his hands behind his back and smiled. "Well, ma'am," he said, "see I'm a member of the Junior Woodchucks—"

"Pete, get in here this minute. I've been worried sick."

The tall man walked into the apartment. He paused for a moment, then he took the girl into his arms and kissed her. She pulled away. "And now, before I go crazy," she said, "will you please tell me what this is all about?"

The tall man smiled. "I'll tell you what it's all about," he promised. "But let's not talk here."

"I want to know if you're all right," Jess said, looking at him. "What's that scar on your face?"

"I'm all right," the tall man said. "Come on, a drink. Get your coat."

Jess went to the closet and pulled out a jacket and slipped it on.

They went out of the apartment.

A cold gray moon spread light across the streets.

"Pete, something is wrong. I know it is."

"No," the tall man said. "Other way around. Something is right, for a change." He held her arm and looked at her and then she saw his smile and stopped talking.

They went into a bar.

At a table, after they ordered, he lit a cigarette for her. Then he lit one for himself. He held the flame of the lighter before his face for a long moment, and he heard her exclaim as he ran his index finger through the flame. Hot pain seared through him. He pulled his finger away, snapped off the lighter and grinned at her.

"What did you burn your finger for, Pete? You did it deliberately . . ."

He laughed. "Couldn't help it. Had to prove something to myself."

"What?"

He shrugged, still smiling. "Had to make sure I was really flesh and blood and not some part of a plastic nightmare . . ."

"I don't understand, Pete."

"Not necessary, honey. Not at all. Everything's ok. The past is gone and for the first time in my life I'm looking forward to the future. In a way I guess we're seeing each other for the first time. What I see is nice."

The waiter brought their drinks. He raised his, wiggled his burnt finger for her to do likewise, and proffered a toast.

Outside the bar an old man in a dirty white raincoat walked up and down, carrying newspapers.

"Subway killer still at large!" the old man shouted.

His voice was a whisper in the wind.

The Jungle

Suddenly it was there. On foxfeet, invisibly, it had crept, past all the fences and traps he had laid, past all the barriers. And now it sat inside his mind, a part of him, like his pulse, like the steady beat of his heart.

Richard Austin became rigid in the chair. He closed his eyes and strained the muscles in his body until they were silent and unmoving as granite; and he listened to the thing that had come again, taking him by surprise even while he had been waiting. He listened to it grow—it *seemed* to grow; he couldn't be sure: perhaps he was merely bringing it into sharper focus by filtering out the other constant sounds: the winds that whispered through the foliage of balloon-topped trees the murmurous insect-drone of all the machines that produced this wind and pumped blood through the city from their stations far beneath the night-heavy streets. Or, perhaps, it was because he was searching, trying to lay hands on it that the thing seemed to be different tonight, stronger, surer. Or—what did it matter?

He sat in the darkened room and listened to the drums; to the even, steady throb that really neither rose nor diminished, but held to that slow dignified tempo with which he'd become so familiar.

Then quickly he rose from the chair and shook his head. The sounds died and became an indistinguishable part of the silence. It was only concentration, he thought, and the desire to hear them that gave them life . . .

Richard Austin released a jagged breath from his swollen lungs, painfully. He walked to the bar and poured some whiskey into a glass and drank most of it in a single swallow: it went down his dry throat like knives, forcing the salivary glands back into action.

He shook his head again, turned and walked back across the living room to the far door. It swung out noiselessly as his hand touched the ornamented circle of hammered brass.

The figure of his wife lay perfectly still under the black light, still and pale, as she had lain three hours before. He walked toward her, feeling his nostrils dilate at the acrid medicine smells, harshly bitter and new to his senses. He blinked away the hot tears that had rushed, stinging, to his eyes; and stood for a time, quietly, trying not to think of the drums.

Then he whispered: "Mag . . . Mag, don't die tonight!"

Imbecile words! He clenched his fists and stared down at the face that was so full of pain, so twisted with defeat, that now you could not believe it had once been different, a young face, full of laughter and innocence and courage.

The color had gone completely. From the burning splotchy scarlet of last week to this stiff white mask, lifeless, brittle as drying paste. And covered over with perspiration that glistened above her mouth in cold wet buttons and over her face like oil on white stone. The bedding under and around her was drenched gray.

Austin looked at the bandage that covered his wife's head, and forced away the memory, brutally. The memory of her long silver hair and how it had fallen away in clumps in his hands within a week after she had been stricken . . .

But the thoughts danced out of control, and he found himself remembering all the terrible steps in this nightmare.

The scientists had thought it malaria, judging from the symptoms, which were identical. But that was difficult to accept, for malaria had been effectively conquered—powerful new discoveries in vaccines having been administered first, and then the primary cause of the disease itself—the Anopheles mosquitoe—destroyed completely. And the liquid alloys which formed the foundations for this new city eliminated all the likely breeding places, the bogs and marshlands and rivers. No instance of re-occurrence of the disease had been reported for half a century. Yet—malarial parasites were discovered in the bloodstreams of those first victims, unmistakable parasites that multiplied at a swift rate and worked their destruction of the red corpuscles. And the chemists immediately had to go about the business of mixing medicines from now ancient prescriptions, frantically working against time. A disquieting, even a frightening thing; but without terror for the builders of the new city; not sufficient to make them abandon their work or to spark mass evacuations. Panic was by now so forgotten by most that it had become a new emotion, to be learned all over again.

It had not taken very long to relearn, Austin recalled. Terror had come soon enough. The stricken—some thirty husky workmen, engineers, planners—had rallied under the drugs and seemed to be out of critical condition when, one night, they had all suffered relapses, fallen into fevered comas and proceeded to alternate between unconsciousness

and delirium. The scientists were baffled. They tried frenz-
iedly to arrest the parasites, but without success. Their medicines were useless, their drugs and radium treatments and
inoculations—all, useless. Finally, they could only look on
as the disease took new turns, developed strange characteristics, changed altogether from what they had taken to be
malaria to something utterly foreign. It began to assume a
horrible regular pattern: from prolonged delirium to cata-
tonia, whereby the victim's respiratory system and heartbeat
diminished to a condition only barely distinguishable from
death. And then, the most hideous part: the swift decom-
position of the body cells, the destruction of the tissues . . .

Richard Austin carefully controlled a shudder as he
thought of those weeks that had been the beginning. He
fingered out a cigarette from his pocket, started to strike it,
then broke the cylinder and ground its bright red flakes into
his palms.

No other real hint had been given then: only the disease.
Someone had nicknamed it "Jungle Rot"—cruel, but apt.
The victims *were* rotting alive, the flesh falling from them
like rain-soaked rags; and they did not die wholly, ever,
until they had been transformed into almost unrecognizable
mounds of putrescence . . .

He put out a hand and laid it gently against his wife's
cheek. The perspiration was chill and greasy to his touch,
like the stagnant water of slew banks. Instinctively his fingers
recoiled and balled back into fists. He forced them open
again and stared at the tiny dottles of flesh that clung to
them.

"Mag!" It had started already! Wildly, he touched her
arm, applying very slight pressure. The outer skin crumbled
away, leaving a small wet gray patch. Austin's heart raced;
an involuntary movement caused his fingers to pinch his own
wrists, hard. A wrinkled spot appeared and disappeared, a
small, fading red line.

She's dying, he thought. Very surely, very slowly, she's
begun to die—Mag. Soon her body will turn gray and then
it will come loose; the weight of the sheet will be enough to
tear big strips of it away . . . She'll begin to rot, and her
brain will know it—they had discovered that much: the
victims were never completely comatose, could not be ade-
quately drugged—she will know that she is mouldering even
while she lives and thinks . . .

And why? His head ached, throbbed. *Why?*

The years, these past months, the room with its stink of
decay—everything rushed up, suddenly, filling Austin's
mind.

If I had agreed to leave with the rest he thought, to run away, then Mag would be well and full of life. But—I didn't agree . . .

He had stayed on to fight. And Mag would not leave without him. Now she was dying and that was the end of it.

Or—he turned slowly—was it? He walked out to the balcony. The forced air was soft and cool; it moved in little patches through the streets of the city. Mbarara, *his* city; the one he'd dreamed about and then planned and designed and pushed into existence; the place built to pamper five hundred thousand people.

Empty, now, and deserted as a gigantic churchyard . . .

Dimly he recognized the sound of the drums, with their slow muffled rhythm, directionless as always, seeming to come from everywhere and from nowhere. Speaking to him. Whispering.

Austin lit a cigarette and sucked the calming smoke into his lungs. He remained motionless until the cigarette was down to the cork.

Then he walked back into the bedroom, opened a cabinet and took a heavy silver pistol.

He loaded it carefully.

Mag lay still; almost, it seemed to Austin, expectant, waiting. So very still and pale.

He pointed the barrel of the pistol at his wife's forehead and curled his finger around the trigger. Another slight pressure and it would be over. Her suffering would be over. Just a slight pressure!

The drums droned louder until they were exploding in the quiet room.

Austin tensed and fought the trembling, gripped the pistol with his other hand to steady it.

But his finger refused to move on the curved trigger.

After a long moment, he lowered his arm and dropped the gun into his pocket.

"No." He said it quietly, undramatically. The word hit a barrier of mucus and came out high-pitched and child-like.

He coughed.

That was what they wanted him to do—he could tell, from the drums. That's what so many of the others had done. Panicked.

"No."

He walked quickly out of the room, through the hall, to the elevator. It lowered instantly but he did not wait for it to reach bottom before he leapt off and ran across the floor to the barricaded front door.

He tore at the locks. Then the door swung open and he

was outside; for the first time in three weeks—outside, alone, in the city.

He paused, fascinated by the strangeness of it. Impossible to believe that he was the only white man left in the entire city.

He strode to a high-speed walkway, halted it and stepped on. Setting the power at half with his passkey, he pressed the control button and sagged against the rail as the belt whispered into movement.

He knew where he was going. Perhaps he even knew why. But he didn't think about that; instead, he looked at the buildings that slid by silently, the vast rolling spheres and columns of colored stone, the balanced shapes that existed now and that had once existed only in his mind. And he listened to the drums, wondering why the sound of them seemed natural and his buildings suddenly so unnatural, so strange and disjointed.

Like green balloons on yellow sticks, the cultured Grant Wood trees slipped by, uniform and straight, arranged in aesthetically pleasing designs on the stone islands between belts. Austin smiled: The touch of nature. Toy trees, ruffling in artificial winds . . . It all looked, now, like the model he had presented to the Senators. About as real and lifelike.

Austin moved like a carefully carved and painted figurine, incredibly small and lonely-looking on the empty walkway. He thought about the years of preparation; the endless red tape and paper work that had preceded the actual job. Then of the natives, how they had protested and petitioned to influence the Five-Power governments and how that had slowed them down. The problem of money, whipped only by pounding at the point of over-population, again and again, never letting up for a moment. The problems, problems . . .

He could not recall when the work itself had actually begun—it was all so joined. Laying the first railroad could certainly not have been a particle as beset with difficulty. Because the tribes of the Kenya territory numbered into the millions; and they were all filled with hatred and fury, opposing the city at every turn.

No explanation had satisfied them. They saw it as the destruction of their world and so they fought. With guns and spears and arrows and darts, with every resource at their disposal, refusing to capitulate, hunting like an army of mad ants scattered over the land.

And, since they could not be controlled, they had to be destroyed. Like their forests and rivers and mountains, destroyed, to make room for the city.

Though not, Austin remembered grimly, without loss. The

white men had fine weapons, but none more fatal than machetes biting deep into neck flesh or sharp wooden shafts coated with strange poisons. And they did not all escape. Some would wander too far, unused to this green world where a man could become hopelessly lost within three minutes. Others would forget their weapons. And a few were too brave.

Austin thought of Joseph Fava, the engineer, who had been reported missing. And of how Fava had coming running back to the camp after two days, running and screaming, a bright crimson nearly dead creature out of the worst dreams. He had been cleanly stripped of all his skin, except for the face, hands, and feet. . . .

But, the city had grown, implacably, spreading its concrete and alloy fingers wider every day over the dark and feral country. Nothing could stop it. Mountains were stamped flat. Rivers were dammed off or drained or put elsewhere. The marshes were filled. The animals shot from the trees and then the trees cut down. And the big gray machines moved forward, gobbling up the jungle with their iron teeth, chewing it clean of its life and all its living things.

Until it was no more.

Leveled, smoothed as a highway is smoothed, its centuries choked beneath millions and millions of tons of hardened stone.

The birth of a city . . . It had become the death of a world.

And Richard Austin was its murderer.

As he traveled, he thought of the shaman, the half-naked, toothless Bantu medicine man who had spoken for most of the tribes. *"You have killed us, and we could not stop you. So now we will wait, until you have made your city and others come to live here. Then* you *will know what it is to die."* Bokawah, who lived in superstition and fear, whom civilization had passed, along with the rest of his people. Who never spoke again after those words, and allowed himself to be moved to the wide iron plateau that had been built for the surviving natives.

Bokawah, the ignorant shaman, with his eternal smile . . . How distinct that smile was now!

The walkway shuddered, suddenly, and jarred to a noisy grinding stop. Austin pitched forward and grasped the railing in order to break his fall.

Awareness of the silence came first. The eerie dead silence that hung like a pall. It meant that the central machines had ceased functioning. They had been designed to operate automatically and perpetually; it was unthinkable that these power sources could break down!

As unthinkable as the drums that murmured to life again beyond the stainless towers, so loud now in the silence, so real.

Austin gripped his pistol tightly and shook away the panic that had bubbled up like acid in his chest. It was merely that the power had gone off. Strike out impossible, insert improbable. Improbabilities happen. The evil spirits do not summon them, they *happen*. Like strange diseases.

I am fighting, he thought, *a statistical paradox. That's all. A storage pile of coincidences. If I wait*—he walked close to the sides of the buildings—*and fight, the graph will change. The curve will* . . .

The drums roared out a wave of scattered sound, stopped, began again . . .

He thought a bit further of charts; then the picture of Mag materialized, blocking out the thick ink lines, ascending and descending on their giant graphs.

Thinking wasn't going to help . . .

He walked on.

Presently, at the end of a curve in the city maze, the 'village' came into view, suspended overhead like a gigantic jeweled spider. It thrust out cold light. It was silent.

Austin breathed deeply. By belt, his destination was only minutes away. But the minutes grew as he walked through the city, and when he had reached the lift, hot pains wrenched at his muscles. He stood by the crystal platform, working action back into numbed limbs.

Then he remembered the silence, the dead machines. If they were not functioning, then the elevator—

His finger touched a button, experimentally.

A glass door slid open with a pneumatic hiss.

He walked inside, and tried not to think as the door closed and the bullet-shaped lift began to rise.

Below, Mbarara grew small. The treated metals glowed in a dimming lace of light. And the city looked even more like the little clay model he had built with his hands.

At last movement ceased. Austin waited for the door to slide open again, then he strode out onto the smooth floor.

It was very dark. The artificial torches did not even smolder: their stubs, he noticed, were blackened and cold.

But the gates to the village lay open.

He looked past the entrance into the frozen shadows.

He heard the drums, throbbing from within, loud and distinct. But—ordinary drums, whose sound-waves would dissipate before ever reaching the city below.

He walked into the village.

The huts, like glass blisters on smooth flesh, sat silent. Somehow, they were obscene in the dark, to Austin. Built to incorporate the feel and the atmosphere of their originals and yet to include the civilized conveniences; planned from an artistic as well as a scientific standpoint—they were suddenly obscene.

Perhaps, Austin thought, as he walked, perhaps there was something to what Barney had been saying . . . No—these people had elected to stay of their own free will. It would have been impossible to duplicate *exactly* the monstrous conditions under which they had lived. If not impossible, certainly wrong.

Let them wallow in their backward filth? In their disease and corruption, let them die—merely because their culture had failed to absorb scientific progress? No. You do not permit a man to leap off the top of a hundred-story building just because he has been trained to believe it is the only way to get to the ground floor—even though you insult him and blaspheme against his gods through your intervention. You restrain him, at any cost. Then, much later, you show him the elevator. And because he is a man, with a brain no smaller than yours, he will understand. He will understand that a crushed superstition is better than a crushed head. And he will thank you, eventually.

That is logic.

Austin walked, letting these thoughts form a thick crust. He felt the slap of the pistol against his thigh and this, also, was comforting.

Where were they now? Inside the huts, asleep? All of them? Or had they, too, contracted the disease and begun to die of it? . . .

Far ahead, at the clearing which represented the tip of the design, a glow of light appeared. As he approached, the drums grew louder, and other sounds—voices. How many voices? The air was at once murmurous and alive.

He stopped before the clearing and leaned on the darkness and watched.

Nearby a young woman was dancing. Her eyes were closed, tightly, and her arms were straight at her sides like black roots. She was in a state of possession, dancing in rhythm to the nearest drum. Her feet moved so fast they had become a blur, and her naked body wore a slick coat of perspiration.

Beyond the dancing woman, Austin could see the crowd, squatted and standing, swaying; over a thousand of them— surely every native in the village!

A clot of brown skin and bright white paint and brilliant feathers, hunched in the firelight.

An inner line of men sat over drums and hollow logs, beating these with their palms and with short sticks of wood. The sounds blended strangely into one—the one Austin had been hearing, it seemed, all his life.

He watched, fascinated, even though he had witnessed Bantu ceremonies countless times in the past, even though he was perfectly familiar with the symbols. The little leather bags of hex-magic: nail-filings, photographs, specks of flesh; the rubbing boards stained with fruit-skins; the piles of bones at the feet of the men—old bones, very brittle and dry and old.

Then he looked beyond the natives to the sensible clean crystal walls that rose majestically, cupping the area, giving it form.

It sent a chill over him.

He walked into the open.

The throng quieted, instantly, like a scream cut off. The dancers caught their balance, blinked, drew in breath. The others lifted their heads, stared.

All were turned to dark unmoving wax.

Austin went past the gauntlet of eyes, to one of the painted men.

"Where is Bokawah?" he said loudly, in precise Swahili. His voice regained its accustomed authority. "Bokawah. Take me to him."

No one moved. Hands lay on the air inches above drums, petrified.

"I have come to talk!"

From the corner of his eyes, Austin felt the slight disturbance. He waited a moment, then turned.

A figure crouched beside him. A man, unbelievably old and tiny, sharp little bones jutting into loose flesh like pins, skin cross-hatched with a pattern of white paint, chalky as the substance some widows of the tribes wore for a year after the death of their mates. His mouth was pulled into a shape not quite a smile, but resembling a smile. It revealed hardened toothless gums.

The old man laughed, suddenly. The amulet around his chicken-neck bobbled. Then he stopped laughing and stared at Austin.

"We have been waiting," he said, softly. Austin started at the perfect English. He had not heard English for a long time; and now, coming from this little man . . . Perhaps Bokawah had learned it. Why not? "Walk with me, Mr. Austin."

He followed the ancient shaman, dumbly, not having the

slightest idea why he was doing so, to a square of moist soil. It was surrounded by natives.

Bokawah looked once at Austin, then reached down and dipped his hands into the soil. The horny fingers scratched away the top-dirt, burrowed in like thin, nervous animals, and emerged, finally, holding something.

Austin gasped. It was a doll.

It was Mag.

He wanted to laugh, but it caught in his throat. He knew how the primitives would try to inflict evil upon an enemy by burying his effigy. As the effigy rotted, symbolically, so would . . .

He snatched the doll away from the old man. It crumbled in his hands.

"Mr. Austin," Bokawah said, "I'm very sorry you did not come for this talk long ago." The old man's lips did not move. The voice was his and yet not his.

Austin knew, suddenly, that he had not come to this place of his own accord. He had been summoned.

The old man held a hyena's tail in his right hand. He waved this and a slight wind seemed to come up, throwing the flames of the fire into a neurotic dance.

"You are not convinced, even now, Mr. Austin. Aiii. You have seen suffering and death, but you are not convinced." Bokawah sighed. "I will try one last time." He squatted on the smooth floor. "When you first came to our country, and spoke your plans, I told you—even then—what must happen. I told you that this city must not be. I told you that my people would fight, as *your* people would fight if *we* were to come to your land and build jungles. But you understood nothing of what I said." He did not accuse; the voice was expressionless. "Now Mbarara lies silent and dead beneath you and still you do not wish to understand. What must we do, Mr. Austin? How shall we go about proving to you that this Mbarara of yours will *always* be silent and dead, that your people will never walk through it?"

Austin thought of his old college friend Barney—and of what Barney had once told him. Staring at Bokawah, at this scrawny, painted savage, he saw the big Texan clearly, and he remembered his wild undergraduate theories—exhuming the antique view of primitives and their religions, their magics.

"Go on, pal, laugh at their tabus," Barney, who was an anthropologist, used to be fond of saying, *"sneer, while you throw salt over your shoulder. Laugh at their manas, while you blab about our own 'geniuses'!"*

He had even gone beyond the point of believing that magic was important because it held together the fabric of culture among these natives, because it—and their religious superstitions—gave them a rule for behavior, therefore, in most cases, happiness. He had even come to believe that native magic was just another method of arriving at physical truths.

Of course, it was all semantic nonsense. It suggested that primitive magic could lift a ship into space or destroy disease or . . .

That had been the trouble with Barney. You could never tell when he was serious. Even a social anthropologist wouldn't go so far as to think there was more than one law of gravity.

"Mr. Austin, we have brought you here for a purpose. Do you know what that purpose is?"

"I don't know and I don't—"

"Have you wondered why you, alone, of all your people, have been spared? Then—listen to me, very carefully. Because if you do not, then what has happened in your new city is merely the beginning. The winds of death will blow over Mbarara and it will be far more awful than what has been." The medicine man stared down at the scattered piles of bones. Panther bones, Austin knew—a divination device. Their position on the ground told Bokawah much about the white people.

"Go back to your chiefs. Tell them that they must forget this city. Tell them that death walks here and that it will always walk, and that their magic is powerful but not powerful enough. It cannot stand against the spirits from time who have been summoned to fight. Go and talk to your chiefs and tell them these things. Make them believe you. *Force* them to understand that if they come to Mbarara, they will die, in ways they never dreamed, of sickness, in pain, slowly. Forever."

The old man's eyes were closed. His mouth did not move at all and the voice was mechanical.

"Tell them, Mr. Austin, that at first you thought it was a strange new disease that struck the workers. But then remind them that your greatest doctors were powerless against the contagion, that it spread and was not conquered. Say these things. And, perhaps, they will believe you. And be saved."

Bokawah studied the panther bones carefully, tracing their arrangement.

Austin's voice was mechanical, also. "You are forgetting something," he said. He refused to let the thoughts creep in. He refused to wonder about the voice that came through closed lips, about where the natives could have found soil or fresh panther bones or . . . "No one," he said to the old man, "has fought back—yet."

"But why would you do that, Mr. Austin, since you do not believe in the existence of your enemy? Whom shall you fight?" Bokawah smiled.

The crowd of natives remained quiet, unmoving, in the dying firelight.

"The only fear you hold for us," Austin said, "is the fear that you may prove psychologically harmful." He looked at the crushed doll at his feet. The face was whole; otherwise, it lay hideously disfigured.

"Yes?"

"Right now, Bokawah, my government is sending men. They will arrive soon. Whey they do, they will study what has happened. If it is agreed that your rites—however harmless in themselves—cause currents of fear—are in *any way* responsible for the disease—you will be given the opportunity to go elsewhere or—"

"Or, Mr. Austin?"

"—you will be eliminated."

"Then people will come to Mbarara. Despite the warnings and the death, they will come?"

"Your magic sticks aren't going to scare away five hundred thousand men and women."

"Five hundred thousand . . ." The old man looked at the bones, sighed, nodded his head. "You know your people very well," he murmured.

Austin smiled. "Yes, I do."

"Then I think there is little left for us to talk about."

Austin wanted to say, No, you're wrong. We must talk about Mag! She's dying and I want to keep her from dying. But he knew what these words would mean. They would sketch his real feelings, his fears and doubts. And everything would be lost. He could not admit that the doll was anything more than a doll. He must not!

The old man picked up a calabash and ran water over his hands. "I am sorry," he said, "that you must learn the way you must."

A slow chant rose from the natives. It sounded to Austin like Swahili, yet it was indistinct. He could recognize none of the words, except *gonga* and *bagana*. Medicine? The man with the medicine? It was a litany, not unlike the Gregorian chants he had once heard, full of overpowering melancholy. Calm and ethereal and sad as only the human voice can be sad. It rode on the stale air, swelling, diminishing, cutting through the stench of decay and rot with profound dignity.

Austin felt the heaviness of his clothes. The broken machines had stopped pumping fresh breezes, so the air was like oil, opening the pores of his body, running coldly down his arms and legs.

Bokawah made a motion with his hand and sank back onto the smooth floor. He breathed wrackingly, and groaned as if in pain. Then he straightened and looked at Austin and hobbled quickly away.

The drums began. Movement eased back into the throng and soon the dancers were up, working themselves back into their possessed states.

Austin turned and walked quickly away from the ceremony. When he had reached the shadows, he ran. He did not stop running until he had reached the lift, even while his muscles, long dormant, unaccustomed to this activity, turned to stone, numb and throbbing stone.

He stabbed the button and closed his eyes, while his heart pumped and roared sound into his ears and colored fire into his mind. The platform descended slowly, unemotional and calm as its parts.

Austin ran out and fell against a building, where he tried to push away the image of the black magic ceremony, and what he had felt there.

He swallowed needles of pain into his parched throat.

And the fear mounted and mounted, strangling him slowly . . .

The Towers of Mbarara loomed, suddenly, to Austin, more unreal and anachronistic than the tribal rites from which he had just come. Stalagmites of crystal pushing up to the night sky that bent above them; little squares and diamonds and circles of metal and stone. Office buildings; apartments; housing units; hat stores and machine factories and restaurants; and, cobwebbing among them, all these blind and empty shells, the walkways, like colored ribbons, like infinitely long reptiles, sleeping now, dead, still.

Or, were they only waiting, as he wanted to believe?

Of course they're waiting, he thought. People who know the answers will come to Mbarara tomorrow. Clear-headed scientists who have not been terrorized by a tribe of beaten primitives. And the scientists will find out what killed the workers, correct it, and people will follow. Five hundred thousand people, from all over the closet-crowded world, happy to have air to breathe once more—air that hasn't had to travel down two-hundred feet—happy to know the Earth can yet sustain them. No more talk, then, of "population decreases"—murder was a better word—; no more government warnings screaming "depopulation" at you . . .

The dream would come true, Austin told himself. Because it must. Because he'd promised Mag and they'd lived it all together, endless years, hoped and planned and fought for the city. With Mbarara, it would begin: the dark age of a sardine can world would end, and life would begin. It would be many years before the worry would begin all over—for half the earth lay fallow, wasted. Australia, Greenland, Iceland, Africa, the Poles . . . And perhaps then the population graph would change, as it had always changed before. And men would come out of their caverns and rat-holes and live as men.

Yes. But only if Mbarara worked. If he could show them his success here . . .

Austin cursed the men who had gone back and screamed the story of what had happened to the other engineers. God knew there were few enough available, few who had been odd enough to study a field for which there seemed little further use.

If they'd only kept still about the disease! Then others would have come and . . .

Died. The word came out instantly, uncalled, and vanished.

Austin passed the Emperor, the playhouse he had thought of that night with Mag, ten years before. As he passed, he tried to visualize the foyer jammed with people in soup-and-fish and jeweled gowns, talking of whether the play had meat or not. Now, its marbled front putting out yellow glow, it looked foolish and pathetic. The placard case shone through newly gathered dust, empty.

Austin tried to think of what had been on this spot originally. Thick jungle growth alone. Or had there been a native village—with monkeys climbing the trees and swinging on vines and white widows mourning under straw roofs?

Now playing: JULIUS CAESAR. Admission: Three coconuts.

Be still. You've stayed together all this time, he thought, you can hold out until tomorrow. Tcheletchew will be here, sputtering under his beard, and they'll fly Mag to a hospital and make her well and clear up this nonsense in a hurry.

Just get home. Don't think and get home and it will be all right.

The city was actually without formal streets. Its plan did not include the antiquated groundcars that survived here and there in old families. Therefore, Mbarara was literally a maze. A very pretty maze. Like an English estate—Austin had admired these touches of vanished gentility—the areas were sometimes framed by green stone hedges, carved into functional shapes.

He had no difficulty finding his way. It was all too fresh, even now, the hours of planning every small curve and design, carefully leaving no artistic 'holes' or useless places. He could have walked it blindfolded.

But when he passed the food dispensary and turned the corner, he found that it did not lead to the 'copter-park, as it should have. There were buildings there, but they were not the ones they ought to have been.

Or else he'd turned the wrong— He retraced his steps to the point where he had gone left. The food dispensary was nowhere in sight. Instead he found himself looking at the general chemistry building.

Austin paused and wiped his forehead. The excitement, of course. It had clouded his mind for a moment, making him lose his way.

He began walking. Warm perspiration coursed across his body, turning his suit dark-wet, staining his jacket.

He passed the food dispensary.

Austin clenched his fists. It was impossible that he could have made a complete circle. He had built this city, he knew it intimately. He had walked through it without even thinking of direction, in the half-stages of construction, and never taken a wrong step.

How could he be lost?

Nerves. Nothing strange in it. Certainly enough had happened to jar loose his sense of direction.

Calmly, now. Calmly.

The air hung fetid and heavy. He had to pull it into his lungs, push it out. Of course, he could go below and open the valves—at least *they* could be operated by hand. He could, but why? It would mean hunching down in a dark shaft— damn, should have made that shaft larger! And, there were, after all, enough openings in the sealing-bubble to keep a breathable flow of oxygen in circulation. If the air was heavy and still outside the bubble, he could scarcely expect it to be different within . . .

He looked up at the half-minaretted tower that was one of the 'copter repair centers. It was located in exactly the opposite direction to the one he thought he'd taken.

Austin sank onto a stone bench. Images floated through his mind. He was lost; precisely as lost as if he had wandered into the jungle that had stood here before the building of Mbarara, and then tried to find his way back.

He closed his eyes and saw a picture, startlingly clear, of himself, running through the matted growths of dark green foliage, stumbling across roots, bumping trees, face grotesque with fear, and screaming . . .

He opened his eyes quickly, shook away the vision. His brain was tired; that was why he saw such a picture. He must keep his eyes open.

The city was unchanged. The park, designed for housewives who might wish to pause and rest or chat, perhaps feed squirrels, surrounded him.

Across the boating lake was the university.

Behind the university was home.

Austin rose, weakly, and made his way down the grassy slope to the edge of the artificial lake. Cultured city trees dotted the banks: the lake threw back a geometrically perfect reflection.

He knelt and splashed water into his face. Then he gulped some of it down and paused until the ripples spread to the center of the lake.

He studied his image in the water carefully. White skin, smooth cheeks, iron-colored hair. Good clothes. A dolichocephalic head, evenly spaced, the head of a twenty-second century civilized . . .

Above his reflection, Austin detected movement. He froze and blinked his eyes. As the water smoothed, the image of an animal appeared on the surface, wavering slightly. A small animal, something like a monkey. Like a monkey hanging from the branches of a tree.

Austin whirled around.

There was only the darkness, the golfing-green lawn, the cultured trees—smooth-barked, empty.

He passed a hand through his hair. It was a trick of the lights. His subconscious fear, the shimmering water . . .

He walked quickly to the darkened boathouse, across its floor, his footsteps ringing against the stone, echoing loudly.

At the end of the miniature pier, he untied a small battery boat and jumped into it. He pulled a switch at the side, waited, forced himself to look back at the deserted bank.

The boat moved slowly, with only a whisper of sound, through the water.

Hurry, Austin thought. *Hurry— Oh God, why are they so slow!*

The boat, whose tin flag proclaimed its name to be *Lucy*, sliced the calm lake with its toy prow, and, after many minutes, reached the center.

The glow was insufficient to make the approaching bank distinct. It lay wrapped in darkness, a darkness that hid even the buildings.

Austin narrowed his eyes and stared. He blinked. It was the fuzziness of the luminescence, of course, that gave movement to the bank. That made it seem to seethe with unseen life.

It was only that his position to the shadows kept changing that made them turn into dark and feral shapes; trees, where buildings surely were, dense growth . . .

It was the milky phosphorescence of the metals that rose like marsh-steam from the nearing water . . .

He thought of stepping off the boat into a jungle, a magical forest, alive and waiting for him.

He closed his eyes and gripped the sides of the boat.

There was a scraping. Austin felt the cement guard, sighed, switched off the battery and leapt from the little boat.

There was no jungle. Only the lime-colored city trees and the smooth lawn.

The university sat ahead like a string of dropped pearls: blister-shaped, connected by elevated tunnels, twisting, delicate strands of metal and alloy.

Austin scrambled up the embankment. It must be very late now. Perhaps nearly morning. In a few hours, the others would arrive. And—

He halted, every muscle straining.

He listened.

There were the drums. But not only the drums, now. Other sounds.

He closed his eyes. The airless night pressed against him. He heard a rustling noise. Like something traveling through dense brush. He heard, far away, tiny sounds, whistlings, chitterings. Like monkeys and birds.

He tore open his eyes. Only the park, the city.

He went on. Now his feet were on stone and the park was behind him. He walked through the canyons of the city again, the high buildings, metal and crystal and alloy and stone.

The rustling noises did not cease, however. They were behind him, growing nearer. Bodies, moving through leaves and tall grass.

Austin suddenly remembered where he'd heard the sound before. Years ago, when he'd first visited this land. They had taken him on a hunting expedition, deep into the wild country. They were going to bag something—he forgot exactly what. Something strange. Yes; it was a wild pig. They had walked all day, searching, through the high tan grass, and then they had heard the rustling sounds.

Exactly like the sound he heard now.

Austin recalled the unbelievable fury of the boar, how it had disemboweled two dogs with a couple of swipes of those razor-sharp fangs. He recalled clearly the angry black snout, curled over yellow teeth.

He turned and stared into the darkness. The noises grew steadily louder, and were broken by yet another sound. Deep and guttural, like a cough.

As the sound behind him came closer, he ran, stumbled and fell, pulled himself from the stone and ran until he had reached a flight of steps.

The coughing noise was a fast, high-pitched scream now, a grunting, snorting, a rush of tiny feet galloping across tamped earth, through dry grass. Austin stared blindly, covered his face with his arms and sank back until the sound was almost upon him.

His nostrils quivered at the animal smell.

His breath stopped.

He waited.

It was gone. Fading in the distance, the rustling, the coughing, and then there was the silence of the drums again.

Austin pressed the bones of his wrist into his throbbing skull to quiet the ache.

The panic drained off slowly. He rose, climbed the steps and walked through the shadowed courtyard onto the campus.

It was a vast green plain, smooth and grassy.

Across from it, in sight, was Austin's home.

He gathered his reason about him like a shield, and decided against taking the other routes. If he had gotten lost before, it could happen again. Certainly now, with his imagination running wild.

He must cross the campus.

Then it would be all right.

He began treading, timorously at first, listening with every square inch of his body.

The shaman's voice slithered into his mind. Chanting.

". . . *you were destroying us against our will, Mr. Austin. Our world, our life. And such is your mind, and the mind of so-called 'civilized' men, that you could not see this was wrong. You have developed a culture and a social structure that pleased you, you were convinced that it was right; therefore, you could not understand the existence of any that differed. You saw us as ignorant savages—most of you did— and you were anxious to 'civilize' us. Not once did it occur to you that we, too, had our culture and our social structure; that we knew right and wrong; that, perhaps, we might look upon you as backward and uncivilized . . .*"

The sound of birds came to Austin; birds calling in high trees, circling impossibly in the night sky.

". . . *we have clung to our 'magic,' as you call it, and our 'superstitions' for longer than you have clung to yours. Because —as with your own—they have worked for us. Whether magic can be explained in Roman numerals or not, what is the difference, so long as it works? Mr. Austin, there is not only one path to the Golden City—there are many. Your people are on one path—*"

He heard the chatter of monkeys, some close, some far away, the sound of them swinging on vines, scolding, dropping to mounds of foliage, scrambling up other trees.

"—my people are on another. There is room in this world
for both ways. But your failure to grasp this simple fact has
killed many of us and it will kill many more of you. For we
have been on our path longer. We are closer to the Golden
City . . ."

Austin clapped his hands to his ears. But he did not stop
walking.

From the smooth stone streets, from the direction of the
physics department, came the insane trumpeting of elephants,
their immense bulks crashing against brittle bark, their huge
feet crunching fallen limbs and branches . . .

The shaman's voice became the voice of Barney Chad-
field . . . He spoke again of his theory that if one could only
discover the unwritten bases of black magic and apply for-
mulae to them, we would find that they were merely another
form of science . . . perhaps less advanced, perhaps more.

The sounds piled up, and the feelings, and the sensations.
Eyes firmly open, Austin thought of Mag and felt needled
leaves slap invisibly against his legs; he smelled the rot and
the life, the heavy, wild air of the jungle, like animal steam;
the odors of fresh blood and wet fur and decaying plants;
the short rasping breath of a million different animals—the
movement, all around him, the approaches, the retreats, the
frenzied unseen . . .

Eyes open he felt and smelled and heard all these things;
and saw only the city.

A pain shot through his right arm. He tried to move it:
it would not move. He thought of an old man. The old man
had a doll. The old man was crushing the doll's arm, and
laughing . . . He thought of reflexes and the reaction of reflexes to emotional stimuli.

He walked, ignoring the pain, not thinking about the arm
at all.

". . . tell them, Mr. Austin. Make them believe. Make them
believe . . . Do not kill all these people . . ."

When he had passed the Law College, he felt a pain wrench
at his leg. He heard another dry-grass rustle. But not behind
him: in front. Going forward.

Going toward his apartment.

Austin broke into a run, without knowing exactly why.

There was a pounding, a panting at his heels: vaguely he
was aware of this. He knew only that he must get inside,
quickly, to the sanity of his home. Jaws snapped, clacked.
Austin stumbled on a vine, his fingers pulled at air, he leapt
away and heard the sound of something landing where he had
just been, something that screamed and hissed.

He ran on. At the steps, his foot pressed onto something
soft. It recoiled madly. He slipped and fell again, and the

feel of moist beaded skin whipped about his legs. The thunder was almost directly above. He reached out, clawed loose the thing around his leg and pulled himself forward.

There was a swarming over his hands. He held them in front of his eyes, tried to see the ants that had to be there, slapped the invisible creatures loose.

The apartment door was only a few feet away now. Austin remembered his pistol, drew it out and fired it into the night until there were no more bullets left.

He pulled himself into the lobby of the unit.

The door hissed closed.

He touched the lock, heard it spring together.

And then the noises ceased. The drums and the animals, all the wild nightmare things—ceased to be. There was his breathing, and the pain that laced through his arm and leg.

He waited, trembling, trying to pull breath in.

Finally he rose and limped to the elevator. He did not even think about the broken machines. He knew it would work.

It did. The glass doors whirred apart at his floor, and he went out into the hall.

It was soundless.

He stood by the door, listening to his heart rattle crazily in his chest.

He opened the door.

The apartment was calm, silent. The walls glowed around the framed Mirós and Mondrians and Picassos. The furniture sat functionally on the silky white rug, black thin-legged chairs and tables . . .

Austin started to laugh, carefully checked himself. He knew he probably would not be able to stop.

He thought strongly about Tcheletchew, and of the men who would come to Mbarara in the morning. He thought of the city teeming with life. Of the daylight streaming onto the streets of people, the shops, the churches, the schools. His work. His dream . . .

He walked across the rug to the bedroom door.

It was slightly ajar.

He pushed it, went inside, closed it softly.

"Mag," he whispered. "Mag—"

There was a noise. A low, throaty rumble. Not of anger; of warning.

Richard Austin came close to the bed, adjusted his eyes to the black light.

Then he screamed.

It was the first time he had ever watched a lion feeding.

The Quadriopticon

I T WAS A DARK musty place, bigger than it had to be and faintly reminiscent of a family crypt. The asbestos-and-cork walls were peeling like the bark of a dead tree, the proscenium drapes were holey rags, the ceiling was covered with a million plastered cracks. But Projection Room # 7 had a nice carpet: rich, thick, crimson.

Like Sherman Boetticher's face. Of course he tried to fake it by putting on his informal smile, but this failed because the smile looked as if it had been drawn on with a burnt match by a small boy. To the assembled crowd stationed in regiments in the tan leather studio chairs, the truth was evident: Sherman Boetticher was coming loose at the hinges.

Finally he looked at his watch, giggled once and trembled forward. "All right," he said, "I guess we'll just have to proceed. I'm sure Rock was unavoidably detained; however, in deference to Mr. Mendel, who is, as we all know, a very busy man—Jimmy! Let's go."

The lights dimmed down to almost absolute blackness. Then a thin blue spot came on and picked around the room for a few seconds before lighting on the mole-faced producer. Boetticher opened his mouth and began: "Ladies and gentlemen, what you are about to witness will take its place as the most unusual, the most startling, the most precedent-smashing advancement in the history of the motion picture. Thanks to a revolutionary—"

"Hands up, *everybody!*" A tall well-built man in a trench coat stepped suddenly into the spotlight and gave Sherman Boetticher a quick hard push. The man held something in his hand that glinted silver. "This is the vice squad! You're all under arrest for violating the Mann Act, the Woman Act, and what is that couple doing in the third row balcony?"

Marcus Mendel, the studio manager, smiled the quickest, smallest, most obligatory of smiles and swiveled his head back toward the screen.

Boetticher's little fists unballed and he took the tall man's arm. "You're just in time, Rock. Now if you'll take a seat . . ."

"Rock, please," Boetticher whined.

The man whose real name was Leroy Guinness O'Shea winked and brought his hand down on a bare and exceedingly freckled back. "Bless me, if it isn't the tail well calculated to keep you in suspense!"

Sheila Tyler smiled gaily. "Hello, doll."

"Darling!"

Rock Jason stumbled across legs to his chair. He sat down next to the corpulent-hipped queen of the columnists, Dolly Dixon, whose sudden kewpie smile gave her face the look of a crumpled balloon. "Rock, you naughty boy—I swear, I mean, you'd be late for your own funeral! Aren't you knocked out?"

"In a sense," Jason said, removing the flask and shaking it disappointedly. Then he leapt up: "I re*fuse* to sit next to this woman!"

Dolly Dixon's face reddened and then exploded in a germ-laden laugh. "Stop, oh stop!"

Boetticher's eyes were now his only mobile feature. "Why?" he asked dutifully.

"Because," Jason said, planting a kiss on the powder-caked cheek, "she gets grabby."

"Stop, Rock, you old rogue, you old liar!"

Jason smiled. He hiccupped. "Well, all right—but no kneesies."

"Ha ha. That's just so deliriously funny!"

He jerked his head around. Only one person in the world would dare to be so openly sarcastic to him: Robbie. Dear Robbie, his co-star, the face that launched a thousand fan magazines.

"Ah," Jason cooed, "America's *other* sweetheart. How are you, love?"

Robin Summers wasn't smiling at all. "Just dandy," she said. "Now does Mr. Box Office think he might shut up long enough for us to see the picture?"

She was indecently beautiful today. Golden brown skin lustrous against the white no-sleeved blouse, wild black hair set off by simple silver earrings . . . and that thin black ribbon around her throat. . . .

"Don't fret, darling," Jason said. "If you miss it now you can catch it at your nearest bagnio."

Dolly dissolved. Her jellyfolds of fat quivered and exuded the powerful aroma of musk. The combination, the perfume and the flask of whisky, made Jason's head float uncomfortably.

Robin Summers threw herself back in her chair. Her round full lips were pulled down in inexpressible anger.

Jason hiccupped again. "On with the production!" he hollered. "I yield the floor."

The lights got dim again and the spot picked up Boetticher's faulty and helpless figure.

"As I was saying," he intoned, "this is an historic occasion. What you are about to watch is the newest innovation, and the greatest, since 3-D—since sound, even! Through a secret process, which we have spent ten years in developing—"

Jason fingered his mustache and snorted lowly. He leaned toward Dolly's ear. "Poor Sherm is a dear sweet thing," he whispered. "Lies so convincingly, don't you agree? I mean, is there *any*one who doesn't know that this little fellow—what's his name, Gottfried, Gottschalk—invented it, by accident . . ."

"—and from now on, all of Galactic's pictures will employ the use of this startling invention, the Quadriopticon. Now, I'm not going to bore you with a lot of technical language at this present instant. But basically, what we have here is a machine that literally puts *you* inside the picture! That's what I said. No glasses are required for this process, no discomfort, no eyestrain. The use of the revolutionary Prismascopic screen not only gives the illusion of third dimension, but makes this illusion stick! Ladies and gentlemen, the 3-D 'flatties' are a thing of the past. No more throwing things at the audience to suggest realism—folks, it's there, all the time! And why? you ask. Because the image is broken up for you by the Quadriopticon, which works exactly like the human eyes. The Prismascopic screen is actually many screens, each overlay representing the effect of each frame of depth on the naked eye." Boetticher tapped his glasses for effect. "Ever try looking through a screen door? What do you see? Wait now —two things, each completely different. If you concentrate on the screen, then you can't see anything else outside; if you 'adjust' your human telescopes, see, then the screen disappears —right? Well, this amazing machine permits us to do just that with our image, in exactly the same identical way."

Boetticher looked proudly disdainful over the blank pond of faces.

"But let's save some surprises. Believe me, please, take my word for it, it's revolutionary. It'll put Galactic Pictures right back into position as the foremost production unit in the world!" Boetticher was warming up; the embarrassment flushed out of him: it was his baby. He began to sound like a bad carny barker, the words most frequently used being *revolutionary* and *tremendous*.

"And so," he said, "it was only natural that the world's first picture in 4-D—"

Ears perked up: these were the magic words. 4-D!

"—should star the inimitable team, Rock 'n Robbie, those grand troupers and America's Sweethearts. Ladies and gentlemen, we give you the most thrilling story ever written, a tremendous follow-through on the current science fiction trend—" Herman Mancini, the writer, sank down in his seat "—*The Conquest of Jupiter!* Starring Rock Jason and Robin Summers! Filmed in fabulous color with the fabulous 4-Dimensional Quadriopticon camera!"

The spot flicked out and the room was dark. Rock Jason smiled: he'd seen the rushes. They were pretty fair. It involved some hocus-pocus with a prismed screen—which he could hear being lowered in the blackness—and some junk sprayed out through a bellows, "to bring not only sight and sound but also *smell* to motion pictures." It was all right. It would kick up some excitement and that would net him more dollars— but it would die out, just as everything had since the big 3-D craze. Then Galactic would be back riding on his shoulders. Which was all right, too.

He could hear Robbie breathing in back of him. The little moron—of them all, he thought, she detests me most. Well, such is Fame's Cross. Great men have ever had their enemies. Didn't she know he could kill it for her, like *that!* Just refuse to play in a picture with her. Then where would the independent Miss Summers be? The independent, beautiful, lovely, desirable Miss Summers . . .

"I'm so excited," Dolly was whispering, "I could just flip. Couldn't you just flip, Rock?"

"Like a trained dog, sweet."

"Well, they're certainly keeping us on edge. Leave it to Sherm. Sherm's a live wire. Sherm's going places."

"Sherm," Jason said truthfully, "stinks."

The lights came on again. Billy Zelmo, the comic, got up and did a Bronx cheer. There were rustlings.

"A little difficulty getting the sync right," Boetticher called nervously from the booth.

Jason swam across the legs and tumbled out into the aisle, stopping only to stick out his tongue at Mendel.

"Fear not!" he hooted. "Fortunately, among my variegated talents, I am a highly skilled projectionist." Still carrying along the flask, he careened up the aisle.

Robbie was furious. He could tell. Why should she get so furious? Her eyes were flashing embarrassedly, those black black eyes.

"Here now boys, let me at it!"

"It's all right, Rock," Boetticher rattled, "it's all right. We got it fixed okay now. Why don't you just—"

"Nonsense. Permit a trained man to make it official."

He didn't exactly know why he was doing it. He could see the agony outside on the faces of the others in the film: Guy Randolph, the old regular, the scared-to-death ex-Shakespearean who once went three years without a picture job;

Burton Mitchell, on his last legs, hungry for the break this seemed to be; the rest, the frightened people who all knew that this roll of celluloid could make or break them, depending upon its outcome. And now Rock Jason was doing his damndest to louse it up for them.

"Rock, this is important. We've got to snag Mendel. *Please* sit down."

The lights had been killed. The Quadriopticon, a weird box that didn't even look like a projector, had begun to hum and warm.

"Don't tell me what to do, you—sycophant! I said I'd fix it and that's what by God I intend to do!"

Jason pushed Boetticher's limpid form away and advanced on the machine.

There was a small door on the back. He opened this.

"Don't touch!" someone said, trying to grab his hands. "You shouldn't touch!" It was little Mr. Gottschalk.

"Avaunt!" he yelled at the bald-headed old man, and gave him a push, too.

Mr. Gottschalk stumbled out of his way.

Behind the tiny door was a pair of electrodes. The ball-pointed shafts of metal crackled and danced white hot light. Beyond the field was an indented knob. Jason started to reach.

"Nein, nein! Wait. I will turn it off—"

His right hand, which held the metal flask, was draped across the bare metal control cabinet; with his left hand, Jason reached far in and felt the sparks tickle and fry his flesh. The whisky container touched metal at the exact moment he grabbed the flying knob.

Rock Jason felt a giant hand pick him up and toss him away, far away, where it was all dark and quiet. . . .

"Commander Carlyle, sir, I—" The man stuttered helplessly, "Sir, how do you keep it up? Sizzling jets, you haven't slept for five nights."

One by one Rock Jason opened his eyes. He shook his head vigorously and said, "Ohhh." He tried to, but somehow could not quite, put things together: he was overcome with the greatest drowsiness he had known since that memorable do in Malibu. Sleep crudded his eyes and brain.

"You're perfectly right, Ronnie. Can't account for it. So tired . . ."

"Beg pardon, sir?"

Jason looked at the young man. Let's see—of course: a binge. Probably with Doris Dulane, the bitch. She'd tanked him up, or let him get tanked up, and now they were pulling one of their idiotic gags. Like Eddie Fritz's famous upside-down room.

"Ronnie, be a dear child and take the ridiculous Mason jar off your head. And steer me to a bed. Quickly."

Ronald Curtis, a fairly typical Sunset Boulevardier and an incurable whiner, stood at strict attention. Pretty cocky, all considered. If it hadn't been for Jason's big heart, the kid would still be perched on a stool at Schwab's dreaming of the movies.

Jason pinched the flesh of his arm. Sleep. Great Oliver, what had he been drinking! "Darling," he said with immense control, "I'm in no mood for jokes. Tomorrow perhaps. A bed is what I'm in the mood for now. A soft bed. Do you understand?"

The young man looked hopelessly bewildered. "But, Commander Carlyle, sir—that is—"

Very well. Tend to the ignoramus later. "Never mind. I'm sure I will be convulsed with the hilarity of this situation by next morning. I am not now amused. So go away, and leave me alone."

Jason's head nodded toward the desk. There was a ringing reverberating clang. He reached up and felt the glass helmet. "And *what*," he moaned, "this is I'd like to know. Goddam it, help me off with it—this minute!" He began to search for clamps, sensing a dizzy blackness clouding his mind.

"Sir, be careful! The rips haven't been repaired yet."

"Ronnie, I love you like a son, genuinely I do. But if you don't get this thing off me and stop this nonsense immediately, I'm afraid I'll have to discuss your future with Mendel. I'm a sick man. What the devil are you talking about—rips?"

"The Mercutians, sir. Their armada surprised us. We were hit."

"Stop that!" We were hit . . . of course. That horrible science fiction thing. These were lines from the movie. They'd rigged up the room to look like the first scene set. INT. ROCKET SHIP—COMMANDER'S CABIN—MED. SHOT. And this was the bit where Jason as Commander Derek Carlyle was supposed to be working day and night because only he knew how to repair the damage to the complex machinery.

"Benson and Carstairs are dead, sir. Their air ran out."

Charming. Now what was the next line? Oh yes. *Very well, Lieutenant. Fix me some black coffee. I'm going out there and finish the job.*

"Yes, sir."

"Oh, shut up."

"Sir?"

"I said—darling, whose captivating idea was this? Doris'?" The young man kept looking confused, standing there quietly looking confused. Well—damn good acting. Give him that. Maybe too good.

Strange, Jason thought, that he couldn't remember *anything* about last night. He knew he was supposed to have appeared for Boetticher's party with the Quadriopticon. But—oh yes— he'd stopped by the Inferno first, for a very short one. Then . . . *then?*

"We got the last one, sir."

"*Last* what?"

"Mercutian. Johnson beamed his forward jets. That wipes them all out. Sir—if we get the damage repaired in time, we're Venus bound!"

"Ronnie, *please*—my head!"

"I'll get the coffee, sir."

The young man saluted smartly, did an about face and marched out of the room.

Must be Doris. Who else would have the money to build such a duplication of the set? The cabin was perfect. To the last detail. They'd even put him in that monstrous spacesuit dear Carpenter had dreamed up, the swine. How un-chic can you get? Next thing they'd be putting him in Indian blankets. Spacesuits. Whither thou, Thespis?

Ohhh. One's head. Well, figure it out later. Get some sleep is the thing now.

He tore viciously at the clamps that secured the helmet. They slipped loose. He lifted off the glass bubble.

He found he could not breathe; the blackness fuzzed up entirely and he fainted promptly.

Very dark . . . very quiet . . .

"Commander Carlyle, sir, I—" The man stuttered helplessly. "Sir, how do you keep it up? Sizzling jets, you haven't slept for five nights."

Jason pulled himself into consciousness. *Now* what was it? The whole idiotic bit again? He tapped upward with tentative fingers. The Mason jar, right back on his head. And he'd taken the thing off. Hadn't he?

"You shall pay for this, Ronnie Curtis. In full."

"Benson and Carstairs are—"

Well, maybe it's part of the gag. Let him pass out and then wake him up and start it again, ad nauseum.

"I know, I know—dead. Wonderful. Fine. At least Benson and Carstairs have got some peace and quiet now. Stop looking so foolish! And *do* for heaven's sake stop saying 'sizzling jets!' What a line!"

"Yes, sir. About the damage, Commander—"

"Fix it yourself. What am I talking about? Say, weren't you just in here a minute ago?"

"No, sir."

"And stop saying 'sir'!" Jason rapped at the helmet perched on his shoulders. "I am dying," he said. "Here, help me up. Get me a Bromo. I'm going to have a word with Doris."

The young man assisted Jason to his feet. They walked out of the cabin.

"For Pete—" Jason stopped and stared. "Just how far does a gag go?"

It was the rocket ship, perfectly done. Except the bars under his hands didn't feel like silver-painted plaster. They felt very real.

The young man thrust some odd looking things into his hands. "Good luck, sir."

Suddenly, he was being helped up a ladder. Below, a number of extras he'd never seen stared in unbelieving admiration. "There goes a *man*," someone whispered. "You couldn't drag *me* out there," commented another.

"Now wait a minute!" Jason cried. Above, the alloy roof was gashed and instruments hung lose. The night looked very black.

A powerful aroma suddenly seemed to permeate the helmet, cutting up through his nostrils. The smell of dryness and deserts, cooked up by Pa Franklin to simulate the odors of far space. If there *were* odors in far space.

He began to feel peculiar. What was all this, after all? Was he actually on the set again, for a remake? He looked for the crew, James the director, Bolana the cameraman—but there was only the ship and these crazy people and the stars.

Then a horrible thought occurred to him: So this is the DT's! Dr. Morris had warned him. Plenty of times.

Delirium tremens. Oh no. No. But what else?

Jason found himself on the outer hull of the rocket. Exactly as in the first scene of *The Conquest of Jupiter*. In fact, everything followed the scene. Now he was supposed to start fixing the airlock or some sort of gimmick and a Mercurian—beg pardon, *Mercutian,* and where did these "science" fiction writers think the planet Mercutio was located?—a Mercutian devil-man was supposed to creep up on him and—

"Look out, sir!"

Jason glanced up dazedly from the twisted machinery and faced a gigantic orange creature with scales and eyes of an alarming protuberance.

"Pinkie, for God's sake don't *do* that!"

The creature came closer, slowly, leering with the pride of the special effects department, three mouths where the eyes should have been but weren't. It said something that sounded like: "Umbawa unbawa, figgg-ouf!"

"What was that, Pinkie? I can't hear a word with this imbecile thing on. Repeat?"

"*Umbawa unbawa, figgg-ouf!*"

"Stop growling. And take off that moldy left-over from *John Carter on Mars* and tell me when the hell this bit is going to end."

The creature was almost upon him, liquid fire oozing from the giant pores between scales. Its body odor suggested that of the Inside Man at the Putrefaction Works.

"Shoot, sir! Oh, sir!"

"He's a cool one, Commander Carlyle. Knows what he's about."

"Pinkie. That is, I wish—Pinkie?"

"UMBAWA UNBAWA, FIGGG-OUF MAGOFU!"

"Good God!"

Jason tried to turn and run but his magnetic shoes held him fast to the hull. He whipped around and permitted his jaw to drop as the creature's arms began to encircle him.

"Please! I've told you a dozen times, I'm not that way. Especially here in front of—Pinkie? I'll have you fired. I will."

Automatically Jason wrenched loose one hand from the steaming tentacles and squeezed the trigger of the gun he'd forgotten about. A beam of light sprang out into the monster's face. "Umbawa unb-a-wa figg—" The monster fell and proceeded to float away in the darkness of space, its stench floating after it, if too slowly for comfort.

"Magnificent! Carlyle knew his gun wouldn't have been any use except at close range. What *guts*."

Jason's fingers seemed to move of their own accord about the broken machinery. He watched with fascination. Then his legs took over and brought him back down the ladder.

"She'll be all right now, men," his voice said.

"Hurrah! Hurrah!"

"Now," said Jason's voice, "Denton, you and Marchelli do the patchwork. I'm going to catch a few winks. Wake me at 0700 promptly."

His legs propelled him along the catwalk and took him back into the cabin.

He lay down on the bunk. "DT's," he said, aloud. "They're murderous."

Sleep came to the courageous commander of the spaceship *Starfire;* sleep well earned by a man who had toiled five days and five nights to bring his craft safely through the greatest space battle of all time.

Jason started to remember something just before unconsciousness set in. "Murderous," he mumbled and closed his eyes.

"Aldridge, you traitorous cur. Court-martialing is too good for you!"

"You mean . . . ?"

"Exactly."

Jason scratched his head. How long, he wondered, does this kind of thing go on? After all, DT's are supposed to wear off, aren't they? Or are they—?

"What do you propose to do about it, earthling?" the uniformed navigator spat. It was the ex-Shakespearean, Guy Randolph. A small part, but plenty dramatic. Well, play along. Scene two, isn't it? You've discovered that the navigator, Aldridge, is really a Venusian in disguise and is the one who alerted the Mercutians and caused—oh Mancini, from the Pulitzer Prize to *this?*—caused the Mercutians to attack and ambush. Now he, Aldridge, had misrouted the *Starfire* and they were headed for Jupiter—the Death Planet. Great. Great little plot. Academy Award.

"What do you propose to do about it, earthling?"

Fight scene. Big fight. Well, delirium tremens only means that you're dreaming. Jacket off. Sleeves up. Sneer. "Get ready, Aldridge—unless you're too yellow."

"You would overrun our world and bring the pestilence of war that ruined your own?" Randolph declaimed in a bad imitation of Maurice Evans. "Never!"

"Take," Jason said, hauling off, *"that,* Venusian filth!"

He carefully missed Randolph's jaw. The man grinned savagely and lunged, his hands snaking up around Jason's neck.

Jason pulled loose the fingers and caught his breath. "What's the big idea, darling?" He started to walk away, massaging the bruised flesh. Very real, he thought, for a dream.

The navigator flung himself upon Jason's back and they fell to the floor. Randolph pounded away, changing form the while: presently, he was a sticky green ameba-like blob.

"Never again," Jason resolved, wishing he had one drink nonetheless. He tore himself free and ran out the door and slammed the door shut. He hurt all over. "Enough," he panted, "is enough!" He went to the airlock and began to pull it open.

Blackness. Inside his head.

Very dark . . . Very quiet . . .

"Aldridge, you traitorous cur! Court mar—"

Like the rushes of a film turned back for editing. Right back to the same damn line. And Randolph wheeling around in his chair.

"You mean?"

Jason remembered how the first scene had gone back. What had done it? Of course. Changing the script. Everything went fine until he did something that Commander Derek Carlyle wouldn't do, something that was impossible to the structure of the story. Then, *zip!* All over again. The dim realization came to him that if he was ever to get out of this he would have to follow the script to the end. But how the hell could that be? No. No no. Not with what was coming up!

"Exactly."

Scene 3: Having beaten Aldridge to death, Commander Carlyle discovers stowaway on board. Beautiful chick. Sweet-smelling, too. Robin Summers. Usual mad-then-glad bit. Robbie is in love with him. Kiss. Headed for peril. Jupiter unknown planet. Maybe hostile. Phew!

"What do you propose to do about it, earthling?"

Bless little Herman. What was this lousy picture about anyway? Earth is being fried by strange ray from space. Authorities send ship to Venus to investigate. Ship has spy. Fight with Mercutians. Land on Jupiter. Turns out Jupiter the real menace. Jovians have Death Ray. Knock it out. Return home. Earth saved. Hotcha.

"You would overrun—"

Well, anyway they cut out those opening scenes. Space battles cost money, be praised. That would have been jolly.

Scene 4: The landing on Jupiter. Jovians appear and my oh my what a fight. Two days to film it. Murder.

Scene 5: They take Robbie hostage.

Scene 6: Commander Carlyle slips inside their temple and is captured.

Scene 7: The *Rakana!*

"Take *that*, Venusian filth!"

Jason fought hard. After all, Randolph was getting along. Sixty if he was a day.

He stomped the greenish blob to a jelly—for the matinee kiddies—and kicked it triumphantly into a corner.

His nostrils filled with the odor of charred flesh. Now, why charred flesh? Oh well. It made him gag. Smells. All the time these smells!

"Commander, we're off our course!"

"Ronnie, you sweet thing. How observant. I mean, how very observant. That is: Very well, Lieutenant—I know all about it. Aldridge was a spy. We're going to have to try for a forced landing on Jupiter."

"*Jupiter!* Screaming asteroids, sir, that planet looks dangerous!"

"Danger is our business, Lieutenant."

"Yes sir. Jupiter it is."

That's it. Just reroute and land on Jupiter. Mancini, you brain, even the schoolboys know better than that. Forget it.

The young man stuck his head in the doorway.

"Stowaway on board, sir."

"All right, I'll have a look."

Wearily, Jason rubbed his head and went with the Lieutenant.

"Robbie, dear!" he said, when they brought the prisoner forward. "How nice to see *some*one human. I'm having a dream, you know." Jason giggled. "You're looking splendid. Smelling splendid, too."

"I told you I'd be with you always, Derek," Robbie said, eyes glistening. "And I meant it."

"Why did you do this foolish thing?"

"Because I love you."

Jason grinned. Little liar. Oh, what a lie. "Say that again, darling."

"I love you, Derek."

"I should be angry, furious—but I'm not. We're in trouble, I suppose you know that."

"I know."

"And I suppose they told you we may not get out of this alive."

"It doesn't matter. Not as long as I'm with you."

Jason felt an impulse. Would Commander Derek Carlyle or would Commander Derek Carlyle not sweep the girl into his arms? It wasn't in the script. But—it was beginning to appear—it was all right if you didn't change it altogether. Revisions didn't hurt. Scripts are always being revised.

He swept her in his arms and kissed her and waited for the old fuzzy blackness to come. It didn't.

"Sweetheart!"

She *was* looking splendid. Carpenter did much better by her costume, such as it was. Some absolutely essential impedimenta, three or four sequined disks of varying shapes and all about the size of fig leaves. The diaphanous gown served only to heighten the effect of the deep cherry nut tan skin and the slender curves. And the scent . . . how could even Galactic's labs come up with a perfume that was so purely the odor of clean fresh woman? The look in her eyes, her black dancing eyes, was of an alarming sincerity.

He was going to suggest that they go elsewhere to chat, say to his cabin, where he could show her his navigational charts, but—Mancini had taken care of that. Commander Carlyle. Good egg. A nonagenarian in a harem. Duty first!

But as he looked at her, Jason felt strangely sad. It was the way she had pronounced the word *love*. Not brittle and lifeless, but—well, as if she really meant it. This part of the dream was not so bad, he decided. Maybe even worth the whole thing.

Nonsense, Jason!

Nonsense, your Aunt Hermione. Why kid yourself? You love the girl, don't you? Admit it in a dream, at least. After you wake up, you can hide in that gin-soaked shell if you want to and keep her from ever knowing . . .

"Jupiter ahead, sir!"

"Tell Michaels to prepare the brakes." Jason put a protective arm around Robbie. Her shoulder trembled. He could not bear to look into her eyes. "We'll make it, men, if we keep our heads!"

"I don't care. You stay here if you want to, Jeff. I'm going in."

"But it's sheer suicide! You don't stand a chance in a million of getting out with your skin—"

"It's a chance I'll have to take."

"Derek, listen to me. There's a thousand of those ugly devils and every one spoiling for a fight. They'd pick you up and—well, you know what happened to Fontaine."

"Yes. I—know."

"Well then, make *sense*, Derek! We can still clear out while there's time."

"Sorry, Jeff. No dice. I've made up my mind."

"You crazy fool. I wonder if that girl knows how much you love her . . ."

"It isn't just for Cynthia, Jeff. Don't you understand—it's our only chance to get at that Death Ray."

"Then I'm going to go with you."

"No. One might make it, not two. You go back to the ship, Jeff—that's an order."

"Yes, sir."

"Shake?"

"I—good luck, Derek. Good luck. We'll be waiting."

Jason watched the figure of Jeff Manning, the engineer, walk off toward the *Starfire*. Burton Mitchell, of course, looking as if he'd never spent a day at the phone praying for a call from Central Casting. Maybe he wasn't such a bad sort. They were all behaving well.

Stop it, you ass. This is a fit of some kind you're having. Burton Mitchell is a pitiful and extremely annoying has-been and if he hadn't pestered you to death—still—What's the story, are you letting these Perils-of-Pauline heroics warp your better judgment?

Twice in the picture Mitchell—Manning—had saved his life. Minor episodes. But he was touched. Couldn't help it. Everybody seemed so damned sincere about their corn. This flea-bitten space opera, running the gamut of emotions, the most basic emotions, simplified down to absurdity. But maybe it was the first time Rock Jason had ever been exposed, or permitted himself to be exposed, to real emotions of any kind. In Hollywood, he guessed, you've *got* to rely on dreams for lasting values. Dreams were the only things with value.

Look at him now. The climax of the picture. The big scene. Hero stuff. And yet he was feeling less like Rock Jason every moment and more like Commander Derek Carlyle, Herman Mancini's brainchild. Or was he merely feeling like Leroy Guinness O'Shea in days long ago, when the stage was a magic world and such things as love and honesty existed . . .

Jason felt the anger surge and he didn't try to check it. Trick-suits or not, pimple-faced extras or no pimple-faced extras, he hated the Jovians for what they had done. They had Robbie, the bastards. Well, they wouldn't have her long, by the holies!

He vaulted with great bounding leaps over the rough terrain and crouched at the marble wall of the temple. A guard slithered toward him, hissing. He let him have it. The guard fell. He wrapped the scarlet cloak about his shoulders and faked his entrance into the hall.

The animal smell almost asphyxiated Jason. Direct from the reptile house—he remembered. Together, for effect, with essence du stable.

The Emperor of Jupiter sat upon his throne, clucking gleefully.

"I thought our little ruse would work, Commander. Ah, don't attempt to shoot me. I am covered by a force field. And fifty *Kranek* pistols are aimed at your heart." It was Toby Bowles. Old Toby, who'd made a fortune playing villains because of his impossible face. Even with the weird makeup there could be no mistaking the kindly character actor. Or could there?

"You scum!" Commander Carlyle raged.

"Scum, eh? We'll see how the heroic commander's song changes after he sees—this!"

The emperor motioned with his hand and two slaves pulled aside a thick purple curtain.

"Cynthia! Robbie!"

"Derek!"

"Ah, a most touching reunion." The emperor laughed gutturally.

Robbie was spread-eagled and chained to the wall. The diaphanous gown was gone: she was as naked as the production code would allow. Bright thin red stripes crisscrossed her shoulders and other inoffensive regions.

Commander Carlyle spluttered out an oath and raced forward. The force field knocked him to his feet.

"Cynthia, what have they done to you?"

"Nothing," the emperor laughed; then he sobered, ". . . yet."

"I'll kill you, you Jovian filth!" Commander Carlyle hurled. "Then I'll have you fired, do you hear me? Blackballed by every studio from here to—"

"Strange talk, earthling. Bold talk. But we have more to show you. Come."

Two burly slaves, both looking alike, both resembling great lizards, pinioned Jason's arms and pushed him along roughly. They went through many halls and finally entered an immense rotunda.

An oversized machine something like a searchlight hummed and droned madly in the center of the room.

"The Death Ray!" Commander Carlyle exclaimed. The next lines of dialogue were lost in his fury.

"I see you recognize our little weapon. I thought perhaps you might be interested. Its effects are slow. But they are lasting. The warmth your earth feels now will be increased in a very short time to a heat so unbearable no life can exist."

"Then you move in. Right?"

"As you say, right. We're becoming rather overpopulous here."

"You cold-hearted—Toby, listen to me. Turn that thing off. And then turn Robbie loose. Immediately. Is that clear?"

"Prepare the prisoner for the *Rakana!*"

"Oh, let's not go through that miserable thing." Jason felt unwell. He had turned green just watching the stuntman. The late stuntman it was now.

"We will test your courage, brave soldier." Right straight out of *Gunga Din.*

"Let's talk it over, shall we?"

The blackness began to fuzz up. Stop it. You're too close to the end now. Keep this up and you'll land smack back at the beginning of reel nine!

"Do your worst to me. But release the girl."

"Ah!" the emperor said. "In accordance with the rules, I make you a promise. It is a fair one. In the event that you are victorious in the arena, both you and the girl will be free to leave unharmed."

There were soft, hissing, laughing sounds.

Commander Carlyle grinned wildly. "You've made yourself a deal, snakeface."

"Take him away."

Jason left happily. The *snakeface* had been his own.

Then he thought of what was to come and he stopped being happy.

The darkness of the cell was oppressive. It pushed in. The smell department had gone crazy here. A whiff from a local dairy, frou frou of abattoir, the gentle aromas of cattle barns, stables, cod-liver oil—every repulsive smell in the world. Jason alternately trembled and squared his jaw. It took thought.

On the one hand, this was a fit of the DT's and so, one way or another, he would wake up by and by and everything would be jimdandy. Plus the fact that according to the script Carlyle is victorious. But there was the other hand. Which was that the great stuntman, Ralph Laurie, who had in his career flown through fiery hoops, leaped into ravines and braved death in every conceivable manner, had been killed in this scene. The gorilla had killed Laurie. Stupid to use a gorilla anyway. Who ever heard of gorillas on Jupiter? Who ever heard of *anything* on Jupiter!

Jason thought about the big ape Bobo, painted a sickening bedroom pink, and he began to tremble more often than he squared his jaw.

He had about decided to give the whole thing up when the wooden gate was pulled open and light cascaded in. Two Jovian lizard men also cascaded in. They dragged Jason into the center of the vast circular arena. The crowd cheered madly.

The Jovians slithered away.

Then Jason remembered. Whirling, he saw Robbie. Tied to a stake in the exact center of the sandy circle. She was breathtakingly beautiful now. He went over to her.

She looked very frightened. The ropes had been carefully placed—Lila, from props, had spent almost an hour getting the rough thick loops just right. One above the breasts. One below them. One around the tummy. One—below.

"Robbie, darling!"

"Derek. Whatever happens, I love you, I love you, I—"

Jason put a hand over her lips. "You mustn't say it," he whispered. "Not after the way I've treated you. But Robbie, if we get out of this—I'll make it up. I swear I'll—"

"Derek, look out!"

The crowd's scream whipped him around. Jason swallowed.

It was Bobo. The gorilla. With that look in his eye.

"Nice Bobo. You remember me, Rocky? *Jungle Goddess*—remember?"

The ape walked on all fours twice around Jason. The crowd hushed.

Bobo stopped and scratched. Jason sighed. His heart was thumping. He noticed the flimsy spear the guard had put in his hand just before abandoning him to this dirty creature.

"Bobo, get back. Get back now. Don't do anything foolish."

Someone threw a heavy rock. It hit the ape's behind. "Aarrrgh!" The ape roared disapproval and began to lope straight for Jason.

They sprinted around the arena a few times, the ape hot on his opponent's heels. Jason started to climb the wall. The black fuzziness. He dropped down. The giant creature was thundering toward him.

He closed his eyes. Nothing happened.

He opened his eyes.

Bobo was beating his villainous old chest and hooting at Robbie.

Jason ran over and delivered a well-aimed kick to the gorilla's hindquarters, which were already tender from the rock. Bobo turned, scratched and leapt, saying "Aarrrgh! Aarrrgh!" They fell thuddingly on the sand. The gorilla's arms were crushing his chest.

"For heaven's sake," Jason managed to gurgle, "you're squashing me, you idiot!" They rolled over. And over. The crowd roared. The gorilla roared. Jason roared.

Then Bobo screamed an unearthly unjovian scream in the suddenly quiet arena.

Jason watched the ape clutching and flailing at the spear shaft, which was buried in soft chest flesh. He heard the thunder of over a ton of life hitting the sand. Then, when Bobo twitched no longer, he walked over, bowed in the direction of the emperor's box and pulled out the spear. As he did so, he wondered briefly what had happened.

The throng went crazy. Guards came galloping into the circle, hissing threats, and the emperor's voice could be heard screeching, "KILL the earthling! Kill him!"

"So," Commander Carlyle cried, "*this* is how the ruler of all Jupiter rewards bravery and keeps his promises!"

"Kill him!"

A *Kranek* gun crackled and Commander Carlyle grabbed at his shoulder. He dropped on one knee, tried to shake the pain from his mind.

Then he saw why the crowd had gone so crazy. The crew of the *Starfire*, stationed at crucial posts, were letting loose the fury of zam guns; the Jovians were falling like ants under a spyglass; the stink and sizzle of death on Jupiter filled the heavy air.

Of course! At this point in the scene they come to rescue him!

Commander Carlyle rose to his feet and raced along to the Royal Box. He reached up and pulled the fatty emperor down into the sand.

Toby fumbled with a pistol.

"Oh no you don't!" Commander Carlyle plunged the already bloodied spear into Toby's quivering throat. Then he ran back to the stake and cut loose Robbie's bonds. She collapsed into his arms; he winced at the pain in his shoulder and lifted her to the waiting, loyal Jeff.

"Thanks, boy."

"Okay, skipper!"

He grabbed a *Kranek* and blasted his way through the disorganized Jovians to the rotunda.

The lizard guard whirled, hissed disdainfully and brought his blaster into play. Commander Carlyle dodged the lethal ray and leapt upon the enraged Jovian.

This part, he recalled vaguely, was played by a particularly scrawny extra, so he directed his blows toward the Adam's apple, together with a few good ones to the belly. The Jovian dropped, hissing and moaning.

Commander Derek Carlyle took careful aim with his *Kranek* pistol. Then he fired. The ray hit the machine dead center. He fired again and again. Soon the Death Ray apparatus was a melted pile of steaming junk.

He smiled inscrutably and turned in time to blast the guards out of the doorway. Then he clutched a conveniently placed velvet cord and swung the length of the hall over the heads of the lizard horde, high over them, in a long graceful arc—then, in the sunlight, he ran, blasting his way to freedom.

There were Jovians waiting at the ship. Loyal, good and true Jeff lay dying on the volcanic soil and a slimy snake on legs was slithering away with Robbie in his stunted arms.

"Wait a second, friend."

The Jovian turned. The blast caught him directly in the face. He screamed.

Commander Carlyle helped Cynthia into the ship. Then he climbed back down.

"Jeff," he said. "Come on, let's—Jeff!"

"Sorry, Derek. This is one hand I'll have to sit out on. You'll—have to—go on without me. This is curtains."

"Jeff!"

More Jovians came barreling for the ship. *Kranek* rays cut through the air. One caught Jason's shoulder. Wait a minute—didn't the script girl catch that? For Pete's sake, that shoulder was supposed to be already hit. Never mind that now. Just get in the ship. Hurry!

The lizard men were battering at the door, slicing the alloy with their pistols.

"Let 'er rip!"

The jets thundered to life.

Commander Carlyle chuckled. "That ought to warm 'em up."

He could smile now.

The *Starfire* rose slowly like a gigantic phoenix; then it flashed off, a silver wink in the black-velvet sky.

Commander Carlyle stood at the starboard port. His eyes were sad. His arm was around the girl. She snuggled closer.

"Goodbye," he said, "Jeff, Harry, Don—all of you down there who didn't make it. You died, but your lives were not given in vain. Earth will never forget your sacrifice!"

"And earth will never forget," said the young lieutenant, "a man named Carlyle. God bless you sir. We all love you."

"Yes," Cynthia said, snuggling still closer as the stars whisked by, "we all love you, Commander Derek Carlyle!"

"Robbie," Jason said, holding her, pressing her nearer. "Robbie. Robbie, darling."

This time the blackness came and Jason didn't fight it. He only tried to hold onto that golden tan arm a little longer. . . .

Whistling. Applause. Cheers. Jason blinked, half expecting to find himself back in the *Rakana* field.

He tensed his body.

He opened his eyes, expecting to see Bobo the gorilla. Instead he saw Sherman Boetticher.

He closed his eyes again. It was almost as bad.

"Rock—you all right? Speak to us. Say something."

"Breeng on de dancing gorls," Jason said. The dream was over. He remembered it all now. Or most of it, anyway.

"That's our Rock. Say, you had us worried, boy!"

"What'd I do, faint?"

"I wouldn't know—you just sort of stood here, watching the picture."

He looked puzzled—

"Is that so unusual?"

"Well, what I mean is, you pulled your hand out before Hymie could switch off the Quad and just—well, you didn't say boo. Just watched the picture."

"Is—is it over now?"

"Is it over? Listen to the man! It's a goddam sensation. It was the smells that did it. Oh, *what* a brainstorm those smells were!" Boetticher was smiling broadly. "Excuse me now. Got to go meet our public."

He went outside, burbling happily. The voices were loud.

"How is your hand, Mr. Jason?" Little Mr. Gottschalk looked anxious.

"Beautiful, an artist's," Jason said, thinking of other things.

"I was afraid did you hurt it. Bad type business. Nobody, not even me, knows all about this machine. But so? Maybe all great inwentions get borned like me, isn't it?" The little man looked quite sad. "I tell you tzegret: what I am working on is not for movie camera. No! At first, I sink I got tzegret to forse dimansion! Is beautiful! But—it wouldn't work. T'ousand times I tried: nossing, wouldn't work." He sighed. "So, I turn it into movie camera. All right?"

Jason nodded slowly, wondering about several things all at once.

The door opened. Dolly Dixon stood puffing. *"Daaar*ling!" she ululated, "but it was the most! I mean, the end! I mean, what'll you just do with all your money?"

"Excuse me." Jason brushed past the confused sphere of columnists and looked around the room and then walked quickly out the doorway, tearing loose from the adoring crowd.

She was walking fast.

"Robbie. Wait."

Robin Summers turned around. "For what?" she said. "It's your show, isn't it?" Her black eyes didn't seem so angry. Why didn't they seem so angry? Jason thought for a moment they looked almost as they did on Jupiter.

"Robbie, I want to say some things to you. Will you listen?"

"If I have to," she said, but not harshly; and her skin was even more shining gold in the lights.

Hair of the Dog

"**A**RTERIO—what was that you said?"

"—sclerosis."

"Bunky?"

"Yes."

"*Our* Bunky?"

"Yes."

"God!"

"*Sic transit gloria mundi*. A rare case. Poor chap—went out like a light. Just like a light."

"But I mean—Bunky, of all people! Up in his studies, young, well off, good looking, everything to live for!"

"*Ave atque vale*, old boy."

"I can't believe it."

"Here today, gone tomorrow."

"God!"

Up until now, Lorenzo Gissing had thought about death, when he thought about it at all, which was practically never, as one of those things one didn't think about. The frequency of its occurrence among the lower classes especially made it impossible. None of his relatives had ever died, to his knowledge. Nor had any of his good chums. In fact, he had never once looked upon a human corpse. The entire subject, therefore, was dismissed as pointless, morbid and not a little scatological, no more to be worried over than the other diseases that came as direct sequels to unclean living habits.

So the news of Bunky Frith's rather pell-mell departure from this world affected Lorenzo as few things had. His reaction was one of total disbelief followed by an angry sense of betrayal. He took to his rooms. He refused to eat. He slept little and then fitfully, leaping to the floor from time to time and cursing, knocking the blue china about and gazing at his image in the mirror.

"God!" he exclaimed every so often.

The funeral was the usual sort of thing, though perhaps a shade more elaborate than most. Lorenzo sat dazed throughout. The flowers made him ill at the stomach. The music was unbearable. And Rev. Bottomly's oration struck a new low.

121

Presently, however, services ended and it was time to line up for a last look at old Bunky.

"Dear old pal!" cried Lorenzo, when his turn had come to stand before the dead man. *"What has happened here?"*

They had to carry him away. His eyes had rolled up in his head, his skin had paled and, all things considered, he looked not quite as good as the late Frith.

His studies immediately took a dip: such had been his scholastic standing at the university that this was fatal. He left the ivied walls and took up residence in the city. He became a changed person. From a happy-go-lucky Pierrot to a fog-bound Raskolnikov. Overnight. He lost touch with his parents, with his friends and even with his tailor. He thought of only one thing: Death. His money went for any literature connected with the subject and when he was not thinking about it he was reading about it. The books were without exception humorless and dispiriting, though the medical publications were the worst of all. They had pictures. In color.

He bought every manner of medicine imaginable. He was inoculated against, or given reason to believe he would not contract, diphtheria, smallpox, chicken pox, elephantiasis, polio, jungle rot, cirrhosis of the liver, Bright's disease, hoof and mouth disease and the common cold. He avoided drafts and stuffy rooms. He checked daily with four doctors to make sure he did not have cancer, heart trouble or perforated ulcers.

Then he read a book on the statistics of death. It floored him. He gave up all thought of travel, almost of movement of any kind. It nearly drove him insane. With disease one could fight back, take precautions, guard one's self—but what chance did one have against accidents? If you went into the streets a safe might fall onto your head, if you stayed at home a thief might murder you and then set the house afire.

Lorenzo was thinking these things one night when he found that he had wandered far from home. The gurgle of the Thames could be heard beyond a fogbank. It was late. He remembered poor old Bunky and how frightful he had looked—like dried paste there in the coffin, and dead, dead, dead. He ran a pale hand through his thick bushy hair.

Why not? Do it yourself and at least you won't have to go on waiting for it. There were worse things than drowning. Arteriosclerosis, for one.

He took a step. A finger tapped his shoulder. He let loose a strangulated cry.

"Mr. Gissing?" The man was dressed in execrable taste: jaunty bowler, plus fours, a dun jacket of reprehensible fit. "Mr. Lorenzo Gissing?"

"Yes. Who are you? What are you going about prodding people for? I might have had a heart attack!"

"I'm sorry—I didn't mean to startle you. But you were about to jump into the river."

Mr. Gissing said "Coo" or something that sounded like coo.

"I represent a firm," the man said, "whose services you may find attractive. Shall we talk?"

Lorenzo nodded dumbly. His armpits discharged cold pellets of perspiration as he became aware of what he had been about to do.

"Very well," the man said. "Now then. Does the thought of death keep you up nights, plague you, torture you, prevent you from full enjoyment of life's rich bounty? Does it?"

"In a manner of speaking."

"And do you wish to be rid of this nagging worry?"

"Good heavens, yes! But how?"

"I'll tell you how, sir. I represent the Eternal Life Insurance Company and—"

"What was that?"

"—and we are in a position to help you. Our plan is roughly this: We offer Eternal Life to our clients. Now, we've been established since—"

"Oh dear, is this some sort of quiz program? Because, if it is—"

"Of course, we'll have to sit down and discuss this in more detail. Get your signature on some contracts and the like. But a run-down of our services may be stated in this way: For a very nominal fee—very nominal indeed, sir—to be paid to us monthly, we give you immortality."

"You're not the de—"

"Oh no. I merely work for the company. Mr. Asmodeus, our president, has given up canvassing. It's a very old firm."

"Well . . ."

"Think of it, Mr. Gissing! No more worry about death! But life—happy, content, healthy, eternal, free to do what you choose without thought to consequences."

"Hmm."

"And all for a very low monthly payment."

"What sort of payment?"

"There will be, of course, the usual waiting period. Then—by the way, which do you prefer, the first or the fifteenth?"

"Oh, I don't know—the first, I guess."

"Then on the first of the month and every subsequent month, you will just slip your payment in the mails to us and, why Mr. Gissing, you'll just go on living, that's all!"

"What *sort* of payment?"

"One hair. Plucked from your head on exactly the day the payment comes due—never before."

"Did you say one hair?" Lorenzo started calculating and remembering his wild heavy brown bush.

"One hair. No more, no less." The man dug in his briefcase for some papers. "Each shall represent a month of life to you."

Lorenzo gulped. "Well now," he said, "that's not exactly eternity."

"Rather close though," the man smiled, "wouldn't you say?"

"Yes," Lorenzo agreed, remembering approximately how many hundreds of thousands of hairs one is supposed to have on one's dome.

"Are you interested?"

"I'm interested. But tell me this—what happens when they're all gone?"

"Then you die."

"Oh."

"It's the best we can do. You won't get a better offer."

"Well, I mean, is that all? I just—die? Where's *your* profit?"

"Ah, Mr. Gissing, I wouldn't have suspected such business acumen in one so young. But you're quite right. There is one other little matter."

"I supposed as much. My soul, eh?"

"You won't miss it. They're sort of like an appendix nowadays."

"Well . . ."

"Shall we talk business? I do have other calls to make."

"All right."

The man spoke for almost an hour. Then he gave Lorenzo the contract to read. It seemed in order. Lorenzo signed all copies in a peculiar reddish ink provided by the man. Then he was given a brochure, a number of self-addressed envelopes, a carbon of the contract and a payment book.

"It will be renewed every hundred years or so," the man said, beginning to put things away. "Well!" he said. "That seems to take care of about everything. We're all fixed up now. I think you'll be quite happy with the arrangement—our firm does quite a volume business. You'd be amazed. Good evening, Mr. Gissing. Remember now, the first payment falls due on the first, which is forty-five days from now."

"Good evening," Lorenzo said. But the man was already gone.

"Lorenzo, you're looking peculiar."

"Peculiar, Mama?"

"So healthy! That *savoir vivre,* that smile, that twinkle in the eye! Is this my boy?"

"It is, Mama. In the flesh. Quick now, what has happened? Father ill?"

"No—worse luck. Dead."

"What? Dad? Dad dead?"

"Quite."

"Oh."

"Last week. Fell off his horse whilst hunting a fox. Cracked his skull, poor thing."

"Well, that's the way it goes. *Sic transit gloria mundi.*"

"You're taking it remarkably well, Lorenzo."

"Here today, gone tomorrow, Mama, I always say. Part of the game, what? Well, at least we shan't have to suffer. I imagine poor old Dad's estate is tidied up. That is—"

"Oh Lorenzo!"

"Yes, Mama?"

"Your father, bless his departed soul, has kept something from us."

"And what might that be, Mama?"

"He—I mean to say, your father—well, he—"

"Yes? Yes? Yes?"

"Stony."

"Oh no!"

"Yes. Not a sou. How he ever managed to keep us in such luxury, why, it must have taken everything! Such a good man, not to worry us."

"Yes, quite so, quite so. Mama, when you say 'not a sou' I assume you're indulging in a slight overstatement of the situation. That is to say, surely—"

"Nothing. Except debts. Whatever shall we do? There's scarcely enough for the funeral expenses."

"Good heavens!"

"What is it, Lorenzo?"

"I've just remembered something. An appointment in the city—business, you know. I must leave at once!"

"But my son, you've just arrived!"

"I know. Well, chin up! I'm off!"

Back in the city, Lorenzo Gissing thrashed a good bit at this blow. How ludicrous, after all. Here one is offered eternal life, or very nearly that, and the next thing one knows, one has no money with which to enjoy it. He took to brooding and might have continued to do so indefinitely, had not a happy thought occurred. He smiled. He visited his tailor.

"My dearest!" he said not long afterwards to the Lady Moseby, formerly of Tunbridge Wells now of London, rich, widowed and lonely. "My very dearest only one!"

Anastasia Moseby had heretofore been spared the attentions of bachelors both eligible and ineligible owing to the genuineness of her despair at the death by his own hand of her husband, Sir Malcolm Peterhenshaw Moseby, Bart. This despair was transmitted by the pallor in her face and the quietness of her speech, which qualities actually made her more attractive and generally desirable. She was known as a woman who had loved and would not love again.

Lorenzo Gissing demonstrated the fallacy of this notion by walking down the old aisle with the now beamingly radiant lady, to the incipient dismay of certain other parties in attendance.

She was a woman transformed.

"Lorenzo, duck," she enthused later, at the proper time and place, "I do love you."

"And I love you," Lorenzo responded.

"I love you more than anyone or anything else on Earth!"

"And I love you more than anyone or anything else in the entire galaxy."

"We shall be so very happy."

"Fantastically, deliriously, I'm sure."

"And will you love me all your life?"

"I resent the question's implication."

"Sweet, we are such a pair, we two. I know and understand you so well, Lorenzo. The others—"

"Yes, what about the others?"

"They are saying—no, I cannot even repeat it!"

"What, what? Is this to be a marriage of secrecy and deception?"

"They're saying, Lorenzo my dearest plum, that you married me only for my money."

"The swine! Who said it? Who? I'll beat him to within an inch—"

"Hush, my duck! You and I know differently, don't we."

"Indeed me do. By the bye, what *does* the bally old bank book come to?"

"Oh, I don't know. A few hundred thousand, I should imagine. What does it matter?"

"Matter? Not at all. Only, well, you see—I've had some baddish luck."

"Not really."

"Yes. Wiped out. Utterly."

"I see."

"Yes. Well, never mind; I've my application in at the terminal for a clerk's position. It won't be much, but by the almighty, we'll make it, and without your having to dip—"

"Lorenzo! Kiss me!"

"There!"

"You'll never have to worry about money, so long as you kiss me like that and are faithful to me. This one must go right."

"I beg pardon?"

"Nothing. Only that just before Sir Malcolm's tragic death, the details of which you must have read, I—well, I discovered he had been faithless to me."

"The fool. Darling, oh my darling!"

It did not consume a great deal of time for Lorenzo to arrange for the account to be put in both their names. As soon as this was accomplished, and he had withdrawn the greater portion of it, there was a marked change in the relationship. Anastasia's fey charm was all well and good for a while, downright pleasant once or twice, but, as Lorenzo put it to her one evening, there were other fish to fry.

The day before he left for Cannes, he received an unstamped letter in the mails, which read:

A FRIENDLY REMINDER!

Your first payment falls
due in exactly two (2)
days.

Thank you.

Asmodeus, Pres.
ETERNAL LIFE INS. CO.
Gehenna

It made him feel good somehow, in a creepy kind of way, and he left whistling. He did not kiss his wife goodbye.

Having plucked one hair from his head, placed it into an envelope and included a covering letter, Mr. Gissing set forth to enjoy himself. He learned rapidly the extent to which this was going to be possible.

Having made certain improper overtures to a bronzed and altogether statuesque beauty sunning herself in the Riviera warmth, he was annoyed at the approach of said beauty's husband: tall, angry and, Lorenzo felt sure, a circus giant. There followed an embarrassing scene. The husband actually hit him. In the mouth.

But he didn't feel a thing. And though he had never previously been athletically inclined, Lorenzo's amazing staying power—this extra dividend—eventually tired the irate husband to a point whereat it was possible to kick him senseless. It made quite an impression on the bronzed statuesque beauty and they subsequently enjoyed a relationship which, though brief, was nothing if not satisfactory.

Mr. Gissing proceeded to cut what may be described as a wide swath. He became increasingly mindless of consequences. He traveled from point to point with the unconcerned purpose of a bluebottle fly, leaving untold damaged reputations and memorable evenings in his wake. Each month on the first exactly, he mailed away the hair, praised his good fortune and went on to newer conquests. He set records for derring-do, performing publicly such feats as diving three hundred feet into a bathtub and wrestling a giant ape to the death.

At length, however, as is often the case with the most adventuresome of hearts, he tired of the gaiety, the lights and the tinsel, and began to long for the comforts of hearth, dog-at-the-feet and wife. He therefore gave up his apartment in Tangier, composed an effusive letter of apology to Anastasia —explaining that the death of his father had sent him temporarily balmy—and returned home.

Nothing had changed. Anastasia was as lovely as ever: forgiving, understanding, loving. She tended to his wants as though he had not been gone for the better part of five years. There was not one word of recrimination at his having spent most of the money. They settled in their cozy little cottage and aside from noticing a slightly peculiar look in his wife's eyes once in a great while, Lorenzo Gissing partook of the pleasures of domesticity, content until the old urges should again assail him.

It was during dinner, with Heine the spaniel lying on his feet and roast beef lying on his plate, that Mr. Gissing dropped his coffee cup to the floor.

"What did you say?" he demanded.

"I merely remarked, dear," answered his wife, "that it's a pity you should be losing your hair so rapidly."

"It's a lie!" Mr. Gissing raced for the mirror and stood transfixed before it, running his hands over his head. "It's a lie!"

"Well, you needn't get so broken up about it. Lots of people lose their hair. I shall still love you."

"No no no, that isn't the point. Do you really think that I am?"

"No question about it."

"God!"

It was quite true. It was going fast. How strange that he hadn't noticed before—

He noticed now. It was as if it were all rotting off, so to speak. "My God!" cried Mr. Gissing, "I'm shedding!"

It thinned first at the front of his head: the hairline receding some ten or fifteen inches. In short order it was reduced to a definite tonsure, giving him the curious appearance of a profane monk. He became frantic, finally to the point of spilling the beans to Anastasia.

"But how dreadful!" Anastasia said, "Oughtn't you to complain to the Better Business Bureau? I'm sure it must be some terrible fraud."

"What shall I do? I'm going bald, don't you understand?"

"Now I wonder," Anastasia said, "if that's what's happening to all the men that go bald? I mean, are they clients of Mr.— what's his name—Asmodeus—too?"

"You don't believe me!"

"Now, dear, you've always had a vivid imagination. But if you insist, I'll believe you. Why not see a scalp specialist?"

"Of course! Yes, I will!"

He did. The specialist, a Dr. Fatt, shook his head sadly. "Sorry, old man. One of those rare things. Nothing we can do."

He went to other specialists. They also shook their heads. He thought of saving the hairs as they fell. But no. In the contract it was clearly put forth:

> "—that this hair shall be plucked from the head on the exact day payment falls due; never before, otherwise client risks forfeiture of his security . . ."

"The fiends!" he groaned. "They're responsible for this! Why didn't somebody warn me I'd go bald?"

Mr. Gissing lived the life of a tortured man, running from scalp specialist to scalp specialist, inundating his almost totally unhirsute head with a great variety of oils, herbs, juices and powders. He submitted to treatments by diet, magnet, X Ray, vibrator and once tried hanging a dead toad from the lattice at midnight. Nothing helped. He grew balder and balder and—

At last, down to no more than twenty single hairs, he waited for the first of the month to roll 'round and then carefully sliced the plucked hair into two sections and mailed one of the sections off. He received a letter the same day.

> Dear Mr. Gissing:
> In Hades, we do not split hairs.
> Very truly yours,
> Asmodeus

He got off the remaining section hurriedly.

Finally, when only one solitary tendril protruded from his

pate, one tiny hair flourishing like a lone palm tree in a gigantic desert, Mr. Gissing, nearly speechless with anxiety, contacted the newly founded Binkley Clinic.

"You've come to the right place," said Dr. Binkley, saturnine of expression and comfortingly beshocked and tressed with carrot-colored filaments.

"Thank God," said Mr. Gissing.

"Not a bit of it," said the doctor. "Thank me."

"Can you really keep me from going bald?"

"My dear sir, the Binkley method will grow hair on a billiard ball." He pointed to a green-felt-covered table, on which rested three billiard balls, each covered with a thick hairy matting.

"That's all quite nice," Mr. Gissing said, "but will it grow hair on *me?*"

"I guarantee that in one month you will begin to feel the effects."

"*Feel the effects*—be specific, man. In one month's time, will there be any growth?"

"My method is expensive, but rightly so. Yes, Mr. Gissing: though slight, there will definitely be hairs upon your head in one month's time."

"You *promise?* That is, you've done it before?"

"With scalp conditions such as yours, which are uncommon, yes, I can say unequivocally, I have."

"Let's begin immediately."

It was necessary for Mr. Gissing to stand on his head for several hours and then submit to having his dome raked with a strange electrical device rather like a combination cotton gin and sewing machine.

"Be careful," he reminded the doctor every few minutes, "do not on your life disturb that last hair. Don't even go near it."

Upon leaving the Binkley Clinic, Mr. Gissing put a band aid over the hair and returned to his cottage, tired but happy.

"It's all right now," he said with jubilance to his wife. "I've this month's payment. And by next month I am guaranteed a new growth. Isn't that *wonderful?*"

"Yes, dear. Supper is ready now."

After stowing away his first undyspeptic meal in some time, Mr. Gissing turned to his wife and was shocked to observe how wan and beautiful she looked in the firelight. He felt a surge of sorts.

"Anastasia," he said. "You're looking fit."

"Thank you, Lorenzo."

"Very fit indeed."

"Thank you, Lorenzo."

"In fact, if I may remark, you're looking positively pretty, somehow."

"You are very gallant."

"Nonsense. See here, you're not angry about what happened as a direct result of poor old Dad's death, I mean my skipping off and all that—"

"Not angry, no."

"Good girl. Good *girl*. It's the way a man's constructed, one supposes. Well, it's all over now. I mean, we were barely getting to know one another."

"Yes . . ."

"Say, pretty sage of the old boy—meaning me—outsmarting the devil himself, what?"

"Very sage indeed, Lorenzo. I'm tired. Do you mind if I go to bed?"

Mr. Gissing smiled archly and delivered a pinch to his wife's backside. "Oh," he exclaimed, "I can feel it growing already. The hair. I can make the payment tomorrow—it *is* the first, isn't it?—and by next month I'll be able to start all over again without any fears. Dr. Binkley says *his* hair won't shed. Think of it!"

They retired and after a certain amount of wrestling and one thing and another, Mr. Gissing dropped off to a very sound sleep. He dreamed.

"Anastasia! Oh my Lord!"

"Yes dear, yes, what is it?"

"You mean *where* is it! It's gone, that's where. *Gone*, you understand?"

"I don't know what you're talking about."

"The hair, you idiot. It fell off. Lost. You must help me look for it."

They looked. Frantically. In the bedroom. In the bed. In the bedclothes. The mattress. The sheets. The pillows. Nothing. No hair.

"Again, we must look again. Carefully this time. Oh, *carefully!*"

They covered every inch of the room, then every other room, on hands and knees.

"Are you sure you had it when you came in?"

"Yes. I checked."

"Well, have you looked in all your pockets?"

"Yes. No—wait. No. Not there."

"Then where did you lose it?"

Mr. Gissing gave his wife a withering look and continued his prayerful search. He inspected his clothes minutely. His shoes, his socks. The bathroom drain. The combs. Everything, everywhere.

"We must find it. It's getting near midnight."

"But dear, we've looked all day and all night. Can't you just sort of forget about it?"

"Anastasia, from the way you talk one would think you *wanted* to see me sizzle!"

"Lorenzo, what a discourteous and utterly unattractive thing to say!"

"Just keep looking."

At last, exhausted, breathless, hungry, his mind a kaleidoscope of fear, Mr. Gissing hurled himself onto the bed and lay there trembling.

"Would this be it?"

He leapt to his feet. He took the hair from his wife's hand. "Yes! Yes, it is! I'm sure of it—see, how brown it is. It isn't yours, yours is all black. Oh Anastasia, we're saved! I'll get it in the mails right away."

He started back from the post office still shaken by the experience and was almost to the door. A finger tapped his shoulder.

"Mr. Gissing?"

"Yes, yes?" He turned. It was the man he'd encountered by the Thames, so long ago. Still badly dressed.

"Well, what is it? Almost had me, didn't you?"

"Come with me," the man said.

"In a pig's eye I will. The payment's already in, old boy, and on time too. According to the con—"

The man's clothes suddenly burst into flame and in a moment Mr. Gissing found himself confronted by a creature unlike any in his experience. He quailed somewhat.

"Come—with—me."

A hand of hot steel clutched Mr. Gissing's arm and they began to walk down an alley where no alley had ever seemed to be before. It was quite dark.

"What," Mr. Gissing shrieked, "is the meaning of this, may I inquire? The contract clearly states that as long as I get a hair off to you on the first of every month everything's in order."

"That is not quite correct," said the creature, exuding the kind of aroma one smells at barbeques. "One of *your* hairs."

"But—but that *was* my hair. I saw it. No one else was in the house. Certainly not in the bedroom. Except my wife— and she's brunette."

The creature laughed. "It was not yours."

"Then what—oh surely not! Anastasia, unfaithful? I can hardly believe it."

They walked in silence. The creature said nothing.

"My heart is broken!" Mr. Gissing wailed. "Another man

in *our* bedroom! What sort of world is this where such iniquity is permitted to exist! Surely it can be no worse where we are going."

They disappeared into the blackness.

Anastasia Gissing never saw her husband again. She was left to seek solace from her thoughts and a small brown-haired spaniel named Heine. She bore up well.

The Beautiful People

MARY SAT QUIETLY and watched the handsome man's legs blown off, watched on further as the great ship began to crumple and break into small pieces in the middle of the blazing night. She fidgeted slightly as the men and the parts of the men came floating dreamily through the wreckage out into the awful silence. And when the meteorite shower came upon the men, flying in gouging holes through everything, tearing flesh and ripping bones, Mary closed her eyes.

"Mother."

Mrs. Cuberle glanced up from her magazine.

"Do we have to wait much longer?"

"I don't think so, why?"

Mary said nothing but looked at the moving wall.

"Oh, that." Mrs. Cuberle laughed and shook her head. "That tired old thing. Read a magazine, Mary, like I'm doing. We've all seen *that* a million times."

"Does it have to be on, Mother?"

"Well, nobody seems to be watching. I don't think the doctor would mind if I switched it off."

Mrs. Cuberle rose from the couch and walked to the wall. She depressed a little button and the life went from the wall, flickering and glowing.

Mary opened her eyes.

"Honestly," Mrs. Cuberle said to the woman, beside her, "you'd think they'd try to get something else. We might all as well go to the museum and watch the first landing on Mars. The Mayorka Disaster—really!"

The woman replied without distracting her eyes from the magazine page. "It's the doctor's idea. Psychological."

Mrs. Cuberle opened her mouth and moved her head up and down, knowingly. "I should have known there was *some* reason. Still, who watches it?"

"The children do. Makes them think, makes them grateful or something."

"Oh. Of course, yes."

"Psychological."

Mary picked up a magazine and leafed through the pages.

134

All photographs, of women and men. Women like Mother and like the others in the room; slender, tanned, shapely, beautful women; and men with large muscles and shiny hair. Women and men, all looking alike, all perfect and beautiful. She folded the magazine and wondered how to answer the questions that would be asked.

"Mother—"

"Gracious, what is it now! Can't you sit still for a minute?"

"But we've been here three hours."

Mrs. Cuberle sniffed.

"Do I really have to?"

"Now, don't be silly, Mary. After those terrible things you told me, of *course* you do."

An olive-skinned woman in a transparent white uniform came into the reception room.

"Cuberle. Mrs. Zena Cuberle?"

"Yes."

"Doctor will see you now."

Mrs. Cuberle took Mary's hand and they walked behind the nurse down a long corridor.

A man who seemed in his middle twenties looked up from a desk. He smiled and gestured towards two adjoining chairs.

"Well, well."

"Doctor Hortel, I—"

The doctor snapped his fingers.

"Of course, I know. Your daughter. Well, I know your trouble. Get so many of them nowadays, takes up most of my time."

"You do?" asked Mrs. Cuberle. "Frankly, it had begun to to upset me."

"Upset? Hmm. Not good at all. But then—if people did not get upset, then we psychiatrists would be out of a job, eh? Go the way of the M.D. But I assure you, I need hear no more."

He turned his handsome face to Mary. "Little girl, how old are you?"

"Eighteen, sir."

"Oh, a real bit of impatience. It's just about time, of course. What might your name be?"

"Mary."

"Charming! and so unusual. Well, now, Mary, may I say that I understand your problem—understand it thoroughly."

Mrs. Cuberle smiled and smoothed the metalwork on her jerkin.

"Madam, you have no idea how many there are these days. Sometimes it preys on their minds so that it affects them physically, even mentally. Makes them act strange, say peculiar, unexpected things. One little girl I recall was so distraught she did nothing but brood all day long. Can you imagine!"

"That's what Mary does. When she finally told me, Doctor, I thought she had gone—you know."

"That bad, eh? Afraid we'll have to start a re-education programme, very soon, or they'll all be like this. I believe I'll suggest it to the Senator day after tomorrow."

"I don't quite understand, doctor."

"Simply, Mrs. Cuberle, that the children have got to be thoroughly instructed. Thoroughly. Too much is taken for granted and childish minds somehow refuse to accept things without definite reason. Children have become far too intellectual, which, as I trust I needn't remind you, is a dangerous thing."

"Yes, but what has this to do with—"

"Mary, like half the sixteen-, seventeen- and eighteen-year-olds today, has begun to feel acutely self-conscious. She feels that her body has developed sufficiently for the Transformation—which of course it has not, not quite yet—and she cannot understand the complex reasons which compel her to wait until some vague, though specific, date. Mary looks at you, at the women all about her, at the pictures, and then she looks into a mirror. From pure perfection of body, face, limbs, pigmentation, carriage, stance, she sees herself and is horrified. Isn't that so? Of course. She asks herself, 'Why must I be hideous, unbalanced, oversize, undersize, full of revolting skin eruption, badly schemed organic arrangements?' —in short, Mary is tired of being a monster and is overly anxious to achieve what almost everyone else has already achieved."

"But—" said Mrs. Cuberle.

"This much you understand, doubtless. Now, Mary, what you object to is that our society offers you, and the others like you, no convincing logic on the side of waiting until nineteen. It is all taken for granted and you want to know why! It is that simple. A non-technical explanation will not suffice. The modern child wants facts, solid technical data, to satisfy her every question. And that, as you can both see, will take a good deal of reorganizing."

"But—" said Mary.

"The child is upset, nervous, tense; she acts strange, peculiar, odd, worries you and makes herself ill because it is beyond our meagre powers to put it across. I tell you, what we need is a whole new basis for learning. And, that will take doing. It will take *doing*, Mrs. Cuberle. Now, don't you worry about Mary, and don't you worry, child. I'll prescribe some pills and—"

"No, no, doctor! You're all mixed up," cried Mrs. Cuberle.

"I *beg* your pardon, Madam?"

"What I mean is, you've got it wrong. Tell him, Mary, tell the doctor what you told me."

Mary shifted uneasily in the chair.

"It's that—I don't want it."

The doctor's well-proportioned jaw dropped.

"Would you please repeat that?"

"I said, I don't want the Transformation."

"But that's impossible. I have never heard of such a thing. Little girl, you are playing a joke."

Mary nodded negatively.

"See, doctor. What can it be?" Mrs. Cuberle rose and began to pace.

The doctor clucked his tongue and took from a small cupboard a black box covered with buttons and dials and wire. He affixed black clamps to Mary's head.

"Oh no, you don't think—I mean, could it?"

"We shall soon see." The doctor revolved a number of dials and studied the single bulb in the centre of the box. It did not flicker. He removed the clamps.

"Dear me," the doctor said. "Your daughter is perfectly sane, Mrs. Cuberle."

"Well, then what is it?"

"Perhaps she is lying. We haven't completely eliminated that factor as yet, it slips into certain organisms."

More tests. More machines, and more negative results.

Mary pushed her foot in a circle on the floor. When the doctor put his hands to her shoulders, she looked up pleasantly.

"Little girl," said the handsome man, "do you actually mean to tell us that you *prefer* that body?"

"I like it. It's—hard to explain, but it's me and that's what I like. Not the looks, maybe, but the *me*."

"You can look in the mirror and see yourself, then look at —well, at your mother and be content?"

"Yes, sir." Mary thought of her reasons; fuzzy, vague, but very definitely there. Maybe she had said the reason. No. Only a part of it.

"Mrs. Cuberle," the doctor said, "I suggest that your husband have a long talk with Mary."

"My husband is dead. The Ganymede incident."

"Oh, splendid. Rocket man, eh? Very interesting organisms. Something always seems to happen to rocket men, in one way or another." The doctor scratched his cheek. "When did she first start talking this way?" he asked.

"Oh, for quite some time. I used to think it was because she was such a baby. But lately, the time getting so close and all, I thought I'd better see you."

"Of course, yes, very wise, uh—does she also do odd things?"

"Well, I found her on the second level one night. She was lying on the floor, and when I asked her what she was doing, she said she was trying to sleep."

Mary flinched. She was sorry, in a way, that Mother had found that out.

"Did you say 'sleep'?"

"That's right."

"Now where could she have picked that up?"

"No idea."

"Mary, don't you know nobody sleeps anymore. That we have an infinitely greater life-span than our poor ancestors now that that wasteful state of unconsciousness has been conquered? Child, have you actually *slept?* No one knows how anymore."

"No, sir, but I almost did."

The doctor breathed a long stream of air from his mouth.

"But, how could you begin to try to do something people have forgotten entirely about?"

"The way it was described in the book, it sounded nice, that's all."

"Book, book? Are there *books* at your Unit, Madam?"

"There could be. I haven't cleaned up in a while."

"That is certainly peculiar. I haven't seen a book for years. Not since '17."

Mary began to fidget and stare nervously.

"But with the Tapes, why should you try to read books . . . Where did you get them?"

"Daddy did. He got them from his father and so did Grandpa. He said they're better than the Tapes and he was right."

Mrs. Cuberle flushed.

"My husband was a little strange, Doctor Hortel. He kept these things despite anything I said. Finally hid them, as I see."

The muscular black-haired doctor walked to another cabinet and selected from the shelf a bottle. From the bottle he took two large pills and swallowed these.

"Sleep . . . books . . . doesn't want the Transformation . . . Mrs. Cuberle, my *dear* good woman, this is grave. I would appreciate it if you would change psychiatrists. I am very busy and, ah, this is somewhat specialized. I suggest Central-dome. Many fine doctors there. Goodbye."

The doctor turned and sat in a large chair and folded his hands. Mary watched him and wondered why the simple statements should have so changed things. But the doctor did not move from the chair.

"Well!" said Mrs. Cuberle and walked quickly from the room.

Mary considered the reflection in the mirrored wall. She sat on the floor and looked at different angles of herself: profile, full-face, full-length, naked, clothed. Then she took up the magazine and studied it. She sighed.

"Mirror, Mirror on the wall . . ." The words came haltingly to her mind and from her lips. She hadn't read these, she recalled. Daddy had said them, 'quoted' them as he put it. But they too were lines from a book . . . "who is the fairest of—"

A picture of Mother sat upon the dresser and Mary considered this now. She looked for a long time at the slender feminine neck, knotted in just the right places. The golden skin, smooth and without blemish, without wrinkles and without age. The dark brown eyes and the thin tapers of eyebrows, the long black lashes. Set evenly, so that the halves of the face corresponded precisely. The half-hearted mouth, a violet tint against the gold, the white, teeth, even, sparkling.

Mother, Beautiful, Transformed Mother. And back again to the mirror.

"—of them all . . ."

The image of a rather chubby young woman, without lines of rhythm or grace, without perfection. Splotchy skin full of little holes, puffs in the cheeks, red eruptions on the forehead. Perspiration, shapeless hair flowing onto shapeless shoulders down a shapeless body. Like all of them, before the Transformation . . .

Did they *all* look like this, before? Did Mother, even?

Mary thought hard, trying to sort out exactly what Daddy and Grandpa had said, why they said the Transformation was a bad thing, and why she believed and agreed with them so strongly. It made little sense, but they were right. They *were* right! And one day, she would understand completely.

Mrs. Cuberle slammed the door angrily and Mary jumped to her feet.

"Honestly, expenses aren't so high that you have to leave all the windows off. I went through the whole level and there isn't a single window left on. Don't you even want to see the people?"

"No. I was thinking."

"Well, it's got to stop. It's simply got to stop. Mary, what in the world has gotten into you lately?"

"I—"

"The way you upset Doctor Hortel. He won't even see me anymore, and these traumas are getting horrible—*not* to mention the migraines. I'll have to get that awful Doctor Wagoner."

Mrs. Cuberle sat on the couch and crossed her legs carefully.

"And what in the world were you doing on the floor?"

"Trying to sleep."

"You've got to stop talking that way! Why should you want to do such a silly thing?"

"The books—"

"And you mustn't read those terrible things."

"Mother—"

"The Unit is full of Tapes, full! Anything you want!"

Mary stuck out her lower lip. "But I don't want to hear all about wars and colonizations and politics!"

"Now I know where you got this idiotic notion that you don't want the Transformation. Of *course.*"

Mrs. Cuberle rose quickly and took the books from the corner and from the closet and piled her arms with them. She looked everywhere in the room and gathered the old brittle volumes.

These she carried from the room and threw into the elevator. A button guided the doors shut.

"I thought you'd do that," Mary said, slowly, "that's why I hid most of the good ones. Where you'll never find them!" She breathed heavily and her heart thumped.

Mrs. Cuberle put a satin handkerchief to her eyes.

"I don't know what I ever did to deserve this!"

"Deserve *what,* Mother? What am I doing that's so wrong?" Mary's mind rippled in a little confused stream now.

"What?" Mrs. Cuberle wailed, *"What?* Do you think I want people to point at you and say I'm the mother of a mutant?" Her voice softened abruptly into a plea. "Or have you changed your mind, dear?"

"No." *The vague reasons, longing to be put into words.*

"It really doesn't hurt, you know. They just take off a little skin and put some on and give you pills and electronic treatment and things like that. It doesn't take more than a week."

"No." *The reasons.*

"Look at your friend Shala, she's getting her Transformation next month. And *she's* almost pretty now."

"Mother, I don't care—"

"If it's the bones you're worried about, well, that doesn't hurt. They give you a shot and when you wake up, everything's moulded right. Everything, to suit the personality."

"I don't care, I don't care."

"But *why?*"

"I like me the way I am." *Almost, almost exactly. But not*

quite. Part of it, though; part of what Daddy and Grandpa must have meant.

Mrs. Cuberle switched on a window and then switched it off again. She sobbed. "But you're so ugly, dear! Like Doctor Hortel said. And Mr. Willmes, at the factory. He told some people he thought you were the ugliest girl he'd ever seen. He says he'll be thankful when you have your Transformation."

"Daddy said I was beautiful."

"Well, really, dear. You *do* have eyes."

"Daddy said that real beauty is more than skin deep. He said a lot of things like that and when I read the books I felt the same way. I guess I don't want to look like everybody else, that's all."

"You'll notice that your father had *his* Transformation, though!"

Mary stamped her foot angrily. "He told me that if he had to do it again he just wouldn't. He said I should be stronger than he was."

"You're not going to get away with this, young lady. After all, I *am* your mother."

A bulb flickered in the bathroom and Mrs. Cuberle walked uncertainly to the cabinet. She took out a little cardboard box.

"It's time for lunch."

Mary nodded. That was another thing the books talked about, which the Tapes did not. Lunch seemed to be something special long ago, or at least different . . . The books talked of strange ways of putting a load of things into the mouth and chewing these things. Enjoying them, somehow. Strange and wonderful. . . .

"And you'd better get ready for work."

Mary let the greenish capsule slide down her throat.

"Yes, Mother."

The office was quiet and without shadows. The walls gave off a steady luminescence, distributing the light evenly upon all the desks and tables. It was neither hot nor cold.

Mary held the ruler firmly and allowed the pen to travel down the metal edge effortlessly. The new black lines were small and accurate. She tipped her head, compared the notes beside her to the plan she was working on. She noticed the beautiful people looking at her more furtively than before, and she wondered about this as she made her lines.

A tall man rose from his desk in the rear of the office and walked down the aisle to Mary's table. He surveyed her work, allowing his eyes to travel cautiously from her face to the draft.

Mary looked around.

"Nice job," said the man.

"Thank you, Mr. Willmes."

"Dralich shouldn't have anything to complain about. That crane should hold the whole damn city."

"It's very good alloy, sir."

"Yeah. Say, kid, you got a minute?"

"Yes, sir."

"Let's go into Mullinson's office."

The big handsome man led the way into a small cubbyhole of a room. He motioned to a chair and sat on the edge of one desk.

"Kid, I never was one to beat around the bush. Somebody called in a little while ago, gave me some crazy story about you not wanting your Transformation."

Mary looked away, then quickly back into the man's eyes. "It's not a crazy story, Mr. Willmes," she said. "It's true. I want to stay this way."

The man stared, then coughed embarrassedly.

"What the hell—excuse me, kid, but—I don't exactly get it. You ain't a mutant, I know that. And you ain't—"

"Insane? No; Doctor Hortel can tell you."

The man laughed, nervously. "Well . . . Look, you're still a cub, but you do swell work. Lots of good results, lots of comments from the stations. But Mr. Poole won't like it."

"I know. I know what you mean, Mr. Willmes. But nothing can change my mind."

"You'll get old before you're half through life!"

Yes, she would. Old, like the Elders, wrinkled and brittle, unable to move correctly. Old.

"It's hard to make you understand. But I don't see why it should make any difference, as long as I do my work."

"Now don't go getting me wrong, kid. It ain't me. But you know, I don't run Interplan. I just work here. Mr. Poole, he likes things running smooth and it's my job to carry it out. And as soon as everybody finds out, things wouldn't run smooth. There'll be a big to-do, y'understand? The dames will start asking questions and talk. Be the same as a mutant in the office—no offense."

"Will you accept my resignation, then, Mr. Willmes?"

"Sure you won't change your mind?"

"No, sir. I decided that a long time ago."

"Well, then, I'm sorry, Mary. Couple ten, twenty years you could be centraled on one of the asteroids, the way you been working out. But . . . if you should change your mind, there'll always be a job for you here. Otherwise, you got till March. And between you and me, I hope by then you've decided the other way."

Mary walked back down the aisle, past the rows of desks. Past the men and women. The handsome model men and the beautiful, perfect women, perfect, all perfect, all looking alike. Looking exactly alike.

She sat down again and took up her ruler and pen.

Mary stepped into the elevator and descended several hundred feet. At the Second Level she pressed a button and the elevator stopped. The doors opened with another button and the doors to her Unit with still another.

Mrs. Cuberle sat on the floor by the TV, disconsolate and red-eyed. Her blonde hair had come slightly askew and a few strands hung over her forehead.

"You don't need to tell me. No one will hire you."

Mary sat down beside her mother.

"If only you hadn't told Mr. Willmes in the first place—"

"Well, I thought *he* could beat a little sense into you."

The sounds from the TV grew louder. Mrs. Cuberle changed channels a number of times and finally turned it off.

"What did you do today, Mother?" Mary smiled, hopefully.

"What *can* I do now? Nobody will even come over! Everyone thinks you're a mutant."

"*Mother!*"

"They say you should be in the Circuses."

Mary went into another room. Mrs. Cuberle followed, wringing her hands, and crying: "Mutant, mutant! How are we going to live? Where does the money come from now? Next thing they'll be firing *me!*"

"No one would do that."

"Nobody else on this planet has ever refused the Transformation. The mutants all wish they could have it. And you, given everything, you turn it down. You *want* to be ugly!"

Mary put her arms about her mother's shoulders.

"I wish I could explain; I've tried so hard to. It isn't that I want to bother anyone, or that Daddy or Grandpa wanted me to."

Mrs. Cuberle reached into the pocket of her jerkin and retrieved a purple pill. She swallowed the pill.

When the letter dropped from the chute, Mrs. Cuberle ran to snatch it up. She read it once silently, then smiled.

"Oh," she said, "I was so afraid they wouldn't answer. But we'll see about this *now!*"

She gave the letter to Mary, who read:

> Mrs. Zena Cuberle
> Unit 451-D
> Levels II & III
> City

Dear Madam:

In re your letter of Dec. 3 36. We have carefully examined your complaint and consider that it requires stringent measures of some sort. Quite frankly, the possibility of such a complaint has never occurred to this Dept. and we therefore cannot issue positive directives at this present moment.

However, due to the unusual qualities of the matter, we have arranged an audience at Centraldome 8th Level 16th Unit, Jan. 3 37, 23 sharp. Dr. Hortel has been instructed to attend. You will bring the subject in question.

Yrs.
DEPT. F

Mary let the paper flutter to the floor. She walked quietly to the elevator and set it for Level III. When the elevator stopped, she ran from it, crying, into her room.

She thought and remembered and tried to sort out and put together. Daddy had said it, Grandpa had, the books did. Yes. The books did.

She read until her eyes burned and her eyes burned until she could read no more. Then Mary went to sleep, softly and without realizing it.

But the sleep was not a peaceful one.

"Ladies and gentlemen," said the young-looking, classic-featured man, "this problem does not resolve easily. Doctor Hortel here, testifies that Mary Cuberle is definitely not insane, Doctors Monagh, Prynn and Fedders all verify this judgement. Doctor Prynn asserts that the human organism is no longer so constructed as to create and sustain such an attitude as deliberate falsehood. Further, there is positively nothing in the structure of Mary Cuberle which might suggest difficulties in Transformation. There is qualified evidence for all these statements. And yet—" the man sighed "—while the Newstapes, the Foto services, while every news-carrying agency has circulated this problem throughout the universe, we are faced with this refusal. Further, the notoriety has become excessive to the point of vulgarity and has resultantly caused numerous persons, among them Mrs. Zena Cuberle, the child's mother, grievous emotional stress. What, may I ask, is to be done therefore?"

Mary looked at a metal table.

"We have been in session far too long, holding up far too many other pressing contingencies of a serious nature."

Throughout the rows of beautiful people, the mumbling increased. Mrs. Cuberle sat nervously tapping her foot and running a comb through her hair.

"The world waits," continued the man. "Mary Cuberle, you have been given innumerable chances to reconsider, you know."

Mary said, "I know. But I don't want to."

The beautiful people looked at Mary and laughed. Some shook their heads.

The man in the robes threw up his hands.

"Little girl, can you realize what an issue you have caused? The unrest, the wasted time? Do you fully understand what you have done? We could send you to a Mutant Colony, I suppose you know. . ."

"How could you do that?" inquired Mary.

"Well, I'm sure we could—it's a pretty point. Intergalactic questions hang fire while you sit there saying the same thing over and over. And in judicial procedure I dare say there is some clause which forbids that. Come now, doesn't the happiness of your dear mother mean anything to you? Or your duty to the State, to the entire Solar System?"

A slender, supple woman in a back row stood and cried, loudly: "*Do* something!"

The man on the high stool raised his arm.

"None of that, now. We must conform, even though the problem is out of the ordinary."

The woman sat down, snorted; the man turned again to Mary.

"Child, I have here a petition, signed by two thousand individuals and representing all the Stations of the Earth. They have been made aware of all the facts and have submitted the petition voluntarily. It's all so unusual and I'd hoped we wouldn't have to—but, well, the petition urges drastic measures."

The mumbling rose.

"The petition urges that you shall, upon final refusal, be forced by law to accept the Transformation. And that an act of legislature shall make this universal and binding in the future."

Mary's eyes were open, wide; she stood and paused before speaking.

"*Why?*" she asked.

The man in the robes passed a hand through his hair.

Another voice from the crowd: "Sign the petition, Senator!"

All the voices: "Sign it! Sign it!"

"But *why?*" Mary began to cry. The voices stilled for a moment.

"Because—Because—What if others should get the same idea? What would happen to us then, little girl? We'd be right back to the ugly, thin, fat, unhealthy-looking race we were ages ago! There can't be any exceptions."

"Maybe they didn't consider themselves so ugly!"

The mumbling began anew and broke into a wild clamour.

"That isn't the point," cried the man in the robes, "you *must* conform!"

And the voices cried: "Yes!" loudly until the man took up a pen and signed the papers on his desk.

Cheers; applause; shouts.

Mrs. Cuberle patted Mary on the top of her head.

"There now!" she said happily, "everything will be all right now. You'll see, Mary, dear."

The Transformation Parlor covered the entire Level, sprawling with its departments. It was always filled and there was nothing to sign and no money to pay and people were always waiting in line.

But today the people stood aside. And there were still more, looking in through doors, TV cameras placed throughout and Tape machines in every corner. It was filled, but not bustling as usual.

The Transformation Parlor was terribly quiet.

Mary walked past the people, Mother and the men in back of her, following. She looked at the people, too, as she did in her room through turned-on windows. It was no different. The people were beautiful, perfect, without a single flaw. Except the young ones, young like herself, seated on couches, looking embarrassed and ashamed and eager.

But, of course, the young ones did not count.

All the beautiful people. All the ugly people, staring out from bodies that were not theirs. Walking on legs that had been made for them, laughing with manufactured voices, gesturing with shaped and fashioned arms.

Mary walked slowly despite the prodding. In her eyes, in *her* eyes, was a mounting confusion; a wide, wide wonderment.

She looked down at her own body, then at the walls which reflected it. Flesh of her flesh, bone of her bone, all hers, made by no person, built by herself or Someone she did not know. . . Uneven kneecaps making two grinning cherubs when they straightened, and the old familiar rubbing together of fat inner thighs. Fat, unshapely, unsystematic Mary. But *Mary*.

Of course. Of course! This *was* what Daddy meant, what Grandpa and the books meant. What *they* would know if they would read the books or hear the words, the good, unreasonable words, the words that signified more, so much more, than any of this. . .

"Where *are* these people?" Mary said, half to herself. "What has happened to *them* and don't they miss *themselves*, these manufactured things?"

She stopped, suddenly.

"Yes! That *is* the reason. They have all forgotten themselves!"

A curvacious woman stepped forward and took Mary's hand. The woman's skin was tinted dark. Chipped and sculptured bone into slender rhythmic lines, electrically created carriage, made, turned out. . .

"All right, young lady. Shall we begin?"

They guided Mary to a large, curved leather seat.

From the top of a long silver pole a machine lowered itself. Tiny bulbs glowed to life and cells began to click. The people stared. Slowly a picture formed upon the screen in the machine. Bulbs directed at Mary, then re-directed into themselves. Wheels turning, buttons ticking.

The picture was completed.

"Would you like to see it?"

Mary closed her eyes, tight.

"It's really very nice." The woman turned to the crowd. "Oh yes, there's a great deal to be salvaged; you'd be surprised. A great deal. We'll keep the nose and I don't believe the elbows will have to be altered at all."

Mrs. Cuberle looked at Mary and grinned.

"Now, it isn't so bad as you thought, is it?" she said.

The beautiful people looked. Cameras turned, Tapes wound.

"You'll have to excuse us now. Only the machines allowed."

Only the machines.

The people filed out, grumbling.

Mary saw the rooms in the mirror. Saw things in the rooms, the faces and bodies that had left, the woman and the machines and the old young men standing about, adjusting, readying.

Then she looked at the picture in the screen.

A woman of medium height stared back at her. A woman with a curved body and thin legs; silver hair, pompadoured, cut short; full sensuous lips, small breasts, flat stomach, unblemished skin.

A strange woman no one had ever seen before.

The nurse began to take off Mary's clothes.

"Geoff," the woman said "come look at this, will you. Not one so bad in years. Amazing that we can keep anything at all."

The handsome man put his hands into his pockets, and clucked his tongue.

"Pretty bad, all right."

"Be still, child, stop, stop making those noises. You know perfectly well nothing is going to hurt."

"But what will you do with me?"

"That was all explained to you."

"No, no—with *me, me!*"

"You mean the cast-offs? The usual. I don't know, exactly. Somebody takes care of it."

"I want me!" Mary cried. "Not that!" She pointed at the image in the screen.

Her chair was wheeled into a semi-dark room. She was naked now, and the men lifted her to a table. The surface was like glass, black filmed. A big machine hung above in shadows.

Straps. Clamps pulling, stretching limbs apart. The screen with the picture brought in. The men and the women, more women now. Doctor Hortel in a corner, sitting with his legs crossed, shaking his head.

Mary began to cry loudly, as hard as she could, above the hum of the mechanical things.

"Shhh. My gracious, such a racket! Just think about your job waiting for you, and all the friends you'll have and how lovely everything will be. No more troubles now."

The big machine groaned and descended from the darkness.

"Where will I find me?" Mary screamed. "What will happen to *me?*"

A long needle slid into rough flesh and the beautiful people gathered around the table.

And then they turned on the big machine.

The Last Caper

"So you're Mike Mallet," I said, feeding him some knuckles. He went down—fast—and began to whimper. When he came back up I got my knee under his chin and teeth flew out like the popcorn they used to pop on those drowsy October porches when I was a kid and Mom and Dad used to say "Ah! Ah!" and we'd drink the lemonade and eat the popcorn and breathe the Illinois air which was like old wine.

"Spill it, Mallet," I snarled, but I guess he thought I meant blood. It wasn't pretty. What is?

I tapped him on the forehead with the chromalloy butt of my blaster, just for kicks, and started through his pockets.

There wasn't much. A ray pistol disguised as a ball point pen, a shiv, a sap, a set of knuckles, a paralyzer, a Monopoly score card, eight candy bars, a bottle of Bromo-Seltzer, a picture of an old dame with a funny look (with *For Mikey, with love, Mommy* scrawled suspiciously underneath in crayon), a paint brush, a ticket to Mars (out-dated), a copy of *Sonnets from the Portuguese,* a can of Sterno and a card marked: HONORARY MEMBER—EAST ORANGE CHAPTER LADIES LEAGUE FOR PRESERVATION OF THE AMERICAN BEAUTY ROSE.

And that was all!

If he had it, if Mallet really did have what I was after—the Chocolate Maltese Falcon—it wasn't on him. I toed at his face and jammed the candy bars into my mouth: they tasted real fine, mostly because I'd had nothing in my stomach except straight rye for over seventeen days. The rest of the junk I tossed out the window.

"Come on, friend," I said, but he just laid there bleeding. It made me a little mad, and I'm kind of ugly when I get mad. I went through the door into his outer office. His secretary was there.

"Next time *open* the door before you come through it, big boy," she spat.

I didn't answer. My eyes were riveted to her body. She was wearing a slinky gold gown that looked like it had been painted on and she was laying on a big leather couch, writhing. I still felt pretty mean, so I moved in—fast.

I've got to admit I was plenty surprised when I found out that the gown really *was* painted on; but it made things easier.

"Get much hot weather around here?" I snapped, my eyes traveling up and down her body like ball-bearings over a washboard.

"Sometimes yes," she said evasively, "sometimes no. It comes and it goes."

"Oh yeah?" She was all right: a little wildcat, and I like wildcats just fine. She threw a vicious kick at my groin but I dodged and grabbed her leg. Then I grabbed her other leg. Then I grabbed her other leg. Oh, she was different, all right. But good!

After I finished with her I jammed her into the typewriter cabinet and let the door slam shut. Dames!

I was feeling a lot better by now, though. Kind of like spring in the air and the first time you carried the books home for that freckle-faced girl next door and goodbye and hello and the dead years of your childhood. I knew I could find that Chocolate Maltese Falcon now, no matter how cleverly Mallet had hidden it.

I stormed back into his office. He was coming to, getting to his knees. This time I used a poker on his head. It cracked. The poker, that is.

I went to work, thinking, it's got to be here, it's *got* to be here! I kicked over the book case, took an ax to the desk, piled the chairs into the fireplace, pushed the safe out the window, cut the carpet into Band-Aides, ripped out the light fixtures, flooded the restroom and wrote a couple things on the walls with some charcoal. Mallet was starting to groan a little so I dropped the bathtub on him: he stopped groaning.

Still no Chocolate Maltese Falcon!

The place was getting pretty untidy by now. I decided I'd better ease up or somebody'd figure there'd been trouble.

Just then a movement caught my eye. I jerked around. A tall blonde was walking by the window. I knew she was tall— Mallet's office was on the ninth floor. She looked all February, silos in the rain, clear lakes full of trout. I started after her and was halfway out when there was a knock at the door.

Rat-tat! Rat-tat!

I jumped to answer it but my foot skidded on some blood and I went down for the ten count, hitting my head on one of the Brancusi statuettes Mallet kept around for laughs. Right away an inky black pool came at me: it splashed over my brain and pretty soon it was like lying on your back high on a hill somewheres on a black night where the stars are coruscating and dancing their cosmic rigadoon. Before I blacked out completely, though, I felt the butt of a blaster hit the side of my face. Then it was curtains. . . .

The voice cut through the brain-fog like a knife going through butter. There was a million firecrackers going off inside my head. Pow!

Pow! Pow!

"You Gunther Awl?" a voice said.

I spit out a couple teeth. "Yeah," I choked, "I'm Gunther Awl." It was a lie. I wasn't Gunther Awl at all. But I figured I'd better play it safe.

"C'mon, snap out of it," the voice ordered. I got up, slow-like, and staggered to a chair.

"All right," the voice said, "let's have it."

I focused my eyes. It was a fat guy, with curly hair and jowls and a tattoo of Botticelli's *Venus on the Half Shell* on his forehead. A fink. A patsy.

"Anything particular in mind, badman?" I drawled. The gun butt came down again with savage force and I found myself spiraling into that inky black pool again. Only this time it was like being inside a kaleidoscope and the kaleidoscope is turning like the Giant Barrel over at Coney and you're trying to stand up but the Barrel keeps turning too fast and you keep falling down and every time you fall you slide a little closer to the sparkling fragments of color at the top of the kaleidoscope and the bright white light filters through like it's a big pool with hundreds of jeweled fishes with bright white teeth swimming around in it. Then suddenly you're at the top . . . and you come to again.

"Where's the Falcon, Awl?" the fat man said. "And don't get funny this time."

"No spikka da Heenglish," I faked, but it wasn't any good— I could see that. It didn't stop him for more than two minutes, three at the outside.

He hawked convulsively and I thought he was going to heave, then I saw that he was laughing. What at? I wondered. He stopped laughing before I could dope it out.

"Don't push it, rocket-jockey," he said. I could tell he wasn't joking. This monkey was playing for keeps.

"Look," I said, "you got the wrong boy. I ain't Gunther Awl. My name's Bartholomew Cornblossom."

"Yeah," he said, grinning, "I know." He shifted the blaster to his left hand and let me have a backsided right across the puss.

When his hand came off and dropped to the floor, I knew *I* was in for some surprises myself.

He started to change form—fast—and in less time than it takes to skin a jackrabbit, like the hick says, I was staring at a lousy Venusian. I hated him right away because I didn't understand him and I always hate what I don't understand. Sometimes I hate what I *do* understand.

I had to stall. "What's your angle, cousin?" I asked. "What good's the Chocolate Maltese Falcon to a Venusian?"

There was that laugh again, coming from one of his ears. I did a quick mental flashback as that green blob of jelly came at me.

How had it all started . . .

I'd been sitting in my office that day playing euchre with 1742-A, my secretary. She was beating me—bad—and that made me plenty sore, because I don't dig getting beat; not by a robot, anyway. 1742-A was a robot. Who can afford real secretaries at fifty credits a caper? Besides, business had kind of slacked off.

Well, I was reaching over to turn her off, when this redhead walks in like she owned the place, which she didn't: I rented from a Mrs. Murfreesboro over in Jersey—a bigmouth dame that liked me okay.

"Hello, Bart," the redhead said. She had on a fur coat. It was dead—murdered. I told her to sit down and she said thanks I will and sat down. So far it figured.

She got out a flask from her purse and gave it to me before I could say boo. I shot her a look and let the rye trickle down my craw. It was good rye, fine rye.

"What's the caper?" I snapped.

Then she told me about this thing, the Chocolate Maltese Falcon. She said it was a family heirloom that her old man left to her when he kicked off. She said not only was it worth plenty scratch on the open market, but it had great sentimental value to boot. She said she hired Mike Mallet as a guard, and that's when the trouble started. Next morning: no Mallet, no Falcon.

My job: Find Mallet, get the Falcon, bring it back.

"I suppose," she said, pulling out some vitamin capsules, "that you're in business for your health." She did big things with her eyes. I was impressed.

"No," I told her, "I ain't in business for my health."

She pouted a little. "All right," she said then, "how'd you like a nice new C-note, Handsome?"

"I'd like it fine, ma'am," I said.

"And if you're successful," she cooed, "maybe—who knows?—maybe there'll be a little bonus. . . ."

"You mean?" I pulled her onto my lap and grabbed some lip. It was plenty great. It made me think of oceans crashing against lonely rocks and cotton candy and the carnival where the man in the bright vest says "Hurry! Hurry!"

Then she scrammed. Without leaving a deposit.

"Are you going to turn over the Falcon peacefully?" the

green snake guy was saying, "or must we resort to measures best described as strong?"

I laughed in his faces. The butt flashed out and I was sinking, sinking into that old inky black pool. . . .

When I woke up, my arms were tied. My legs were tied. I was sitting in a straight-back chair. It wouldn't have been so bad, maybe—except I was hanging upside down.

"We shall see now how bravely the Earthling struts!" The Venusian slithered over toward the radio. I wondered: What's his pitch? How come he's so interested in a family heirloom?

"You'll never get nothing out of me," I snarled.

The radio hummed into life.

"What the—" I began, lamely.

The Venusian crammed a gag into my mouth. "Listen!" he said.

I listened. . . .

"Monday . . . Monday . . . *Monday!*"

"No, David, please—don't touch me. I came to see you tonight to say . . . goodbye."

"Goodbye?!"

"Yes! For a few blind, crazy—wonderful—hours, you made me forget that I'm over thirty-five, a married woman and mother of six. But now—"

"Now?"

"—Lord Henri is back. He's—brought the children. I—oh David! Don't touch me! Hold me close!

"Monday!"

"David!"

Then I got it. Leave it to a stinking wet-belly Venusian to think up the *real* tortures. A soap-opera!

I listened to the electric organ's moo. Maybe I shouldn't admit it, but I can't stand soap operas. Oh, I know, *One Man's Cosmos* is mainly what's kept the planets from all-out war, but . . . well, they give me a pain in the gut.

I tried to shut my ears, but it was no dice. . . .

". . . Will Monday be able to make David understand? *How* can she explain to him that she remains loyal to her husband, Lord Henri Winthrop, *not* because she loves him but because he has come back from the Erosian uprising a hopeless paralytic? And what of David? How can he tell Monday that her husband is really dead—murdered—and that his, Lord Henri's, neurotic twin brother, Hugo Winthrop, is playing the part of the invalid husband? How can David let her know that the portals to their happiness lie open—when Hugo threatens to expose David's lurid past as a privateer and *tsi- tso* frond smuggler for the Martians? . . . and the children! Will the operation actually restore little Tuesday's eyesight? Will Wednesday be able to exorcise the Uranian bandit who has inhabited her body? Will Friday regain her memory in time to stop Nick Branzetti's evil plan? . . . Tune in tomorrow at this time to see what Fate has in store for—OUR GAL MONDAY: *The Real Life Story that Asks the Question*: *Can a Girl from a Little Lunar Rocketport Find Happiness with Jupiter's Richest, Most Handsome Queek?* . . . And now, a word from—"

"Would you care to tell me the location of the Falcon *now*, Mr. Cornblossom?" asked the Venusian, removing the gag.

"I don't know where it is," I snapped. "I don't know. I don't know!"

"Very well . . ."

He turned the radio higher. And I thought: My God—it might have been television. . . .

". . . your dishes and thurpets sparkling bright, dazzling white, with the new washday miracle that requires no rinsing, in fact, requires no water: STAR-FLAKES! . . . Just open the cage, let out a few flakes, turn them loose on those greasy pots and torgums and—just watch 'em eat up that grime! PRESTO! The job is finished. Then all you have to do is drop the dead flakes into a handy container and bury them somewhere. Remember! STAR-FLAKES are 99.44 per cent ALIVE! . . ."

"Where is the Falcon?"
"I don't know! I don't know!"

". . . and now stay tuned for the program that follows: The best loved, most respected program in the world: ONE MAN'S COSMOS: *The Story of Just Plain Gratch, the Friendly Tendril-Tender of Betelgeuseville—*"

"All right, you damned fiend!" I screamed. "All right! I'll tell you!"

"Ah." The Venusian turned the program off just as my mind was beginning to go. He let me down.

"Before I give it to you," I said, "would you mind letting me know why you're so interested? After all, even if the statue's worth money, you don't need—"

"Statue!" The snake guy chortled and choked. "Statue!" I thought he'd break up; then he sobered—fast. "The bird with the whimsical cognomen," he hissed, "happens to contain enough D-plus-4-over-X grains to blow up a planet!"

Well, that was a kick in the pants, all right.

The government had been going ape trying to figure out who'd stolen the secret D-plus-4-over-X grains. Now I had the picture. Redhead. My beautiful employer. A lousy spy. She'd lifted the bomb from the government and then somebody'd lifted it from her.

Real sweet. Where did it leave me, Bart Cornblossom, Private Orb? At the short end of the stick, that's where.

"The planet I refer to," the Venusian was saying, "is, needless to remark, your own."

"Not," somebody said, "if I can help it!" It was Mike Mallet —groggy, but still plenty tough. He got a half-nelson around the Venusian, grabbed the blaster and in a second Mr. Venusman was out of the story.

"Hiya, Bart—" Mallet said, then he seemed to remember. "You son of a—"

"Drop the gun, Mallet," a voice said. Mallet whirled around in time to catch three good blasts in the belly. I could smell it clear across the room.

"Hello, Baby," I snarled.

"Hello, Bart," she said. "Now be a good boy and play ball. I know you've got the Falcon."

"Come and get it."

She ripped off her clothes and sat in my lap. I started to think of July when I saw that she was wavering, changing. She wasn't no redhead—she was a Martian!

"Mallet was going to turn the Falcon back over to your government," she said, nibbling at my schnoz. "I had to do it. You can see that, can't you?"

"Sure," I said. "I can see that."

"But you're not like that, Bart. You're smart—I can tell. Look—" She twiddled her antennae like a couple castanets "—you've always made a mess out of me inside. Ever since that first kiss. Miscegenation be damned, that kiss was for real! So listen—with the money my government'll pay me for the D-plus-4-over-X grains, we could really live it up."

"Sure, baby," I said, "but I ain't going nowhere all tied up in this chair."

She planted one on my kisser and I felt all May and golden fields of ripe wheat and barefoot in soft river mud. She undid the ropes.

"We've got to hurry, though," she whispered. "The grains explode—or, I should say, implode—every 36 hours: we have just barely enough time to ship them away. But first—oh darling, squirrel, my own Bart—we're going to be so very happy. . . ."

She was beautiful, green hair or no green hair, and I held

her body—close—and felt her breathing and thought about her next to me at night and the dough and—

I hated it. It made me sick, deep down where it hurts.

"Darling—"

I let her have it in the gut. She sprawled. I grabbed the blaster and pretty soon there was some jam on the floor instead of a dame.

"I'm sorry, baby," I whispered to the sticky heap, "really sorry . . ."

I don't know—maybe I cried, maybe I laughed. I only know I went crazy mad for a few seconds.

Then I straightened up and thought: so, it's all over. End of the caper. Back to the office and a few straight shots and a couple lousy credits.

But wait. Good gravy, I thought: The Falcon! If she was telling the truth and those D-plus-4-over-X grains really were inside—and getting ready to explode, I mean implode . . .

I could hear them coming. Lots of them. I ran to the window—big ones, armed, none of them smiling. Venusians, Martians, Jovians—

There was a wild chuckling then. "Heh heh heh!" I took the lunky out of my mug and snapped it away and went through the door.

The chuckling was coming from the typewriter cabinet. I opened it. I should've known better than to be nice to any chick with three legs. They're poison with two—but with three! "What's the gag?" I snarled.

She told me. I couldn't believe it—I made her go through it four times. Then fear started to tear up my stomach muscles.

Mallet had had the Chocolate Maltese Falcon, all right. But he'd been smart. Yeah, smart.

He'd had it melted down into candy bars!

And I'd been hungry, so—

It wasn't easy to take. All the bums in the Galaxy were after the Chocolate Maltese Falcon. Which meant that all the bums in the Galaxy were after me. Because—

Now I *was* the Chocolate Maltese Falcon!

Sweat Niagaraed down my face. The D-plus-4-over-X grains had been missing for—how long? No, no, I thought. Jeez!

I belted the nutty dame a good one on the smeller and listened to her yell until it got boring. Then the door burst open. The big Jovian started to ankle over, hate in his five little pig eyes.

I squeezed the trigger and turned the Jovian into a blood pudding like they used to serve in those English places with names like Seven Oaks and Ukridge.

Then the Venusians came in and I figured the better part of valor was to blow. A couple squeezes of the trigger and I blew.

I got behind Mallet's desk and loosened my tie and pushed my hat back on my head, thinking, this is it, Bart boy, this is it.

They were getting ready. That door would fly open in a second—

All of a sudden I felt something happening inside my gut, a rumbling like you get after a slug of rye. It started to ache —bad—and the second the scum of the universe spilled in, it came up.

Fast.

And then I wasn't Bart Cornblossom any more. I was Christmas and the smell of afternoon turkey and playgrounds where you fall down and scab up your knees and have to run home to Mom and Dad and hello how are you and a piece of the sky just fell Chicken Little and now it's falling falling and how long is eternity Gramp? and Gramp saying it's a right smart piece o' time boy and don't cry son because worse things than blowing up can happen to a man lots worse things and you're floating floating out there with the whole world for a teeter-totter for ever and ever and ever. . . .

Mother's Day

HIS HAIR WAS red, but his face was redder and I never saw such sadness in the eyes of a man before. Not a new sadness either, but something old and strong and buried deep inside. He sat down at my table.

"Good evening to you," I said, smiling.

He looked up, wrenched off his helmet and rubbed his sweaty face into an even brighter red brightness.

"Good evening," I said again, but without the smile.

"Beer!" he said to the little Venusian who had rolled up. "Earth beer. American beer—understand?" The waiter shook his tendrils angrily and made motions in the air: *"Please use Accepted Signs, wise-fellow."*

The sad red man did so, following a gigantic shrug. He sat quiet as death until the beer arrived, and the waiter had rolled away. He swigged loudly and belched louder still. He looked at me. "Cop?" he said.

"No."

"It would be my luck. I practically live with these overgrown spiders, and the first Earthman I see, what is he: a goddam cop." He snorted disgustedly.

"You're wrong," I said, and offered him a cigarette. He examined it carefully, saw it was a Terran make. He lit up, sighing.

I extended my hand. "Looks like we're going to be together a while," I said. "The *Ginger* isn't due for three more hours. I suppose you're headed for Earth? My name is—"

"Stop play-acting, sonny! You know who I am and you're about to wet your pants over it. Well, I don't care, understand? Not one little bit. Go ahead and laugh your fool head off!"

"I'm sorry. I've not been in touch with Earth for quite a while. Why *should* I laugh at you?"

He examined me with a beady eye; then he sank back in the booth. "Reasons," he said.

"Care to talk about them?" I poured him another beer.

"I only thank the Lord my dear sweet mother—bless her bones—was spared the shame," he murmured. "It would have killed her dead."

158

"Tell me about it," I said.

"I will, by God!" he said, and he began to talk.

They never would have found out I killed that jasper (*the man with the red hair said*) if it hadn't been my black Irish luck to leave fingerprints all over the house. Of course, there was the fact that it was well known that this here particular fella had announced his intention to marry my youngest sister, Amarantha, which made it look pretty suspicious, I suppose, considering my public sentiments. Besides which, three people seen me do it. But otherwise, who would have known? Nobody, that's who.

So they caught me—not without the best kind of fight I want you to know—and in less time than it takes, Mrs. McCreigh's favorite son was thrown in the pokey.

Now there is no worse place on the face of the earth, nor elsewhere for that matter, than these new-fangled jails. Used to be they had bars made of steel and so you was spared temptation: Nowadays it looks just exactly like you're in a swell apartment with the windows wide open. Course, you *touch* them windows and you get enough charge to knock you back to yesterday. I know. I tried.

Well, sir: "Gavin McCreigh," the judge says to me, "for the willful murder of Edgar Johnson, we hereby sentence you to spend the rest of your natural life in exile upon the asteroid *Spartanburg.*"

Sent a chill right through my stummick. Spartanburg! On that mess of mud, a man's 'natural life' couldn't be expected to exceed a day and a half at the outside!

But being Irish-American and a human being of the White race, I took her on the chin. Says I: That's how the cards fall! That's how the big ball bounces!

Spartanburg, as you well know, or ought to if you've ever looked inside a micronews, is crawling with giant bugs and disease of the absolute worst kind. A body would be dead before he started.

So, I mean to say, me loving life and brooking no desire to perish out in the middle of space any more than the next one, maybe you can see why I give her some thought when they come to me with their proposition.

"Gavin McCreigh," says they, "choose. Life or death—which'll you have?"

"Life," says I enthusiastically.

"Come with us."

It almost shook the teeth out of my head when they told me what it was all about—me, of all people, me: Gavin Mc-Creigh: American!

(*Give me some more to drink. Get that hoppin' toad over here with some beer!*)

"For the advancement of science," they said. I truly thought they was joking, swear I did, but it was no joke.

I, Gavin Patrick Quentin McCreigh, was to be the first Earthman to marry a Martian!

Needless to say, I told them where they could put *that* noise. "Let's go," says I. "Let's go to Spartanburg. I'll walk if need be or you can tie me with a rope at the jet-end and *drag* me—anything, my buckos, anything; but not this."

Some choice they give me, wouldn't you say? Die of a lingering disease a million miles from home or take the Holy Vows with an outsize cockroach!

"If it's such an honor," says I, "then why don't you do it yourself?"

They shoveled me back into my hole, and I set there ticking off the days. You ever hear stories about Spartanburg? Man don't have a chance. Longest *anybody* was known to last in that slime was two weeks. They watch you on the screens—everybody does—sitting at home with their TVs. All over the world. Watch you take sick and die.

They put a TV in my room so as I could watch old films of that ax murderer—what was his name—Buechner?—going stark raving crazy mad. Poor fella run around nutty as a squirrel until finally the bugs got him. Took the varmints two minutes by the clock and poor old Buechner was just parched bones.

Well, that did her. I swallowed my fierce Irish pride and give them a buzz and told them all right, by God, I'd marry their Martian beetle and would they please get the thing over with in a hurry.

What a change! You'd think I was the King of England the way they puttered and spit over me, getting me this, getting me that—never letting me out of the cell, you understand, but treating me to cocktails and squab under glass and—it was okay. That part of it was all right.

'Course the papers was coming out with their headlines all about it, like and similar with TV and ekcetra. All the high mucky-mucks from Mars was here and twice as happy about the whole thing as we was, mainly because they had been angling to move in on us before their country went plumb dry. Dis*gust*ing the way them creechures sucked around!

For myself, I always figured we had enough race problem as it was, but I guess you know what happened. It had started even when I was there: They flooded in like crickets, took over and set up their housing projects, messing up the land with big old glass bubbles. Ha! Guess maybe they was sorry they used glass, hey? Imagine some of our boys threw a couple of stones that just accidentally landed somewheres.

But then, I warned them. Said, looky: It ain't as if we don't have enough trouble trying to live on the same planet with all the yellow ones and black ones and the rest, we got to 'adjust' to people who ain't even people in the first place but more like common roaches. I asked, ain't we got enough of a burden as it is?

They wouldn't listen. Deef and dumb. Now look what they got on their hands. Earth ain't even Earth no more. Swear, I'm glad I didn't stick around to see what happened *afterwards . . .*

I mean, referring to after the day when it all really begun.

They got me out and decked me in finery from my neck to my toes and, keeping guard, waltzed me into the Prison Hospital. It was crowded to the living rafters with folks: reporters, newsboys, diplomats and ekcetra.

And then—I fainted. Swear I did—fainted. Or like to. I was introduced to my future wife!

"This is Jane of Mars," the warden says to me. "Shake hands," says he with a frown.

Ever shake hands with a Martian? It's like taking holt of a wet sponge. But I thought of Buechner and grabbed on.

This Jane—she wasn't no different from any of the others. Big as I was, standing there on four legs, twittering them aunt-emmies. "How do you do," says she with her thumbs.

By a stroke of good fortune, I managed not to throw up right then and there, you may be sure.

Well, the officials come and told me as how Jane was elected by unanimous decision—Miss Mars!—and what we was supposed to do, why we was gathered together and the rest of the malarkey.

Then they got a Martian and one of our own men and, next thing I knew, they was saying (one aloud, the other in this sign language):

"Blahblahblah and ekcetra: Do you, Jane of Mars, take this Earthman to be your lawful wedded husband?"

"I do," says the cockroach.

"Do you, Gavin Patrick McCreigh, take this girl, Jane of Mars, for your lawful wedded wife?"

My intruls was boiling with the shame and the humiliation. "I do," says I.

"I now pronounce you man and wife."

"Well?" says the warden.

"Well?" says I.

"Aren't you going to kiss the bride?"

I'll make a long story short right about here, because it's a matter of considerable pain for me to go into the details of what followed then.

We was given a house, a regular house, but specially treated so we could both live in it—which must have cost a pretty penny. Half of it was hers, though, and this here part was full of rocks and stuff and all that stuff the Martians live around like lizards.

They kept a strict watch. Guess because maybe they knew I'd hightail it the minute I could. Particularly at night we was kept tabs on. I don't know what they expected—but I just kept my mouth shut and talked civil as I could to this Jane and stayed out of her way.

She stayed out of mine too. Always looking sad and forlorn like, always telling me how we had to make a go of it for the sake of this and the sake of that. But when I let her know I had hid the meat cleaver, well, she just says: "I don't understand, I don't understand." But she steered clear after that.

After a week of this misery and hell, with me halfway wishing I *had* of gone to Spartanburg to begin with and upheld to the limit my honor and dignity as a white man, the boys trouped in.

Says: "Gavin McCreigh." Says: "Jane of Mars. We must talk to you."

And when they told me what it was they wanted to talk *about*, what they demanded and insisted on, for the 'interests of science'—well, this was one healthy red-blooded American male who wished he'd of been borned a eunuch.

What could I do? What chance did I have?

It was essential, we was told, to find out what would happen. No other way of telling. And since these here Martians looked like cockroaches only to *me* (due no doubt to the manner in which I was brought up)—aside from all them legs and aunt-emmies they pretty well resembled human beings—and there'd be a lot of mixing going on—well, this was really, says they, the whole point of marrying me off to one!

I let 'em all know what I thought about it, you can bet your bottom credit on that. I let 'em know they was going against every natural law and that they'd be punished sure as there's a hell below.

But they told me: "We'll be watching, Gavin McCreigh!"—which any way you look at it is downright obscene—"and unless you want a vacation on a certain asteroid, we suggest you follow through."

So—because an Irishman can do anything he's got to do and do it well—I followed through.

Next week afterwards a peculiar thing happened.

They sent me back to jail.

Talk about your reliefs! I lazed around watching the TV and reading newspapers and wondering in a sort of vague way about it all. What was next? Would I get to stay here smarting from my shame, or would they toss me back with that Martian? But I figured, well, I've done my bit, the good Lord knows, so maybe they'll leave me alone.

Everything went jimdandy until about, oh, I'd say about two-three weeks had gone by. Then I woke up one morning feeling like the last rose of summer pulled up by the roots and stomped on. Got out of bed and fell flat on my face just exactly like I was Lord High. Dizzy I was, and fuzzheaded. When they brought in the breakfast, damn if I didn't heave all over the floor!

Now I want you to understand that for Gavin McCreigh, who'd never seen a sick day in his whole life, this here was mighty peculiar indeed. I didn't say nothing, and it passed and I felt fine for a while—until the next morning.

'Twas the same thing, only twice as bad. Couldn't even keep boiled eggs down.

Then the pains begun.

I set there cramped up, the pains shooting through me like lightning bugs for quite a spell. Finally I got to the visiscreen and hollered for help.

The doctors all come on the double, almost like as if they was waiting for just such a thing to happen. I wouldn't know. Anyway, they rolled me over and punched and poked and shook their heads and give me some slimy stuff to take and the pains stopped so I said: "Leave go of me, I'm all right!"

But they wouldn't. They made X-Ray pictures, and drew up charts and I didn't spend fifteen minutes to myself all that day.

And that's the way it went. They took away my TV. They took away my reading newspapers. The tapes—everything, every touch with the outside. Put me to bed, too, they did and said, "Now don't you get alarmed, now don't you get alarmed."

Alarmed!

By damn, I near like to fell out of the bed when I seen the weight I was putting on. When you're sick, thought I, you're supposed to get all thin and piney; and here I was pooching out like a fed hog.

"Amazing!" says they. "Fantastic!" Then: "The gestation period seems to be the same as with the ordinary Martian."

Fortunately, I didn't know the meaning of that word then, or I would probably of killed myself since there were numerous sharp things still left laying around.

But I see the word ain't new to you. You're wondering, are you?

All right. Come about five weeks, with me looking like the blue ribbon sow—only sicker'n a dog—and *still* not understanding at all, they come in, their old lips drawn back in Chessy smiles a yard wide—but worried too.

"Gavin," says the warden, "we got a little news for you."

Then they told me.

I, Gavin Patrick Quentin McCreigh, son of Mrs. Samuel Denis McCreigh, Irish-American from Atlanta, Georgia, forty-two years of age, male and in my right senses—was about to have a baby.

You don't remember none of this? Well then, maybe you just don't believe, is that it? All right, by Neddie Jingo, you see this here scar? I didn't get it in no duel, sonny.

I got it when three days later they rushed me to the hospital—and me in agony—for what is known as a see-sarian section.

Don't ask me how it happened. I ain't no damn doctor. They went on about 'backwash' or something and talked about a lad named Gene, but it didn't make no sense to me at all, at all.

All I knew was, I was under that ether a long old time, and when I got out I had this scar and I was normal size again.

"This puts a new shading on our relations with Mars," says the warden.

"Puts a new shading," says I, "on a whole hell of a lot of things."

Says he: "Well, my bucko, that's the way she goes."

Says I quick as a wink: "That may be the way she goes now, but that sure ain't the way she used to go."

Then they brought it in.

Now understand. I don't and never did hold with the common notion that any newborn young'n is necessarily the prettiest sight on this here earth. But when they toted *this* thing in, thought I: Gavin, you should have been borned a bald-headed Englishman. Because it was—and I don't color the facts—far and away the ugliest piece of meat ever beholden on the face of the globe.

All red it was and bellering to the top of its lungs—if it had lungs.

Didn't have no aunt-emmies, and right down to the waist could have been a healthy normal child. Except for the fact it had twice the healthy normal number of legs: four to be exact. Four little cockroachy legs and them kicking and flailing in my face till I had to scream to get the crawly thing off of me.

It was an experience.

Well, I thought, anyway this'll sure as the devil put a crimp into the idea of intermarriage if the whole shooting match don't come to nothing else. But you know what? They claimed it was *cute*. You hear me?

"As beautiful a child as anyone could wish" was the way I heard it put.

It takes a lot to sour an Irishman on his own home soil, that it does, but this did the trick, you may bet your spaceboots. I had to do something and do it mighty quick, or it'd be curtains for Gavin McCreigh.

Do you know what they had planned? Planned to put us back in the house and see if it worked out! Just like that: one-man's-family style!

Says I: "You can't make me do it."

Says they: "Spartanburg is reached in two weeks by the direct route."

Says I: "If I may call your gentlemen's kind attention to one fact: According to law, and tradition, only women have babies—correct?"

"Well. . ."

"And according to lawful records, one Gavin Patrick Quentin McCreigh, *male*, was found guilty of murder and sentenced to The Rock. Correct?"

"Well. . ."

"All right. Inasmuch as *I* have just given birth to a bairn, and inasmuch and notwithstanding as men can't have children, that makes me a mother. Correct?"

"Hmmm," says they.

"And being as how I'm a mother and therefore no longer the same person, and the thought of sending a *mother* to Spartanburg is unconstitutional on the grounds of being against God and law—"

Thanks be for my golden Irish tongue, is all I can say. For when I was finished, they was so screwjeed they didn't know whether to shoot me or send me a Mother's Day card.

Anyway, they dropped the charges against me and—legally anyway—I was a free man.

Free to endure my shame. They came after me like buzzards: Sign this; sign that; would I make a testimonial? Would I endorse two dozen and fifty things, from high chairs (with an extra foot rest) to oatmeal. You wouldn't believe it! I had half the diaper laundries in town after me.

Well, I saw it was financially to my good to stay a spell in the same house with this Martian woman Jane. Wasn't easy, but the big hurt had been done, and so I acted out the part of the changed man: pretended I was right in love with my little family. Phew! Some family—three people and eight legs!

Finally though I had enough money from these testimonials

and digest articles and lectures in Denmark and ekcetra to make my move. Junior never did have a name: they was having a contest at the time—he was exactly one year old and according to the rest of the damfool world the cutest tyke that ever was, but according to me a blooming four-legged monsterosity.

The Irish don't forget, laddie-buck. And this Irishman had endured more pain and torment than St. Patrick with the snakes—though on the whole I'd say they was more agreeable creechures. I waited until I knew for fair we weren't being watched in any of the secret ways they'd cooked up. Then I got me a good stout shillelagh and went into the bedroom and woke up that Martian shrew that was palming herself off as my wife and working it through me and my unfortunate situation that her whole damn race of bugs could infest our world.

"Get up!" says I.

"I'm not asleep," says she.

I told her what I aimed to do, but it didn't seem to scare her none: these Martians don't know fear nor any other decent emotion. Just stared at me with them crocus-eyes full of confusion and sorrow, all calculated to make me drop my shillelagh and leave her be.

Made me so dingdong mad I let out a cuss that turned the air blue and hove to. But she wouldn't yell, damn her! Just—took it. If she'd yelled or asked me to quit—anything *human*—maybe it wouldn't of happened.

When I seen what I'd done, I looked around and there was this other little brute, little four-legs, standing up in his crib, wiggling all over and glaring out at me with the fires of Hades in his eyes. Then he begun to bawl fit to wake the whole block. So I left, pretty fast.

It didn't take long for me to grab a ride on a space scow headed far away.

I escaped some things. But some things I didn't. I been give scars I'll never get over, never if I live to be a hundred years. I can't go back. And even if I could, I wouldn't. Not back to my shame—not to a world that ain't my world any more, crawling with the filth of the universe.

They got no room for me there now. They gave me an eternal shame and cast me out and Gavin McCreigh will never have a home again . . .

The man whose name was Gavin McCreigh got to his feet. "Forget what I told you, sonny," he said. "It was stoppered up; now it's out and I'm better for it. But you forget. And if you want my advice, stay away from Earth—just remember it the way it was before they all went crazy with this brother-hood business."

He started to leave, putting on his helmet, pressing the restaurant's inner air-lock button. I called to him: "Wait."

He turned around.

"I'm sorry, Gavin," I said, "but you're right. An Irishman *can't* forget, not even if he wants to. You're a dead thing now, the last of your kind in all the Galaxy; but I've looked for you a long time. A very long time . . . Mother."

He started to run, but it wasn't difficult to overtake him.

After all, four legs are better than two.

Träumerei

A T THE SOUND, Henry Ritchie's hand jerked. Most of the martini sloshed out over his robe. He jumped up, swabbing furiously at the spots. "Goddam it!"

"Hank!" His wife slammed her book together.

"Well, what do you expect? That confounded buzzer—"

"—is a perfectly natural normal buzzer. You're just terribly upset, dear."

"No," Mr. Ritchie said, "I am *not* 'just terribly upset, dear' —for seven years I've been listening to that banshee's wail every time somebody wants in. Well, I'm through, do you understand? Either it goes, or I—"

"All right, all *right*," Mrs. Ritchie said. "You don't have to make a production out of it."

"Well?"

"Well what?"

Mr. Ritchie sighed ponderously, glared at his wife, set what was left of the martini down on a table and went to the door. He slipped the chain.

"Be this the marster of arfway ouse?"

Mr. Ritchie opened the door. "Max—what the devil are you doing up at this hour?"

A large man, well built, in his forties, walked in, smiling. "I could ask you the same question," he said, flinging his hat and scarf in the direction of a chair, "but I'm far too thoughtful and considerate."

They went back into the living room. Mrs. Ritchie looked up, frowned. "Oh swell," she said. "Dandy. All we need now is a bridge four."

"Ruth's just terribly upset," Mr. Ritchie said.

"Well," the large man said, "it's nice to see unanimity in this house for once anyway. Hi, Ruth." He walked over to the bar and found the martini mix and drained the jar's contents into a glass. Then he drained the glass.

"Hey, take it easy!"

Max Kaplan turned to face his hosts. He looked quite a bit older than usual: the grin wasn't boyish now. "Dear folkses," he said, "when I die, I don't want to see any full bottles around."

"Oh ha ha, that's just so very deliriously funny," Mrs. Ritchie said. She was massaging her temples.

"I am glad to see her ladyship amused." Kaplan followed Mr. Ritchie's gaze. "Hickory dickory dock, the mice looked at the clock . . ."

"Oh shut up."

"Oop, sorry." The big man mixed up a new batch silently, then refilled the three glasses. He sat down. The clock's tick, a deep sharp bass sound, got louder and louder in the room. Kaplan rested his head on the couch arm. "Less than an hour," he said. "Not even an hour—"

"I knew it." Mrs. Ritchie stood up. "I knew it the minute you walked in. We're not nervous enough, oh no, now we've got to listen to the great city editor and his news behind the news."

"Very well!" Kaplan rose shakily. He was drunk; it showed now. "If I'm not welcome here, then I shall go elsewhere to breathe my last."

"Never mind," Mrs. Ritchie said. "Sit down. I've had a stomach full of this wake. If you two insist on sitting up until X-hour like a couple of ghouls, well, that's your business. I'm going to bed. And to sleep."

"What a woman," Kaplan muttered, polishing off the martini. "Nerves of chilled steel."

Mrs. Ritchie looked at her husband for a moment. Then she said "Good night, dear" and started for the door.

"See you in the morning," Mr. Ritchie said. "Get a good sleep."

Max Kaplan giggled. "Yeah, a real good sleep."

Mrs. Ritchie left the room.

The big man fumbled for a cigarette. He glanced at the clock. "Hank, for Chrissake—"

Henry Ritchie sighed and slumped in the chair. "I tried, Max."

"Did you? Did you try—I mean with everything?"

"With everything. Might as well face it: the boy's going to burn, right on schedule."

Kaplan opened his mouth.

"Forget it. The governor isn't about to issue a commutation. With the public's blood up the way it is, he knows what it would mean to his vote. We were stupid even to try."

"Lousy vultures."

Ritchie shrugged. "They're hungry, Max. You forget, there hasn't been an execution in this state for over two years. They're hungry."

"So a poor dumb kid's got to fry alive in order for them to get their kicks . . ."

"Wait a second now. Don't get carried away. This same poor dumb kid is the boy who killed George Sanderson in cold blood and then raped his wife, not too very long ago. If I recall, your word for him then was Brutal Murderer."

"That was the paper. This is you and me."

"Well, get that accusatory look off your face. Murder and rape—those are stiff raps to beat, pal."

"You did it with Beatty, you got him off," Kaplan reminded his friend.

"Luck. Public mood—Beatty was an old man, feeble. Look, Max—why don't you stop beating around the bush?"

"Okay," Kaplan said slowly. "They—let me in this afternoon. I talked with him again."

Ritchie nodded. "And?"

"Hank, I'm telling you—it gives me the creeps. I swear it does."

"What did he tell you?"

Kaplan puffed on his cigarette nervously, kept his eyes on the clock. "He was lying down when I went in, curled up tight. Trying to sleep."

"Go on."

"When he heard me, he came to. 'Mr. Kaplan,' he says, 'you've got to make them believe me, you've got to make them understand—' His eyes got real big then, and—Hank, I'm scared."

"Of what?"

"I don't know. Just him, maybe. I'm not sure."

"He carrying the same line?"

"Yeah. But worse this time, more intense somehow . . ."

Ritchie tried to keep the smile. He remembered, all right. Much too well. The whole story was crazy, normally enough to get the kid off with a life sentence in the criminally insane ward. But it was a little *too* crazy, so the psychiatrists wouldn't buy.

"Can't get his words out of my mind," Kaplan was saying. His eyes were closed. " 'Mister, tell them, tell them. If you kill me, then you'll all die. This whole world of yours will die . . .' "

Because, Ritchie remembered, *you don't exist, any of you, except in my mind. Don't you see? I'm asleep and dreaming all this. You, your wives, your children, it's all part of my dream—and when you kill me then I'll wake up and that will be the end of you . . . .*

"Well," Ritchie said, "it's original."

Kaplan shook his head.

"Come on, Max, snap out of it. You act like you never

listened to a lunatic before. People have been predicting the end of the world ever since year 1."

"Sure, I know. You don't have to patronize me. It's just that—well, who *is* this particular lunatic anyway? We don't know any more about him than the day he was caught. Even the name we had to make up. Who is he, where'd he come from, what's his home?"

My home . . . a world of eternities, an eternity of worlds . . . I must destroy, hurt, kill before I wake always . . . and then once more I must sleep . . . always, always . . .

"Look, there's a hundred vagrants in every city. Just like our boy, no friends, no relatives. It means nothing."

"Then he doesn't seem in the least odd to you, is that it? Is that what you're telling me?"

"So he's odd! I never met a murderer that wasn't!" Ritchie recalled the lean hairless face, the expressionless eyes, the slender youthful body that moved in strange hesitant jerks, the halting voice.

The clock bonged the quarter hour. Fifteen to twelve. Max Kaplan wiped the perspiration from his forehead.

"And besides," Ritchie said, somewhat too loudly, "it's plain ridiculous. He says—what? We're a dream he's having, right? Okay—then what about our parents, and their parents, everybody who never heard of the kid?"

"First thing I thought of. And you know his answer."

Ritchie snorted.

"Well, think it over, for God's sake. He says *every* dream is a complete unit in itself. You—haven't you ever had nightmares about people you'd never seen before?"

"Yes, I suppose so, but—"

"All right, even though they were projections of your subconscious—or whatever the hell it's called—they were complete, weren't they? Going somewhere, doing something, all on their own?"

Ritchie was silent.

"Where were they going, what were they doing? See? The kid says every dream, even ours, builds its own whole world —complete, with a past and—as long as you stay asleep—a future."

"Nonsense! What about *us*, when *we* sleep and dream? Or is the period when we're unconscious the time *he's* up and around? And keep in mind that everybody doesn't sleep at the same time—"

"You're missing the point, Hank. I said it was complete, didn't I? And isn't sleeping part of the pattern?"

"Have another drink, Max. You're slipping."

"Hell no I'm not slipping. It makes sense, dammit."

"What will you wake up to?"

"*My home. You would not understand.*"

"*Then what?*"

"*Then I sleep again and dream another world.*"

"*Why did you kill George Sanderson?*"

"*It is my eternal destiny to kill and suffer punishment.*"

"*Why? Why?*"

"*In my world I committed a crime; it is the punishment of my world, this destiny . . .*"

"Then try this on for size," Ritchie said. "That kid's frozen stiff with fear. Since he's going to have to wake up no matter what, then why not sit back and enjoy it?"

Kaplan's eyes widened. "Hank, how soundly do you sleep?"

"What's that got to do with it?"

"I mean, do you ever dream?"

"Of course."

"Ever get hold of any particularly vivid ones? Falling down stairs, being tortured, anything like that?"

Ritchie pulled at his drink.

"Sure you have." Kaplan gazed steadily at the clock. Almost midnight. "Then try to remember. In that kind of dream, isn't it true that the pleasure—or pain—you feel is almost as real as if you were actually experiencing it? I remember once I had a nightmare about my old man. He caught me in the basement with a cigarette—I was eight or nine, I guess. He took down my pants and started after me with his belt. Hank —that hurt, bad. It really hurt."

"So what's the point?"

"In my dream I tried to get away from my old man. He chased me all over that basement. Well, it's the same with the kid—except his dream is a hundred times more vivid, that's all. He knows he'll feel that electric chair, feel the jolts frying into him, feel the death boiling up in his throat just as much as if he were honest-to-God sitting there . . ."

Kaplan stopped talking. The two men sat quietly watching the clock's invisible progress. Then Ritchie leaped up and stalked over to the bar again. "Doggone you, Max," he called. "You're getting *me* fidgety now."

"Don't kid me," Kaplan said. "You've been fidgety on your own for quite a while. I don't know how you ever made the grade as a criminal lawyer—you don't know the first thing about lying."

Ritchie didn't answer. He poured the drink slowly.

"Look at you and Ruth, screaming at each other. And then there was the other tip-off. The way you defended the kid— brilliantly, masterfully. You'd never have done that for a common open-and-shut little killer."

"Max," Ritchie said, "you're nuts. Tell you what: at exactly 12:01 I'll take you out for the biggest, juiciest, rarest steak you

ever saw. On me. Then we'll get loaded and fall all over ourselves laughing—"

Ritchie fought away the sudden picture of steak, rare steak,
with the blood sputtering out, sizzling on an electric stove.

The clock began to strike. Henry Ritchie and Max Kaplan
stood very still.

He uncoiled. The dry pop of hardened joints jabbed wake-
fulness into him until finally the twenty foot length shell lay
straight upon the steaming rocks. He opened his eyes, all of
them, one by one.

Across the bubbling pools, far away, past the white stone
geysers, he could see them coming. Many of them, swiftly,
giant slithering things with many arms and many legs.

He tried to move, but rock grew over him and he could not
move. By looking around he could see the cliff's edge, and he
remembered the thousand bottomless pits below. Gradually
the rest formed, and he remembered all.

He turned to the largest creature. "Did you tell them?" He
knew this would be a horrible punishment, worse than the
last, the burning, far worse. Fingers began to unhinge the
thick shell, peel it from him, leaving the viscous white tender-
ness bare to the heat and pain. "Tell them, make them understand, this is only a dream I'm having—"

They took the prisoner to the precipice, lingered a moment
to give him a view of the dizziness and the sucking things far
below. Then nervous hands pressed him forward into space.

He did not wake for a long time.

The Monster Show

"IS IT SOCK?" the Big Man inquired nervously, flicking a tablet into his mouth.

"It is sock," the Official Coordinator of TV Production replied. "It is wham and boff. I give you my word."

"I give it back to you. Words mean nothing. It's pictures that count. Flap?"

"Sure; flap, flap," the Official Coordinator said, and slipped a small needle into a large vein. "But I tell you, B. P., there is nothing to worry about. We have got thirty cameras regular and sixty in reserve. For every actor, two stand-ins. In fact, we have even got stand-ins for the stand-ins. Nothing can go wrong. Nothing-O."

The Big Man collapsed into a chair and moved a handkerchief rhythmically across his neck. "I don't know," he said. "I am worried."

"What you should do, B. P.," the Official Coordinator said, "is you should relax."

The Big Man belched a picture off the wall. "Relax!" he shouted. "The most expensive TV production in history and he tells me to relax!"

"B. P., flap this. Everything is scatty-boo, A through Z. We absotively and posilutely cannot miss."

"I just don't know," the Big Man said, shaking his head.

The Official Coordinator removed a red pellet from an onyx case and tossed it into his mouth. "Boss, listen to me for a double-mo. Listen. Close the eyes. Now: You are no longer the Chief and Commander of Production of the World's Largest TV Studio—"

The Big Man trembled slightly.

"You are, instead, Mr. Average World Family, 1976 A. D. Flap?"

"Flap, flap."

"Kay. You are sitting in front of your two-thirds-paid-for 150-inch non-curved wall T-Viewer. You are in your undershirt. The missus has poured you a beer and you are munching Cheese Drackles. Reety-O. Suddenly you see that it is two minutes to eight. You jab the auto-ray and switch channels

174

right away, if you are sucker enough to be on another channel, which, thanks to those lousy feebs at OBC, maybe you are. But not for long! Because for six months you have been hearing about it. The biggest, the greatest, the most spectacular, the *most expensive* production ever to hit the screen. Said I biggest? Said I greatest? Said I most spectacular? Father-O, this is a veritybobble *monster* of a show! So what do we call it? Natcheroony: *The Monster Show!* 'EVERYBODY WILL BE WATCHING IT—WILL YOU?' These words, Mr. Average World Family, are stamped into your brain. You've seen them everywhere: billboards, leaflets, sky-writing, magazine ads, the regular 15-minute daily commersh: and you've *heard* them everywhere, too: in busses and planes and cars, from your children—"

"Meant to tell you," the Big Man interrupted, "getting at the children was a good move."

"What about the parrots?"

"The parrots was also a good move."

"I blush, B. P. But hearken-O: There you are. Are you there?"

"Proceed on. I am ears."

"Kay. It is one minute to eight. You are shaking with excitement. Just like all the rest of the Folks everywhere else. In the bars, in the theatres, in the homes. Some with 90-foot curvo screens, some with modest 40-inchers, some even—like the cops and all—with nothing but their wrist-peeps. But they're with ya: you know that. Get the image, B. P. All over the world, everything stopped, everybody staring at their sets, waiting, waiting . . ."

"What about the competition?"

The Official Coordinator stuck his hands in his pockets and did a sort of dance. "B. P., Uncle-O—there isn't any!" He grinned widely. "And *that* is my surprise."

The Big Man opened his eyes. He clutched the arms of the chair. "How's that, how's that?"

"You tell me no stories, I'll tell you no untruths," the Official Coordinator smirked. "Baby, they have scratched themselves. Us they do not choose to buck. They are offering to the folks in place of their usual maloop a kitty of our own show—which I got a hefty slap for which, Mother-O . . ."

"Now, now," said the Big Man, smiling slyly, "you did not muscle the OBC boys a little, I hope?"

"Truth-O, Uncle. Nay. They plain quit. The eight spot is *ours!*" The Official Coordinator slapped his hands together. "And who's to blame them? What *The Monster Show* has not got you can mount on the sharp end of an isotope. Flap this: We begin with a two-hour commercial round-up, advertising the products of our 57 sponsors: General Turbines, Sleep-

Neat Capsules, Chewey-Flakes, the Komfy-Kool TV Furniture
line and ek-cetera. But are these ordinary commershes? Noo.
We have them tricked out so they look prezactly like the show.
Excavate?"

"Yo."

"Kay. Then: into the show. And *what* a show! I ask you,
Mr. Average World Family, at night when you're all blasted
out and ready for the old air-matt do you like to get spooned
a lot of maloop you have got to *think* about, or do you like
to get *round?*"

The Big Man made a solemn circle with his finger.

"And what is the roundest? Something long and complex
and all drawn out? Nay. *Variety*: that's what is the roundest.
So we give you a variety show. Starting things off with a
kronch, we have a half-hour trained dog act. Then right into
fifteen minutes of old Western movie footage, with the middle
reel of a British mystery for the capper. Then a full hour of
wrestling, male and female. Ears?"

"Ears."

"A mere starteroo, B. P. We punch 'em with twenty minutes
of hillbilly-style Used Car commersh, and then we *really* start
fighting. A right cross with Rev. Vincent Bell on *How to Live
Up to the Hilt*: a left jab with the first installment of a new
detergent-opera, *Jill Jackson, Jet-Wife*: an uppercut to the jaw
with *Who's Zoo*—keep moving; don't give 'em a chance to
think, see—followed by a flurry of lightning blows to the face
and body: *Chef Gaston Escargot's School of Cookery! Mike
Tomerist, Private Op! A Ten-Year Roundup of Stock Turbo
and Jaloppy Racing!* A musical remake of the old motion
picture *Waterloo Bridge*, now called *London Derriere!*" The
Official Coordinator was warming to his topic: his eyes were
wide and his lower lip moist. "Do we swing?"

The Big Man nodded. "Speaking as Mr. Average World
Family," he said, "I am getting slightly interested. Wing on."

"Well, we got 'em dizzy now, flap? Kay. We ease off with
a handcream commersh: you know, the voodoo dance rou-
tine? Thirty minutes. Then, quos! Right in the old schwan-
zola!"

"What do we do, what do we do?" the Big Man asked.

"We let 'em have it. POW!" The Official Coordinator
needled a vein ecstatically, and exploded: "The old haymaker.
The slamboreeno. *Twenty* of the world's greatest comedians
on-stage, going through their most famous routines, *all at the
same time!*"

There was a pregnant pause.

Then the Big Man shot from his chair, extruded a hirsute
hand and laid it gently on the Official Coordinator's shoulder.
"One thing," he said, with genuine concern.

"Yes?" the Official Coordinator quavered.

"Do we have *enough*?"

"B. P., I think we do. I really and truly think we do." The Coordinator quickly rolled three pellets into his mouth and grimaced.

"Then," said the Big Man, "I feel that we ought to be mighty proud. And, flap me, mighty humble, too. Because we are giving the world public the thing they want and need most: *Entertainment*." He winked gravely. "Also, we are making for ourselves a few drachmae. Excavate?"

The Official Coordinator brushed a tear of satisfaction from his cheek. "Boss," he said, in cathedral tones, "I promise you this. This I promise you. *Everybody* on Earth is going to be watching *The Monster Show* tonight. It is going to be an experience no one will forget. In fact, I will far-enough-go to say that it will be the most important moment in history!"

The Big Man squeezed the Coordinator's fleshly digits and smiled. "Screech," he said. "You've done poo-goo. Now powder: the mind must rest."

The Coordinator nodded, tugged at his forelock, and exited through the bullet-proof sliding door.

When it was firmly shut, the Big Man went over and locked it; then he removed from his pocket a flat disc with three knobs. He twiddled the knobs.

There was a humming.

"As planned," the Big Man said, and put the triple-knobbed disc back into his pocket.

His face was curiously devoid of expression. There was perhaps a trace of amusement about the mouth-ends as he went to the chromium bar and poured himself a shot of amber; perhaps not. He tilted the glass, swallowed, hiccoughed, set the glass down and punched the inter-office audiobox. "Miss Dovecoat," he said, "please flap me good. I will see no one between now and the show. Out?"

"And over," the voice of Miss Dovecoat crackled.

The Big Man sat in the chair, silent and unmoving, expressionless as a barracuda, for four and a half hours.

At ten minutes to eight he pressed seventeen levers on his desk and listened to seventeen yessirs.

"Report?" he barked.

"Scatoreeny, sir," came the answer like a celestial choir somewhat off-key.

"Sure?"

"Absotive and posilute."

"Everything moving?"

"With an 'o'. With a 'k'."

"Unbad, gentlemen."

"You snap the whip, we'll take the voyage."

"Ears out, now. *Coverage?*"

"One-hundred-percent."

"100% one hundred-percent?"

"100% one-hundred-per*cent* 100%!"

"Kay. Gentlemen: Proceed on."

The Big Man turned off all the levers and touched a concealed desk button. The three walls of the room seemed to shimmer and reshape themselves into a perfect curve; then they became clear. The image of a man fifty feet tall appeared. He was smiling and pouring a hundred gallons of beer into a gigantic glass.

" *. . . so get those taste buds unlimbered, folksies, and treat yourselves to the world's favorite brew: Rocky Mountain! Yes! That's absotively right! I said Rocky Mountain! And . . ."*

In moments the giant man faded, and there was a portentous pause.

Then, the sound of a thousand trumpets, and an aerial shot of 70 hand-picked chorus girls, so arranged as to spell out:

THE
MONSTER
SHOW

The Big Man waited a moment, until the Emcee had come on-stage, then he snapped the concealed button and the walls became walls again.

He removed the triple-knobbed disc. "Now," he said, and slumped into a chair.

Hours passed, but he did not move.

Finally, there was a sharp knock at the bullet-proof sliding door.

The Big Man went to the door and opened it, cautiously. Eight lavender creatures with slimy skin and no noses at all were at the threshold.

"Well?" the Big Man said. "How did it go?"

One of the creatures, slightly more lavender than the rest, stepped forward. "Extremely well," it said. "In fact, perfectly. The Earth people are all dead. Thanks, Volshak, to you."

"Nonsense," the Big Man said, turning into a lavender creature with slimy skin and no nose at all. "I have had quite enough idolatry. I prefer to think of myself as an agent who tried to do his job."

"Volshak, Volshak," the creature hissed, "Such modesty is touching, and a credit to our race; but there is no getting around it. You are a hero. Why, if there had been the slightest resistance, we would have failed. We had few weapons, a bare handful of warriors—frankly, we were very nearly ready to descend into The Great Abyss. But even the gulfs are full of vanquished invaders: we did not have, so to speak, a pit to pass in. But now we may revel in the sunlight and enjoy the blessings of propagation on a new world without having lost a single thrimp." The creature put a boneless tentacle forward. "How did you manage it? Volshak, *how* did you manage to put *all* the Earth people to sleep at the same time?"

But Volshak was blushing. He turned his unproboscidean face to the wall and muttered, in a small, proud voice: "It was easy."

The New Sound

O F ALL THE squirrels in a world full of squirrels Mr. Goodhew was by far the squirreliest. That is, he collected things. But whereas once it had been masks and postage stamps and colored rocks and bits of twine, now he collected death. Vigorously, fanatically, lovingly. He would pluck it out of the air and seal it inside plastoid and listen to it at night. It made him very happy.

But things were not always so. It had come by degrees, beginning with Mozart and Bach and ending with the mollusks and the bats—which was, of course, the real beginning. As a common audiophile he had filled his apartment with a mushroom growth of phonographs and speakers and attachments and he was kept busy reproducing fidelitously the *tutti* passages of the more violent composers. But then, one day, he happened to purchase an album entitled *A World of Sounds*. Its cover was of modern design and it had been manufactured in the interests of science. It contained such items as recordings of seals at play, the death cry of a wounded ibex and a horsefly's heartbeat. Bonus-wise it offered the sound of a squid thrashing in waters described as *lonely* and *unfathomable* and the somewhat unnerving (though not to Mr. Goodhew) chitter of a vampire bat.

Sounds, wonderful and strange; sounds you could get your teeth into, sounds like none he had ever heard . . .

Promptly he was lost and the collection was on its way.

It was crude at first, as all collections are: a higgledy-piggledy potpourri entirely without organization. Hasty purchase followed hasty purchase—today a windstorm over Reykjavik, tomorrow an alligator's yawn, the next day the weary groan of bordello couchsprings . . .

In time, however, Mr. Goodhew tired of such easily come by items and developed a less universal attitude: he narrowed his field. The purchases became less frequent and it was soon necessary for him to dip into capital—a commodity of which, fortunately, he enjoyed a plenitude owing to an inheritance left by his father who had been a used car salesman. He hired Sound Scouts to record the really bizarre, unusual, outré, the near-fantastic. But still, though interesting, the collection was not sufficiently homogenous to please Mr. Goodhew. He listened eveningly to the rustle of unborn infants, to the perspiration afall from thieves' foreheads, to the sound of trap doors swinging against gallows platforms, and he thought as he listened: I must specialize, yes, I must specialize!

But how? In what way?

He thought about it carefully, sorting, eliminating, eliminating. Then he called in his employees and gave them their orders.

It was at that moment that Mr. Goodhew became the first necroaudiophile.

Throwing out all but the death cry of the ibex, he attended scrupulously to his specialty. The first report brought him recordings of crushed mice, immolated earwigs, the gasps of a mongrel lying beneath two tons of truck—a very nice rudimentary start. He listened to them, catalogued them, crossfiled them and put them away. And waited.

He had not long to wait. Presently his apartment bulged with records, and the air was forever alive with the cries, groans, gasps, screams, screeches, whimpers and whines of sundry animals; all dying, each in a different way. Upon that point Mr. Goodhew stood adamant: there must be no repetitiousness.

And all went swimmingly until, for numerous reasons, he found it necessary to change quarters. For one thing, the apartment was becoming incommodious for his needs; for another, he was weary of making explanations to the neighbors and to the policemen summoned by the neighbors. He moved, records and all, to a redwood villa high upon the highest hill, and there he stayed.

And the collection grew. Despite world conditions, which could best be described as taut, each day's mail would bring from all corners something new: the death throes of an armadillo; the shrills, flutings and flutterings of a disemboweled canary; the hysterical hiss of an anaconda dropped into a wood stove . . . Mr. Goodhew had scarcely a moment free, so busy was he listening, filing, recording, processing: only in the evening could he fall into an easy chair, flip on the phonograph and actually enjoy his collection. Then the lights would be turned off and he would sit there, tense, expectant, mouth open, brain a moving image to the sounds. He would listen in the manner of many another collector fingering rare delft or polishing sea shells or putting first folios in line upon library shelves. And he was a true, a real collector, for he enjoyed every phase of it: the preparation, the labor, and, most important, the sounds themselves.

One day, however, after many years had passed, the inevitable happened. His specialty reached completion, or nearly that, very tragically nearly that. No species of animal existed of which at least one member had not died for Mr. Goodhew. He had them all. From aardvark to zebra, from the suba-queous leave-taking of a single cell to the room-filling choke of a giant whale. All there, in Mr. Goodhew's house, filed and stored: complete.

Except—

Once determined, Mr. Goodhew breathed as a prisoner granted pardon. It took adjusting, screwing up of the courage, but he was a collector and he could think of nothing worse than a collector with nothing to collect.

So it was settled.

The first batch arrived one week from the time of his de-cision. It contained one perfect jewel and several of declining quality. But that first! Mr. Goodhew listened to it again and again. He listened to the woman's scream as it echoed through the rooms of his house. What pain! What suffering! What *bel canto!*

She had been strangled, the Sound Scout—an extremely ambitious fellow—had explained, though failing to append any note regarding certain other details which occurred to, but did not overlong remain with, his employer. The rest was chaff, an unhappy mish-mash of hoots and bellows and throbbing guttural wrackings—all obviously spurious.

Which made Mr. Goodhew furious.

He discharged all the men save Mr. Hurke, who had pre-sented him with the initial gem; and thenceforth the Sound Collection flourished—slowly, it is true, what with world tension, the bombs, et al., but quite surely.

At night now, Mr. Goodhew scarcely ever made reference to any of what he termed his Mesozoic period, preferring to concentrate on this latest phase of the collection. Into the weeest hours he would listen and thrill to the death rattles of stilettoed merchants, the last bubblings of drowned spinsters, the dry croaks of nonagenarians, the windcrushed screams of falling eunuchs . . . Terror and anguish and honesty, the sounds of honesty; of souls laid open—this is what he listened to.

And surely, he thought, there is no limit to my collection now! A sound for every soul in a universe overrun with souls. It would last forever; he would go on collecting and collecting and—

On a humid evening high upon his hill Mr. Goodhew got up, walked over to his phonograph and snapped off the seven hundredth shriek of a university student who had yet three hundred to go (the Death of a Thousand Cuts—Mr. Hurke had instituted certain refinements). And so doing, Mr. Goodhew sighed, paced a bit and then proceeded to a hall mirror whereat he stood in contemplation for fifteen minutes. It was difficult to believe; almost, it seemed, impossible to believe. Yet, as he saw those eyes, those lines and wrinkles, that runny scratch of mouth, he knew it was true.

He had become jaded. He had been living off marginalia for years, and now he faced it: he was a Des Esseintes at the end of the trail. There were no more new sounds, none to excite the smallest interest.

His collection was—complete.

He sighed again, and was alarmed at the sudden receipt of a highly whimsical idea. If it is complete, he thought, why then do I feel frustrated? Where is the satisfaction? No. It is *not* complete; there is yet one more, one last sound.

My own!

Nonsense. He spoke aloud now, even as he played with the special tape recorder. If I shoot myself or swallow prussic acid or what have you, and then play it back . . . but stop! That is ridiculous and what is worse, it is grossly literary.

But if not his own death—which, as he reasoned, he would scarcely be able to enjoy afterwards—what then? He began to pace at a faster clip. Searching his mind. The New Sound, the Ultimate Sound, the only one he lacked . . .

Mr. Goodhew stamped his foot upon the Japanese floormat and flung himself onto a large divan and cogitated until his temples ached.

What could it be? What had he overlooked to account for this feeling of incompleteness?

It was at this point of chaotic frustration when thought unravels and trails into a knotted tangle that Mr. Goodhew felt the concussion. Like a silent explosion, the loosing of fantastic pressures, a vast cosmic hemorrhage, assailing the nerves of his body, causing him to roll onto the floor and blink.

What—He rose and rushed directly to the window, the east window which commanded an imperial view of the light-laced city. It was midnight. And yet, from afar, he could see the great inverted orange glow deepening, spreading in the sky like a drop of color in the transparent water of a fishbowl.

He watched it grow and thought about it. Thought about the alarmists and their perpetual pulings of world cataclysm, the C-Bomb, the O-Bomb—

The explosion began, a soft rumble of drums in the bloated black overhead clouds. Mr. Goodhew flinched and trembled as understanding came. Then he snapped his fingers and said of course; he sprang backward and raced to his recording apparatus, fastened the attachments, set it all humming. Hurry, hurry! He brought the special microphone to the open window, held it high, tested it: One, Two, Three, Four.

And then there was the ripping and the crashing and the thunder like no other thunder, loud, so loud, a frenzied tourbillon of sound—but still soft enough to permit the screams to wriggle through, like tiny frightened snakes.

Mr. Goodhew held the microphone high out the window and chuckled: even when the fires began, he chuckled. He breathed fast, waiting . . . A little more, a little longer, two more seconds: Now! He snapped a switch and watched the glistening tanness of tape hiss in fast reverse. He snapped another switch, stopping it.

Mr. Goodhew pressed the playback button and shivered in wild anticipatory glee.

Then the lights went out. He bent closer, listening—he craned his neck and conched his ears; and then he let loose one small strangulated cry of anguish. He shook the dead recorder and did not stop shaking it until the world had burst and split and blown away in a billion flaming specks.

He had missed it. He had missed the ultimate sound.